Earth in the

You are Falcon, special agent of the Temporal, Investigative and Monitoring Executive, one of a highly-trained cadre of operatives with exceptional talents and skills.

Your job is to identify and neutralize threats to the very fabric of history, travelling back and forwards through time on missions that call for a combination of ingenuity, stealth, force and surgical precision. One slip and you could change the course of events beyond repair - and even delete your own existence!

# Gamebooks from Fabled Lands Publishing

*by Jamie Thomson and Dave Morris:*

Fabled Lands 1: The War-Torn Kingdom
Fabled Lands 2: Cities of Gold and Glory
Fabled Lands 3: Over the Blood-Dark Sea
Fabled Lands 4: The Plains of Howling Darkness
Fabled Lands 5: The Court of Hidden Faces
Fabled Lands 6: Lords of the Rising Sun

Fabled Lands Quests: The Keep of the Lich Lord

*by Dave Morris:*

Heart of Ice
Down Among the Dead Men
Necklace of Skulls
Once Upon a Time in Arabia
Crypt of the Vampire
The Temple of Flame
The Castle of Lost Souls

*by Oliver Johnson:*

Curse of the Pharaoh
The Lord of Shadow Keep

*by Dave Morris and Oliver Johnson*
Blood Sword 1: The Battlepits of Krarth
Blood Sword 2: The Kingdom of Wyrd
Blood Sword 3: The Demon's Claw
Blood Sword 4: Doomwalk

IN PREPARATION
Blood Sword 5: The Walls of Spyte

*by Jamie Thomson and Mark Smith:*

Way of the Tiger 1: Avenger
Way of the Tiger 2: Assassin
Way of the Tiger 3: Usurper
Way of the Tiger 4: Overlord
Way of the Tiger 5: Warbringer
Way of the Tiger 6: Inferno

FALCON

# THE RENEGADE LORD

Jamie Thomson and Mark Smith

Cover painting by Peter Andrew Jones

*Fabled Lands Publishing*

First published 1985 by Sphere Books

This edition published 2015 by Fabled Lands Publishing,
an imprint of Fabled Lands LLP

ISBN 978-1-909905-22-1

# CONTENTS

# EARTH 3033 AD

A third of the land's surface is populated with cities which stretch miles up towards the ionosphere and are also tunnelled deep into the Earth's crust.

The world is united – war within the atmosphere of a single planet can only lead to total destruction. Government is carried out by Executives, each having full powers within a certain area. The Food, Health, Pleasure and Enforcement Executives are centred in Alpolis, a city covering what was once an independent country, Switzerland, and it is here that the most recent Executive, TIME, exists.

People live for fun, not to work. Most tasks are performed by robots, so life is quite easy. Only 10% of the population still works, and then only for fun or out of a sense of social duty. Food is plentiful, the main source being a fungus grown in huge vats under artificial light. Luxury foods, such as meat, are a rarity. Communications have improved so as to transform society: holophones connect everyone across the Space Federation so it is possible to be in direct contact with many alien species light years across space. Travel on earth is by hovrail, jetcopter or stratocruiser, so that the longest journey need take no more than an hour.

The average Earther lives for two hundred and fifty years and the ageing process only begins during the last fifty years of life. Life-prolonging drugs, called anagathics, are freely available, and transplant surgery is now a simple operation. Unfortunately, because people live longer, there are many problems. There is overcrowding and very little to do, which has resulted in a rapid increase in violent crime. With so many people needing new hearts, lungs and other organs there is a shortage of spare parts for use in transplant surgery, so the Enforcement Executive has passed a Termination Code. All violent crimes are punishable by painless death. The Enforcement Executive has had sensors set up to catch criminals, especially bodybrokers who deal illegally in organs for surgery. If energy weapons are used by criminals, for instance, a police jetcopter will be there in seconds.

Using hyperdrive – faster-than-light travel – Earth has established itself as head of the Space Federation, which includes all the earth colonies and alien planets. The Navy patrols the colonies: Lastlanding, Proxima Centauri, Ascension and so on, as well as the alien worlds: Kelados, Sundew, Dyskra, Clyss, Rigel Prime, the Hive and others. Contact with alien life forms is commonplace and colony ships sent out in the twenty-fourth century are still approaching the centre of the galaxy.

## HOW TO TRAVEL IN TIME

Travel through time involves crossing a fourth dimension, 'Null-space' or the 'Void' as it is known. This dimension joins all points in time and space from the beginning of the universe to its end. Imagine time as a cable. Earth's timeline (or past, present and future) is a single strand of this cable stretching from Earth's beginning to the end of time. The timelines of other planets run alongside this and weave around each other, because events on one planet affect things on another. These strands, or timelines, are insulated from the fourth dimension in the same way that an electrical wire is insulated. At certain points there are holes in the insulation allowing travel from one point on the wire through this hole to a different point on this or another wire. In this way a time machine may move from one 'timehole' to another and from one point in space to another via Null-space.

The timeholes are formed when the fabric of time is damaged by unknown forces. They are usually less than five miles across, but can be larger. Timeholes come and go as new damage occurs and older timeholes close up naturally. The Monitoring Section is responsible for keeping the map of current timeholes. Your up-to-date map is at the beginning of the book. At least one hole has been there for a long time – the Eiger Vault, near the TIME Building in the Alps. It is thought to be a permanent timehole and your time machine, Falcon's Wing, is kept there along with those of the Lords of TIME and other agents. Some timeholes are safer than others and it is possible to go back in time only to find that the hole through

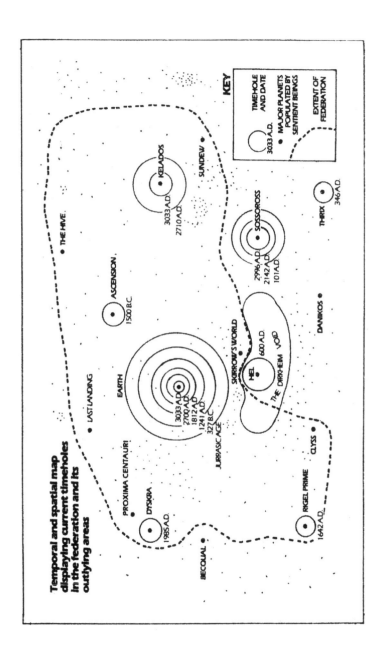

Temporal and spatial map displaying current timeholes in the federation and its outlying areas

KEY

TIMEHOLE AND DATE
3033 A.D.

MAJOR PLANETS POPULATED BY SENTIENT BEINGS

EXTENT OF FEDERATION

THE HIVE

KELADOS
3033 A.D.
2710 A.D.

SUNDEW

SOSSOROSS
2996 A.D.
2142 A.D.
101 A.D.

THIRX
346 A.D.

ASCENSION
1500 B.C.

LAST LANDING

EARTH
3033 A.D.
2700 A.D.
1812 A.D.
1241 A.D.
327 B.C.
JURRASIC AGE

SORROW'S WORLD

HEL
600 A.D.

THE DIRRI-EEM VOID

DANIKOS

PROXIMA CENTAURI

DITSKRA
1985 A.D.

CLYSS

RIGEL PRIME
1642 A.D.

BECQUAL

which you travelled has closed up, trapping the unfortunate traveller in the past. Time passes at the same rate in all timeholes as on Earth. If you begin a journey to a timehole ten minutes after somebody else does you will arrive ten minutes later than them. Only those with Psi Sense can navigate across Null-space.

## GAME RULES

ATTACK
In certain paragraphs you will have the chance to attack an enemy. When you choose to do so, you will be asked to make an Attack Roll. To do this, roll two dice and add the numbers together. You will be told which paragraph to turn to next, depending on your score. In all combats you are more likely to succeed if your score is high than if it is low.

ATTACK MODIFIER
Whenever you make an Attack Roll you must add or subtract your Attack Modifier to the dice score. Your Attack Modifier may change as the adventure unfolds and you should keep a note of this on your Agent Profile (at beginning of adventure). To begin with your Attack Modifier is zero.

EVASION
In certain cases you may need to avoid the attack of an enemy or escape from a difficult situation. You will be asked to make an Evasion Roll, to which you must add or subtract your Evasion Modifier. This works in the same way as the Attack Roll and Attack Modifier as described above. Your initial Evasion Modifier is also zero.

POWERS OF THE MIND
Some paragraphs will offer you the chance to make a mental attack, either a Thinkstrike or Power of Will. Make an Attack Roll, just as if you were attacking normally, but add or subtract your Thinkstrike or Power of Will Modifier, not your Attack Modifier. In all other ways mental attacks work in the

same way as a physical attack. To begin with your Thinkstrike and Power of Will Modifiers are zero, as noted on your Agent Profile.

PSI SENSE
Your Psi Sense operates at all times and you will be told when you have discovered anything of interest.

ENDURANCE
You start the adventure with 20 points of Endurance. If you are wounded in combat, become exhausted, or suffer something unpleasant such as exposure to an acid atmosphere without a space suit, you will lose Endurance points. Keep a running total of your Endurance on your Agent Profile. If at any time you fall to zero Endurance or less you are dead and your adventure is over. Endurance points can be regained by visiting the autodoc in your time machine (see equipment list) and you will be told when you can use your autodoc.

SCORING
You will notice as you use this book that certain paragraph numbers are followed by a letter in brackets. If you wish to score your performance as Special Agent Falcon, you will need to make a list of the letters following these numbers on the box provided on your Agent Profile every time you come to one of these paragraphs. If you should be killed or fail in your adventure, delete your current recorded letters *except for all the Qs,* which must be kept, and then begin again. Each letter corresponds to a score, and you will be given a rating depending on what the total of your scores is. The letter scores can be found at the back of the book. But do not look at the scores until you have replayed this book to a satisfactory conclusion, as seeing the scores before then would reveal the right decisions to take in this adventure!

# EQUIPMENT
## Standard issue for TIME special agents

ITEM1: MODEL A3 TIME MACHINE [see accompanying specifications]

Your own time machine, Falcon's Wing, is silver with bright scarlet markings and is the eleventh machine capable of travel through time ever built. Its cost cannot be computed, since it involves the use of certain materials and scientific skills which are priceless. The silver and scarlet hull will withstand enormous pressure, heat and exposure to harmful gases and liquids, as well as providing protection from radiation.

The six hydraulic legs which support the machine are extended when it materialises in a new timehole, to provide stability on uneven ground. The main access is operated by invisible tractor beams (directional force fields that can be used to grip and lift) that will draw the time traveller up into the cabin to rest on the access disc. This disc is matter but is changed to air as you move through it by the molecular converter (see item 4). The pressurised cabin is lined with instruments and gadgets. The crash couch is moulded to fit your shape and can be moved up to the command console or up into the flyer (see item 6). The air inside the machine is kept pure by the life support unit and can be flushed out and replaced within ten seconds. The main access will work only when its memory scanner recognises your own brain patterns. Specially sensitive cameras and power floodlights are mounted on top of the machine. The Variac drive, which forces the machine into null-space, is housed beneath the deck and is controlled through your computer (CAIN, see item 7).

ITEM 2: HOLOGRAM GENERATOR

Each time machine is equipped with a hologram generator, which is essential if the First Law of TIME is to be observed. The generator changes the appearance of the machine by projecting a hologram around it, so the computer can make the machine look like a copse of trees, a hayrick, a grassy knoll, etc. The image appears realistic to any observer more than two metres away.

# TIME MACHINE

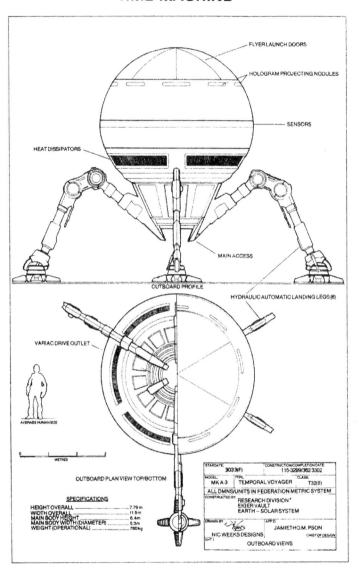

FLYER LAUNCH DOORS

HOLOGRAM PROJECTING NODULES

SENSORS

HEAT DISSIPATORS

MAIN ACCESS

OUTBOARD PROFILE

HYDRAULIC AUTOMATIC LANDING LEGS (6)

VARIAC DRIVE OUTLET

AVERAGE HUMAN SIZE

0        1        2        3
METRES

OUTBOARD PLAN VIEW TOP/BOTTOM

## SPECIFICATIONS

HEIGHT OVERALL ............................ 7.79 m
WIDTH OVERALL ............................. 11.5 m
MAIN BODY HEIGHT ........................ 6.4 m
MAIN BODY WIDTH (DIAMETER) ...... 5.3m
WEIGHT (OPERATIONAL) ................. 780kg

| STARDATE: 3033(F) | | CONSTRUCTION/COMPLETION DATE: 115-3299/362 3302 | |
|---|---|---|---|
| MODEL: MK A-3 | TYPE: TEMPORAL VOYAGER | | CLASS: T32(II) |
| ALL DMNS/UNITS IN FEDERATION METRIC SYSTEM | | | |
| CONSTRUCTED BY: | RESEARCH DIVISION EIGER VAULT EARTH – SOLAR SYSTEM | | |
| DRAWN BY: NIC WEEKS DESIGNS | | APP'D: JAMIE THO.M. PSON | CHIEF OF DESIGN |
| SHT 1 | OUTBOARD VIEWS | | |

# TIME MACHINE

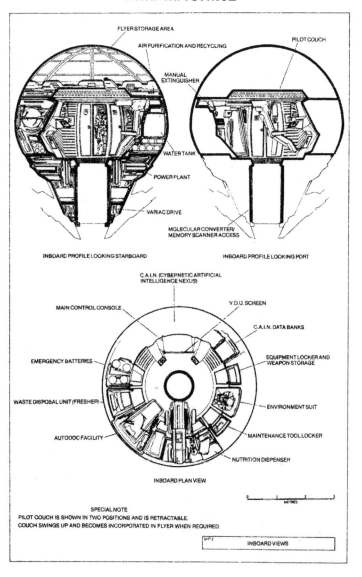

FLYER STORAGE AREA

AIR PURIFICATION AND RECYCLING

PILOT COUCH

MANUAL EXTINGUISHER

WATER TANK

POWER PLANT

VARIAC DRIVE

MOLECULAR CONVERTER/ MEMORY SCANNER ACCESS

INBOARD PROFILE LOOKING STARBOARD

INBOARD PROFILE LOOKING PORT

C.A.I.N. (CYBERNETIC ARTIFICIAL INTELLIGENCE NEXUS)

MAIN CONTROL CONSOLE

V.D.U. SCREEN

C.A.I.N. DATA BANKS

EMERGENCY BATTERIES

EQUIPMENT LOCKER AND WEAPON STORAGE

WASTE DISPOSAL UNIT (FRESHER)

ENVIRONMENT SUIT

AUTODOC FACILITY

MAINTENANCE TOOL LOCKER

NUTRITION DISPENSER

INBOARD PLAN VIEW

METRES

SPECIAL NOTE
PILOT COUCH IS SHOWN IN TWO POSITIONS AND IS RETRACTABLE.
COUCH SWINGS UP AND BECOMES INCORPORATED IN FLYER WHEN REQUIRED.

SHT 2  INBOARD VIEWS

## ITEM 3: HOLO-DETECTOR

Owing to the existence of hologram generators you may find it difficult to spot other time machines. As a member of the Time Police you have been given a hologram detector which is portable and operates to a range of fifty metres. This will reveal the presence of a hologram disguising another time machine.

## ITEM 4: MOLECULAR CONVERTOR

Each time machine is equipped with a molecular converter, a device which uses the rarest of all elements, polybdenum, as its fuel. Small articles placed in the converter are transformed into whatever the computer decides. In this way, time travellers have disguises which allow them to pass undetected amongst the intelligent beings of other times. CAIN, your computer, carries information about the timeholes shown on your map so that the blueprints, required by the converter to make the disguises accurate, are usually available. Your psionic helmet, for instance, can be turned into a legionary's helmet, while keeping its modern powers.

## ITEM 5: AUTODOC

This is a couch-like device which has needles, a drip, a blood supply and surgical robo-arms. You may lie in the autodoc during the time taken to travel from one timehole to another, for instance, and come out healed, restoring your Endurance by up to twelve points. You will be told when you can use your autodoc.

## ITEM 6: FLYER

Your crash-couch swivels up onto the platform of your flyer when you wish to use it. The flyer is a small hover-raft which is catapulted out of the time machine through the launch doors, two sections on top of the hull that slide apart. Once safely away from the machine the ion drive can be cut in, giving the flyer a top speed many times the speed of sound (Mach 6). It can hover, allowing you to use it as an observation platform, but it is too small to carry a hologram generator and

# FLYER

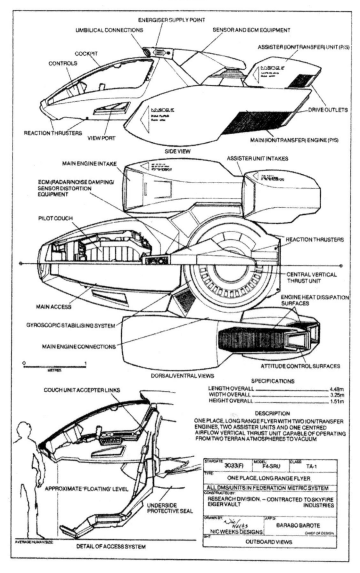

ENERGISER SUPPLY POINT

UMBILICAL CONNECTIONS

SENSOR AND ECM EQUIPMENT

ASSISTER (ION/TRANSFER) UNIT (P/S)

COCKPIT

CONTROLS

DRIVE OUTLETS

REACTION THRUSTERS

VIEW PORT

SIDE VIEW

MAIN (ION/TRANSFER) ENGINE (P/S)

MAIN ENGINE INTAKE

ASSISTER UNIT INTAKES

ECM (RADAR/NOISE DAMPING/
SENSOR DISTORTION
EQUIPMENT

PILOT COUCH

REACTION THRUSTERS

CENTRAL VERTICAL
THRUST UNIT

ENGINE HEAT DISSIPATION
SURFACES

MAIN ACCESS

GYROSCOPIC STABILISING SYSTEM

MAIN ENGINE CONNECTIONS

ATTITUDE CONTROL SURFACES

0                1

METRES

DORSAL/VENTRAL VIEWS

SPECIFICATIONS

LENGTH OVERALL .................... 4.48m
WIDTH OVERALL ...................... 3.25m
HEIGHT OVERALL ..................... 1.51m

COUPLE UNIT ACCEPTER LINKS

DESCRIPTION

ONE PLACE, LONG RANGE FLYER WITH TWO ION/TRANSFER
ENGINES, TWO ASSISTER UNITS AND ONE CENTRED
AIRFLOW VERTICAL THRUST UNIT CAPABLE OF OPERATING
FROM TWO TERRAN ATMOSPHERES TO VACUUM

APPROXIMATE 'FLOATING' LEVEL

UNDERSIDE
PROTECTIVE SEAL

AVERAGE HUMAN SIZE

DETAIL OF ACCESS SYSTEM

| STARDATE 3G33(F) | MODEL F4-SRU | CLASS TA-1 |
|---|---|---|
| TYPE ONE PLACE, LONG RANGE FLYER | | |
| ALL DMS/UNITS IN FEDERATION METRIC SYSTEM | | |
| CONSTRUCTED BY RESEARCH DIVISION. – CONTRACTED TO SKYFIRE EIGER VAULT INDUSTRIES | | |
| DRAWN BY Nic Weeks NIC WEEKS DESIGNS | APP'D BARABO BAROTE CHIEF OF DESIGN | |
| SHT | OUTBOARD VIEWS | |

# FLYER

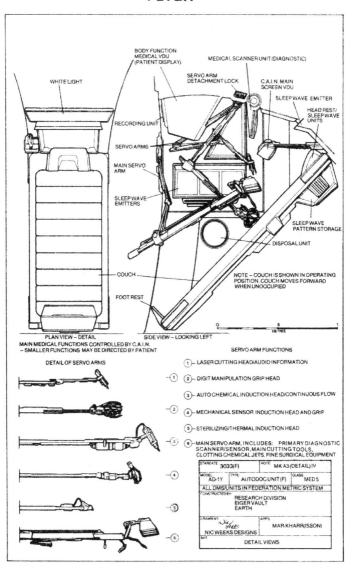

WHITE LIGHT

BODY FUNCTION MEDICAL VDU (PATIENT DISPLAY)

MEDICAL SCANNER UNIT (DIAGNOSTIC)

SERVO ARM DETACHMENT LOCK

C.A.I.N. MAIN SCREEN VDU

SLEEP WAVE EMITTER

HEAD REST/ SLEEP WAVE UNITS

RECORDING UNIT

SERVO ARMS

MAIN SERVO ARM

SLEEP WAVE EMITTERS

SLEEP WAVE PATTERN STORAGE

DISPOSAL UNIT

COUCH

NOTE – COUCH IS SHOWN IN OPERATING POSITION. COUCH MOVES FORWARD WHEN UNOCCUPIED

FOOT REST

PLAN VIEW – DETAIL

SIDE VIEW – LOOKING LEFT

MAIN MEDICAL FUNCTIONS CONTROLLED BY C.A.I.N.
– SMALLER FUNCTIONS MAY BE DIRECTED BY PATIENT

DETAIL OF SERVO ARMS

SERVO ARM FUNCTIONS

1 – LASER CUTTING HEAD/AUDIO INFORMATION

2 – DIGIT MANIPULATION GRIP HEAD

3 – AUTO CHEMICAL INDUCTION HEAD/CONTINUOUS FLOW

4 – MECHANICAL SENSOR INDUCTION HEAD AND GRIP

5 – STERILIZING/THERMAL INDUCTION HEAD

6 – MAIN SERVO ARM, INCLUDES: PRIMARY DIAGNOSTIC SCANNER/SENSOR, MAIN CUTTING TOOLS, CLOTTING CHEMICAL JETS, FINE SURGICAL EQUIPMENT

| STARDATE 3033(F) | NOTE | MK A3 (DETAIL) IV | |
|---|---|---|---|
| MODEL AD-1Y | TYPE AUTODOC UNIT (F) | | CLASS MED 5 |
| ALL DMS/UNITS IN FEDERATION METRIC SYSTEM | | | |
| CONSTRUCTED BY: RESEARCH DIVISION EIGER VAULT EARTH | | | |
| DRAWN BY: Nic Weeks NIC WEEKS DESIGNS | | APPD MAR-KHARR(ISSON) | |
| SHT | DETAIL VIEWS | | |

# BLASTER

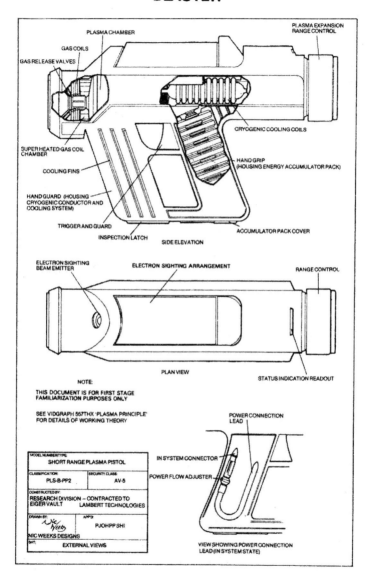

PLASMA EXPANSION RANGE CONTROL

PLASMA CHAMBER

GAS COILS

GAS RELEASE VALVES

SUPER HEATED GAS COIL CHAMBER

COOLING FINS

HAND GUARD (HOUSING CRYOGENIC CONDUCTOR AND COOLING SYSTEM)

TRIGGER AND GUARD

INSPECTION LATCH

CRYOGENIC COOLING COILS

HAND GRIP (HOUSING ENERGY ACCUMULATOR PACK)

ACCUMULATOR PACK COVER

SIDE ELEVATION

ELECTRON SIGHTING BEAM EMITTER

ELECTRON SIGHTING ARRANGEMENT

RANGE CONTROL

PLAN VIEW

STATUS INDICATION READOUT

NOTE:

THIS DOCUMENT IS FOR FIRST STAGE FAMILIARIZATION PURPOSES ONLY

SEE VIDGRAPH 557THX 'PLASMA PRINCIPLE' FOR DETAILS OF WORKING THEORY

POWER CONNECTION LEAD

IN SYSTEM CONNECTOR

POWER FLOW ADJUSTER

| MODEL NUMBER/TYPE: | |
|---|---|
| SHORT RANGE PLASMA PISTOL | |
| CLASSIFICATION: | SECURITY CLASS: |
| PLS-B-PP2 | AV-5 |
| CONSTRUCTED BY: | |
| RESEARCH DIVISION – CONTRACTED TO EIGER VAULT LAMBERT TECHNOLOGIES | |
| DRAWN BY: | APP'D: |
| *Nic Weeks* | PJOHPP SHI |
| NIC WEEKS DESIGNS | |
| SHT: | |
| EXTERNAL VIEWS | |

VIEW SHOWING POWER CONNECTION LEAD (IN SYSTEM STATE)

should only be used when strictly necessary. Fortunately its ion drive is almost soundless. You are also issued with a homing beacon, which, when activated, will make the flyer move to its location as quickly as possible. The flyer is then piloted by its micro computer. The beacon is magnetic, and about the size of a coin.

ITEM 7: CAIN [Cybernetic Artificial Intelligence Nexus]
CAIN is one of the most advanced computers known to man. Its data banks offer information on all subjects and historical data on all Federation and alien planets. Its memory banks are continuously updated with information concerning the timeholes and it is able to link with the massive memory banks of the TIME Service Computer at the Eiger Vault. A holophone, through which you can contact any other holophone in the Federation, is built into CAIN and you also have access to most of the files kept by TIME. CAIN answers to your spoken commands and runs the time machine for you. It can display information visually, via the terminal screen, or verbally, using its melodic chimes.

ITEM 8: BLASTER
This is your standard SAT issue plasma pistol. It fires superheated plasma to a range of one hundred metres, and the energy pack is sufficient for ten minutes' continuous use. You have more energy packs in your weapons locker. Your blaster is labelled, 'For use in exceptional circumstances only'.

ITEM 9: PSIONIC ENHANCER
This helmet boosts your mind powers by damping all other thoughts. Neural sensors detect when you want to use your power and activate the device automatically.

ITEM 10: ENVIRONMENT SUIT
A light, pressurised suit for use in vacuum, inhospitable atmospheres and extreme ranges of temperature which monitors your life signals such as pulse and temperature. It is compatible with your psionic enhancer.

# PSIONIC ENHANCER

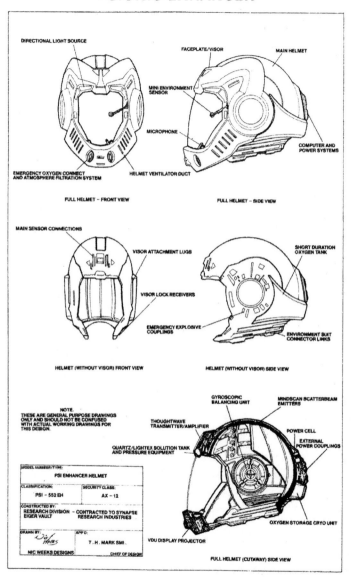

DIRECTIONAL LIGHT SOURCE

FACEPLATE/VISOR

MAIN HELMET

MINI ENVIRONMENT SENSOR

MICROPHONE

COMPUTER AND POWER SYSTEMS

EMERGENCY OXYGEN CONNECT AND ATMOSPHERE FILTRATION SYSTEM

HELMET VENTILATOR DUCT

FULL HELMET – FRONT VIEW

FULL HELMET – SIDE VIEW

MAIN SENSOR CONNECTIONS

VISOR ATTACHMENT LUGS

SHORT DURATION OXYGEN TANK

VISOR LOCK RECEIVERS

EMERGENCY EXPLOSIVE COUPLINGS

ENVIRONMENT SUIT CONNECTOR LINKS

HELMET (WITHOUT VISOR) FRONT VIEW

HELMET (WITHOUT VISOR) SIDE VIEW

NOTE.
THESE ARE GENERAL PURPOSE DRAWINGS ONLY AND SHOULD NOT BE CONFUSED WITH ACTUAL WORKING DRAWINGS FOR THIS DESIGN.

GYROSCOPIC BALANCING UNIT

MINDSCAN SCATTERBEAM EMITTERS

THOUGHTWAVE TRANSMITTER/AMPLIFIER

POWER CELL

EXTERNAL POWER COUPLINGS

QUARTZ/LIGHTEX SOLUTION TANK AND PRESSURE EQUIPMENT

| MODEL NUMBER/TYPE: | |
|---|---|
| PSI ENHANCER HELMET | |
| CLASSIFICATION: | SECURITY CLASS: |
| PSI – 552 EH | AX – 12 |
| CONSTRUCTED BY: | |
| RESEARCH DIVISION – CONTRACTED TO SYNAPSE EIGER VAULT – RESEARCH INDUSTRIES | |
| DRAWN BY: | APP'D: |
| NIC WEEKS DESIGNS | T . H . MARK SMI .   CHIEF OF DESIGN |

OXYGEN STORAGE CRYO UNIT

VDU DISPLAY PROJECTOR

FULL HELMET (CUTAWAY) SIDE VIEW

# ENVIRONMENT SUIT

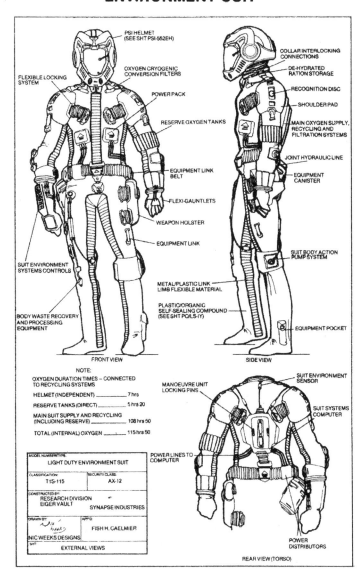

PSI HELMET
(SEE SHT PSI-552EH)

OXYGEN CRYOGENIC
CONVERSION FILTERS

FLEXIBLE LOCKING
SYSTEM

POWER PACK

RESERVE OXYGEN TANKS

EQUIPMENT LINK
BELT

FLEXI-GAUNTLETS

WEAPON HOLSTER

EQUIPMENT LINK

SUIT ENVIRONMENT
SYSTEMS CONTROLS

BODY WASTE RECOVERY
AND PROCESSING
EQUIPMENT

FRONT VIEW

COLLAR INTERLOCKING
CONNECTIONS

DE-HYDRATED
RATION STORAGE

RECOGNITION DISC

SHOULDER PAD

MAIN OXYGEN SUPPLY,
RECYCLING AND
FILTRATION SYSTEMS

JOINT HYDRAULIC LINE

EQUIPMENT
CANISTER

SUIT BODY ACTION
PUMP SYSTEM

METAL/PLASTIC LINK
LIMB FLEXIBLE MATERIAL

PLASTIC/ORGANIC
SELF-SEALING COMPOUND
(SEE SHT PO/LS-IY)

EQUIPMENT POCKET

SIDE VIEW

NOTE:
OXYGEN DURATION TIMES – CONNECTED
TO RECYCLING SYSTEMS

HELMET (INDEPENDENT) _____ 7 hrs

RESERVE TANKS (DIRECT) _____ 5 hrs 20

MAIN SUIT SUPPLY AND RECYCLING
(INCLUDING RESERVE) _____ 108 hrs 50

TOTAL (INTERNAL) OXYGEN _____ 115 hrs 50

SUIT ENVIRONMENT
SENSOR

MANOEUVRE UNIT
LOCKING PINS

SUIT SYSTEMS
COMPUTER

POWER LINES TO
COMPUTER

POWER
DISTRIBUTORS

REAR VIEW (TORSO)

| MODEL NUMBER/TYPE: LIGHT DUTY ENVIRONMENT SUIT | |
|---|---|
| CLASSIFICATION: T1S-115 | SECURITY CLASS: AX-12 |
| CONSTRUCTED BY: RESEARCH DIVISION EIGER VAULT | SYNAPSE INDUSTRIES |
| DRAWN BY: Nic Weeks NIC WEEKS DESIGNS | APP'D: FISH H. GAELMIER |
| SHT EXTERNAL VIEWS | |

# PERSONAL BACKGROUND

Special Agent (TIME)
Codename: Falcon

For three years you have studied at the Academy as a cadet attached to TIME: the Temporal, Investigative and Monitoring Executive, and you have passed the difficult training programme with flying colours. You have been selected from the Academy to be a Special Agent because of your unusual talents, having been born with psionic aptitude. You can sense things that others can't and even influence their actions through thought alone. These powers have been strengthened and focussed during your training and you have been issued with a psionic enhancer, a helmet which increases these mental powers. You have been taught to attack the minds of others with a blast of mental energy you call Thinkstrike. Your Power of Will allows you to control the minds of those weaker than you, and your Psi Sense allows you to sense things that others cannot, including the presence of another with such mental powers. This Psi Sense also lets you navigate your time machine through time and space. Few have such powers and even fewer are trusted with one of the small number of time machines in existence.

You are expert in survival and in combat, armed and unarmed. History and detective powers of deduction have also been major subjects of study. You are now a Special Agent in the Time Police, whose job is to guard the timelines of the past and to ensure that no-one tampers with past events in any way that would change things as they are now.

TIME, the Temporal Investigative and Monitoring Executive, was set up in Alpolis forty years ago shortly after time travel was discovered. The realisation that anyone with access to time travel could change the past so that the entire human race might cease to exist was worrying, so time machines were built for the Time Police in their crystal domed TIME headquarters, in order to stop this. TIME is headed by five Lords, representing the most powerful groups in the

Space Federation. Each of these has Powers of the Mind, and their own time machine.

The Executive is divided into four sections: Administrative, Research, Monitoring and the Special Agent Section (or SAS). The Monitoring Section, headed by Section Chief Jobanque, is responsible for noting any disturbances in the past, or timelines, of the planets in the Federation. The Research Section, headed by Section Chief Skirrow is responsible for all equipment used by Special Agents and is also examining the possibilities of travel into the future, as yet impossible. Your own Special Agent Section is headed by Section Chief Agidy Yelov, a Siriun humanoid from the Federation member planet, Sirius Secundus. Agidy Yelov and others have told you the importance of the First Law of TIME when on active service: 'A TIME Agent must, in all cases, act naturally according to the time in which he or she is currently operating, thus minimising any disruption of the timelines his or her presence might be causing'. As Yelov once said to you: 'There's no point in coming back to 3033 if you have left an atomic hand gun near Hitler's bunker, because this would change the present – in fact, you'd probably find you had never existed!' As with all Special Agents, your bloodline has been traced back as far as surviving records permit, in your case to the French Revolution in 1789 AD. Should any one of your ancestors fail to produce the next in line it would be as if you had never existed.

### HINTS ON PLAY

Your mission to find the renegade lord is a race against time, Falcon. You must catch up with the lord before history can be changed or you will have failed, perhaps never have existed at all. You may find it useful to make a note of the places and times to which you travel so that you can form an idea of where to go next.

The rules are very simple – you could almost play this book without reading them at all. But reading the Personal Background and of course, the Mission Briefing will help you to understand what is happening as you begin the adventure.

If you come across something you don't understand, don't worry, check the Equipment List and this may give you a clue. If not, carry on anyway, it will probably come clear later.

Good luck, and remember, the fate of the Space Federation rests in your hands.

## MISSION BRIEFING

Touching the pad which changes the walls of your home to tranquil white you casually note how smart you look in your dress uniform in the mirror wall. It is less than an hour to your graduation ceremony, when you will stand before the Lords of TIME in the Hall of Honours and, taking these moments to relax, you remember the excitement of simulated ship-to-ship combat, the long hours of concentration as you worked on your Powers of the Mind, and the fascinating vid-lectures on history that were part of your course at the Academy. Though you excelled in all of these things, you are well aware that the job which you began officially today as a Special Agent of the Time Police will be the most challenging of any Federation citizen. The responsibility of guarding the past for all who live today weighs heavily but such sobering thoughts are interrupted by the quiet tone of your holophone.

You click your fingers and the remote accepts contact. Your section commander, Agidy Yelov, seems to appear in the room before you. The slitted pupils of his amber eyes narrow as they adapt to the white light. Tall, lean and cat-like, Yelov looks imposing in his steel grey uniform, his blue-black hair framing a face which betrays nothing. 'Falcon, I must see you before the ceremony. Come straight to my office.' He taps his desk, breaking the hob-link and vanishing before you can reply. Seconds later, you are on the moving pedway leading to his office in the Security Wing of TIME headquarters. As you leave the domed apartment, the blue sky is clear, and it is due to remain so for a further 4.5 days.

The door to Yelov's office slides open at your touch – the building's service computer recognises your fingerprints. Agidy Yelov, standing before his com-console, beckons you in. 'Your pardon for this untimely intrusion, please be seated.' It is only as you step through the doorway that you notice Yelov is not alone. Jobanque, head of the Monitoring Section, is lying on a couch, a welcoming smile stretching his black features. You sit and the chair expands with a hiss to fit you snugly. Looking at Yelov, you might think him nervous if you didn't believe he is unable to feel anxiety. 'I have no time for the usual pleasantries.' His voice is hard. 'I know that this is your first mission, but Jobanque and I have picked you because you're the best person I've got. The fate of every being in the Federation and billions beyond will depend on you. We have lost an Agent. Q has been killed while on active service, investigating a disturbance of the timeline of the planet Kelados. It seems he had found out who was responsible.'

Jobanque speaks next. 'His final transmission reported that he had identified the culprit as a Lord of TIME.' He pauses to watch your reaction to this incredible news. 'Unfortunately, Q died before he could tell us which one of the Lords is trying to change the past in order to gain power here and now, in 3033.'

Yelov continues brusquely: 'Of course, we can't arrest them all. They are our superiors and it is a difficult situation, particularly as far as the alien Lords of TIME are concerned. Because of this your mission has to be completely unofficial, but we must arrest or terminate the renegade Lord as soon as we have proof and before anything disastrous occurs. When you have proof, do whatever you feel is necessary, Falcon. Is that understood?'

'Understood,' you reply.

Yelov continues: 'It will be a race against time. You may need to deal with an attempt to change the past within the next few hours.'

'Yes,' Jobanque breaks in, 'Q had already foiled one attempt in the Kelados timeline, in 2710 AD. He was a fine agent. It is too late for you to do anything to save him. Time passes in the timeholes at the same rate as it passes in the present and if you travelled back to the same hole you would arrive after his death. I have identified an even earlier timehole on Kelados, but Skirrow's men in the Tech Section say we can't send you back there and put you into cold sleep, to awaken at the time of Q's arrival, because of the rapid ageing effect of being away from your own time for extended periods.'

'Your machine is ready in the Eiger Vault,' Yelov goes on. 'We have no idea what the renegade Lord's next move will be but all the Lords will attend your graduation ceremony. All five of their time machines are logged in at the Vault, so none of them are meddling with the past as we speak. Go to your ceremony but remember, one of them is a traitor, a traitor to TIME and to the Space Federation. Good luck, Falcon. If you are not successful we may never meet again…'

As you turn to the door, Jobanque rises and says: 'We'll be seeing you. Falcon.' You salute and leave, to begin your search for the renegade Lord, wondering whether in fact you will ever see them or any of your friends again. The fate of worlds rests on your shoulders.

Now turn to **1**.

# AGENT PROFILE

## Codename: FALCON

Attached to TIME Executive, Special Agent Section
Security Clearance Code: EPSILON

### Attack modifier

| 0 | | | | | | | | | |
|---|---|---|---|---|---|---|---|---|---|

### Evasion modifier

| 0 | | | | | | | | | |
|---|---|---|---|---|---|---|---|---|---|

### Endurance

20

### Standard Issue field equipment

Model a3 time machine
Plasma pistol
Universal translator
Spacetime map
Hologram detector
Psionic enhancer helmet
Environment suit

## Powers of the mind

### Thinkstrike modifier

| 0 | | | | | | | | | |
|---|---|---|---|---|---|---|---|---|---|

### Power of Will modifier

| 0 | | | | | | | | | |
|---|---|---|---|---|---|---|---|---|---|

## Special Items

## Notes

## References

| | |
|---|---|
| FILE NO: | FILE NO: |
| FILE NO: | FILE NO: |
| FILE NO: | FILE NO: |

## 1

### [score a Q]

The door hums closed behind you as you step out of the high security wing which houses Section Chief Yelov's offices. Boarding the pedway you request the time. The service computer responds from a nearby speaker: 'It is three minutes, fifteen seconds to your appointment with the Lords of TIME at 10am, Falcon. If you would care to step into Lane 9, I can see that you arrive in time.' Realising that you have only a few moments to prepare, you transfer lanes and open a link to CAIN, punching in your security clearance code on your Remote Access Terminal (RAT), a flexible keyboard and visual display incorporated into the left forearm of your uniform which you can use to communicate with CAIN via the building's service computer. The link opens. Do you:

| | |
|---|---|
| Ask to see Special Agent Q's Termination Report? | Turn to **14** |
| Ask to see the last transmission that Special Agent Q submitted to Agidy Yelov? | Turn to **36** |
| Ask CAIN why Section Chief Yelov gave you so little warning about your mission prior to your ceremony? | Turn to **60** |

## 2

You leap across Ogedei's bed, putting the older general between yourself and the Emperor's guard. Make an **Attack Roll** as they rush at you with swords drawn.

If you score 8-12, turn to **113**

If you score 2-6, turn to **356**

If you score 7, roll again.

## 3

Your blow lands and the bear retreats into its cave, grunting with pain. You quickly board your flyer and decide to fly over the city.

Turn to **63**.

Lord Speke's mind falls under your control. You hold him there as Alexander, exhausted, drops his sword again. Some of his men arrive in time to defend him. Within moments the tide of battle is turned completely and the Macedonians, driven wild by the danger to their king, begin to massacre the townspeople. Alexander is borne away by several soldiers to be tended by the doctors in his tent. When the danger is past and the battle moved on, you take Lord Speke up to the hills. Looking into his mind you see that he has been breaking the First Law of TIME and living as an ancient Greek. He has always been careful not to upset the timelines seriously, but he knows he has been acting wrongly. His collection of ancient Greek weapons in his time machine is authentic and he has even buried ancient artifacts in places where he could 'discover' them as archaeological finds in the 31st century.

Speke is not the renegade Lord, and you release him from your control. Tears run down his face as he realises his hobby is over. 'At least', he says, 'I can say I saw the man whose people thought he was a god.' He asks you how you discovered him and you tell him about your mission. He is shocked by the news of a traitor Lord but offers a few words of advice: 'It is not likely to be either Pilota or myself. We are both Earther stock and interference with Earth's past might mean that we had never existed.'

You thank Speke but feel obliged to order him to return to 3033 AD and give himself up. Downcast, he agrees and returns to his time machine while you continue with your mission.

Turn to **272**.

He leaps at you. You grab for your blaster and trigger it just in time. A white bolt of superheated plasma eats into his chest. To your surprise, sparks fly and there is the unmistakable tang of vaporised metals. A nearby plasma sensor begins to flash and the siren of a Citpol jetcopter wails as the 'cydroid' buckles, short-circuiting in a sea of sparks, before falling inert.

You have been fighting a machine. You examine it, but the damage is too severe for you to gain a clue as to its origins before two Enforcers alight from their 'copter, pointing their stun-lances at you. 'Let's see your ID'. You produce your ID chip and hand it to the one who spoke, still covered by the other. He clips it into the Remote Access Terminal (RAT) on his arm and a look of disappointment crosses his features as he realises who you are. 'What's been going on here?' he says. You report exactly what happened and he returns your chip and turns to examine the cydroid.

Turn to **137**.

## 6

Knowing that Lynx is trained in the use of powers of the mind, you make a special effort to try to overcome her mental defences. Make a **Thinkstrike Roll:**

If you score 7-12, turn to **118**
If you score 2-6, turn to **85**

## 7

The ambulance trundles on towards Napoleon and you sense that the renegade Lord is reaching out to control the Emperor's mind. You can no longer see Bloodhound and decide to attack when Napoleon begins to order the Imperial Guard to advance. As you do so, the renegade Lord becomes aware of you and a wave of mental energy flows into you – your brain goes haywire. You seem to feel hot, cold, rain and fire all at once. It is as if you can see all colours at the same time and myriad voices speak every word in every language you have ever studied. Your brain overheats, literally burning itself out like a faulty electric motor. You are a zombie, incapable of thought, gurgling like a baby. You have failed.

## 8

A hand-axe, thrown by one of the Imperial Guardsmen strikes the back of your knee and you fall to the floor and are taken. The fate of the Khan's assassin is not a pleasant one. They discuss your punishment, which will be to have molten silver poured into your eyes and ears before you are boiled alive – a death reserved for their respected enemies. You have failed and the Space Federation will never be.

### 9

Your attack fails and is returned by a mental blast far more powerful than your own. You sink to the ground feeling as if your brain is boiling. Your brain is about to burn out like a faulty electric motor when the renegade Lord's attention is shifted to Bloodhound who is making an attack of his own, saving your life as he does so. You fall unconscious and your powers of Thinkstrike will never again be what they were. *Subtract one from your Thinkstrike Modifier.*

When you awake, Bloodhound is coming round, lying next to you. You shake your head to clear the pain and look up to see that the Imperial Guard are marching to the attack. The renegade Lord is changing history. You both begin to run up the hillside and the ambulance comes into view a hundred yards away from the Emperor.

Turn to **344**.

### 10

You step from the pedway at an interchange but dart into a construction tunnel leading down to Old Geneva on the lower levels. As you emerge into the lowlife area of the city the stench of sewers bathes you. The dark, squat buildings are made of old-fashioned concrete. A few even are of bricks, which you have only seen before in architectural museums. The Enforcers of Citpol seldom penetrate to these depths, preferring to leave the lowlifers to their own devices. There are no pedways or plasma sensors down here, just graffiti and cracked tarmac. You plunge into a blank-eyed crowd of leisure zombies, milling around the sim-combat booths, unnoticed, and unfollowed. You search for a different way back to the upper levels.

Turn to **201**.

## 11

You splash your way into the pond and grab for the rope ladder which is hanging from your flyer. Shouts ring out behind you and an arrow hits you in the bottom as you climb. You pull it out but are losing blood. *Lose 4 Endurance points.* Panting, you kneel in the cockpit and fire up the flyer's drive and the ladder slowly retracts. The flyer rocks unsteadily as if the stabilisers were malfunctioning. Looking down, you see the dark eyes, wide with fright, of a Mongol guard swinging from the ladder, a torch burning in his hand. You dip the flyer down across the pool, plunging him into the water and the flyer bucks skyward as he falls from the ladder. Realising that all of the guards on the ground are now alerted you decide to risk hovering above the palace roof, hoping to find the balcony on which Ogedei appeared earlier. Turn to **28**.

## 12

The Creche are weakened. There are only five of them left alive, and you are combining your powers. Make a **Thinkstrike Roll**.

If you score 7-12, turn to **83**
If you score 2-6, turn to **204**

## 13

You cannot control Speke, his mind is too strong, but he has realised you are here. Alexander, exhausted, drops his sword and Speke, picking it up, defends him from attack. Within moments, the tide of battle is turned completely and the Macedonians, driven wild by the danger to their king, begin to massacre the townspeople. Alexander is borne away by several soldiers to be tended by the doctors in his tent. When the danger is past and the battle moved on, Lord Speke approaches carrying Alexander's sword and gives himself up. You walk up into the hills, and he explains that for some time he has been breaking the First Law of TIME and living as an ancient Greek. He has always been careful not to upset the timelines seriously but he knows he has been acting wrongly. His collection of ancient Greek weapons in his time machine is authentic and he has even buried ancient artifacts in places where he could 'discover' them as archaeological finds in the 31st century. You look into his mind, with his consent, and see that it is all true – Speke is not the renegade Lord. Tears run down his face as he realises his hobby is over. 'At least,' he says, 'I can say I saw the man whose people thought he was a god.' He asks you how you discovered him and you tell him about your mission. He is shocked by the news of a traitor Lord but offers a few words of advice. 'It is not likely to be either Pilota, or myself – we are both Earther stock and interference with Earth's past might mean that we had never existed.' You thank Speke but feel obliged to order him to return to 3033 AD and give himself up. Downcast, he agrees and returns to his time machine while you continue with your mission.

Turn to **272**.

## 14

You give your Epsilon security code and the micro-display on your wrist lights up. The report on Q's death seems surprisingly brief:

| | |
|---|---|
| Termination Report: | TIME Special Agent Q. Born: 1/9/2890 AD – Lastlanding (Outer Colonies). Killed on active service |
| Cause of death: | Autodoc malfunction |
| Mission brief at time of death: | Monitor disturbance in Kelados timeline 2047 AD |
| Last known action: | Transmission to Sector Chief Yelov, Security Code Epsilon, interrupted subject: Kelados timeline disturbance. |

End of Report
Message Ends

To your certain knowledge, there has not been an officially recognised autodoc malfunction in seventeen years. As you approach the Hall of Honours you realise there is still time to call up Agent Q's last, interrupted, report. You re-open your link with CAIN.

Turn to **36**.

## File

| | |
|---|---|
| SUBJECT: | Yelov, Agidy |
| POSITION: | Head of Special Agent Section, TIME |
| SPECIES: | Siriun |
| BORN: | Sirius Secundus, 2940 AD |
| LIVES: | TIME Headquarters, Alpolis, Earth |

## Personality

Efficient, calm, and a good leader. Yelov is sparing with words but what he says usually counts. He has had a glittering career in the Siriun Navy as a test pilot for time travel and now within the Temporal Investigative and Monitoring Executive. He is ambitious and dedicated to his work. His close friends all belong to the small community of Siriuns living on Earth. He is much respected, if not well liked and his standing within TIME is high. He is extremely deadly, proficient in most forms of combat and was personally responsible for the training of Special Agent Lynx in this area.

## Homeworld

Sirius Secundus. Population: 12.576 billion. Sirius Secundus is a world similar to Earth but cooler, rich in minerals, and with a strong economy. As the sun, Sirius, gradually wanes the Siriuns are beginning to emigrate in increasing numbers from their dying world.

## Diplomatic History

The Siriuns are fiercely independent members of the Space Federation, which they joined in order to gain the secrets of space travel. Trade between Sirius and other worlds is now flourishing.

**End of File**

## 16
### [score a K]

The flyer hovers above the darkest part of the palace gardens and you release the rope ladder from its edge. You climb down cautiously, unable to see the ground; it is black as pitch. You step down off the ladder and catch your breath as you find yourself waist deep in freezing water. You have climbed down into the ornamental pond. You stand still, waiting to see if you've been heard, then wade out trying not to splash and walk stealthily between cherry trees towards the torch-lights of the palace. Pausing to take stock of your surroundings you notice two guards at the rear of the palace, guarding a small wooden door. Nearby is a low wooden building with several horses tethered to posts outside it. Do you:

| | |
|---|---|
| Thinkstrike the two guards? | Turn to **369** |
| Try to control them both, using your Power of Will? | Turn to **377** |
| Pull out your blaster and fry them? | Turn to **387** |

## 17

Your mind is gripped like a vice and there is nothing you can do as your hand is forced inside your jacket. Sweating with effort, you try to stop yourself aiming your blaster at Bloodhound. Your arm quivers as you line him up in your sights. Bloodhound realises what is happening and reaches for his own blaster. Too late. The lightning bolt of plasma hurls him into the wheel of the ambulance and his corpse slumps, a grotesque travesty of a human being. Your eyes are riveted on the muzzle of your death-dealing blaster as, inch by inch, you are forced to point it at yourself. Your hand is still shaking but your finger closes on the trigger and the left half of your face and head is wiped away. You have failed.

Your opponent's reactions are even faster than yours. He catches your leg in his hand and then, with amazing strength, begins to crush it slowly. Pain overcomes you and you pass out, never to come round. You have failed.

You bank and dive as twin laser pulses from the Phocian flash past your ship into the blackness of space. Then the Phocian increases speed. A third, larger ship appears on the scanner, beyond an asteroid belt, and the Corsair changes course to intercept. You match course and increase speed as a second message reaches you, this time from the larger ship: 'This is the clanship *Keladan III*. We are on a priority diplomatic mission. Do not attack; repeat, do not attack. Change course. We are Keladi. Do not attack.'

You realise that this is the convoy ship carrying Korakiik, and that they will soon be within the attack range of the Phocian Corsair. Do you:

| | |
|---|---|
| Open fire on the Phocian Corsair with your ship's pulse lasers? | Turn to **141** |
| Wait to see what happens? | Turn to **104** |

The battle is fierce but soon Bloodhound is attacking your mind and before you can recover he has blasted you again. You double up as the plasma bolt hits your side – *lose 13 Endurance points.* If you are still alive, you find yourself too stunned to do anything. Bloodhound walks over to your stricken body and levels his weapon for the final blast.

'Wait, Bloodhound! Kill me and the population of all Earth and the colonies may perish. I am helpless, but look at CAIN's memory banks before you void me.'

He hesitates, then drags you into Falcon's Wing and ties you up. Examining CAIN's records, it soon becomes obvious to him that you are on a vitally important mission and that his mission to kill you must be abandoned. He unties you, but your wounds are so bad you must *subtract one from your*

*Evasion Modifier.* Bloodhound says, 'I'm sorry, Falcon. Somebody's been using me – somebody who wants the timelines to be changed.'

'Who gave the order to kill me?'

'Our Section Chief, Agidy Yelov. He told me you had killed Lord Kirik.'

'But Kirik has only been dead a matter of minutes,' you tell him.

Bloodhound pauses, then says, 'Yes, of course, Falcon, how can he know of Kirik's death so soon? Either he was responsible or he is in league with the traitor that did it.'

Your Section Chief is working with the renegade Lord. Turn to **99**.

## 21

Bloodhound shouts: 'No, Falcon, Thinkstrike!' Too late, you realise you have made a mistake, for the Creche, although reduced in number to five, are masters of mind control. They take you over, and you draw your blaster and kill Bloodhound before he realises what is happening. Staring in horror at what you have done, you feel your hand turning the blaster towards your own head. The last thing you see before you kill yourself is Agidy Yelov stepping from behind the time machine of the Creche. Only Lynx is left to defeat him and the renegade Lord. You have failed.

## 22

You leave the Hall of Honours *en route* for the Eiger Vault and your time machine, and approach the hovrail, calling a car to the nearest embarkation point using CAIN and the service computer.

Stepping from the TIME building pedway, you emerge into the cityscape, to be dwarfed by the tiered office blocks surrounded by housing for the workers and the prodmarkets which supply them. Jetcopters hum overhead like streams of flies, each one darting or circling, its pilot intent on reaching particular destinations. The lower level streets and pedways are thick with people. Those streets which curve up to the higher levels and along the buttresses of the larger buildings bear a steady flow of skimmers, runners sparking as they contact the electrified streetmetal.

Some way from the embarkation point you realise that you are being followed. You step from the pedway onto the deserted bay of a warehouse. The anonymous figure of an office worker in a one-piece suit steps off the pedway behind you. Do you:

| | |
|---|---|
| Use your Power of Will to control your follower? | Turn to **44** |
| Duck into a doorway and wait to confront him at close quarters? | Turn to **81** |
| Slip through the warehouse and lose your pursuer in the lowlife area, Old Geneva? | Turn to **10** |

### 23

The din of the battle is like a maelstrom around you. Swept on towards Alexander and Speke, you concentrate your mind. You hurl a blast of mental energy at Lord Speke remembering, too late, that his mental defences against Thinkstrike are almost invincible. Speke is unaffected. You lose confidence in your Thinkstrike ability; *subtract one from your Thinkstrike Modifier.* Do you:

| | |
|---|---|
| Use your blaster to kill Lord Speke? | Turn to **41** |
| Use your Power of Will to control Lord Speke? | Turn to **32** |

### 24
#### [score a K]

Clone's mind is a maze of violent and selfish impulses, easily controlled. You make him call off his gang and in amazement they goggle as you force Clone to let you climb up behind him. 'But Machine is dead,' cries one of the women.

Before they can protest further, Clone whisks you away to the edge of Old Geneva and you relinquish control of his mind as you step onto the pedway once more. 'I'll get you for this, mutie mind-scrambler. They'll never follow me now. I'll remember you…'

He is still raving as you near the hovrail embarkation point. Turn to **169**.

## 25

You concentrate your will in a great effort to overcome Lynx, knowing that she has trained for these forms of mental combat and that she will put up a hard struggle. Make a **Power of Will Roll.**

If you score 7-12, turn to **135**
If you score 2-6, turn to **184**

## 26

You concentrate on an infantry man who has just reloaded his musket and is passing nearby, and try to control him. Make a **Power of Will Roll**.

If you score 5-12, turn to **35**
If you score 2-4, turn to **411**

## 27

A lancing white bolt of superheated plasma misses your target and smashes a hole in the end wall of the corridor. One of the guards fires his laser rifle as the other runs towards you. He wings you in the side: *lose 4 Endurance points.* Then two security droids arrive and your assailants run back down the corridor, darting out of sight. You give your Security Clearance Code and identify yourself. Satisfied, the security droids chase the two would-be assassins and you return to the safety of Falcon's Wing. Turn to **336**.

## 28

The flyer hovers above the palace roof and you jump down from it onto the wood slats, then swing over the edge of the roof and drop to the torch-lit balcony below. As you do so you are noticed by some people in the palace courtyard. There is an uproar. You see that silk curtains are spread across the entrance to the room. Parting them you enter a bedchamber. Inside, sitting on a large litter, swaddled in silks and furs, is

Ogedei Khan, still weak from his illness. He looks up, his narrow eyes questioning your purpose. Golden statues, treasure chests and tapestries line the walls. The door opens and two men burst in brandishing swords, alerted by the noise of the crowd. One is a member of the Khan's Imperial Guard, dressed immaculately in black and gold lacquered armour, the other an older man, a general or 'noyan', wearing a simple wrap-around leather cloak lined with fur. You have no time to draw your blaster as they close to attack. Do you:

| | |
|---|---|
| Try to Thinkstrike them both? | Turn to **54** |
| Use your skill at unarmed combat? | Turn to **2** |

### 29

You flip the safety on your blaster and the charge light registers. You take aim. Make an **Attack Roll**.

If you scored 2-5, turn to **162**

If you scored 6-12, turn to **108**

### 30

You dismount and walk towards the new mental presence, looking carefully around. Suddenly a drummer boy who had been wandering forlornly up the hillside turns to you and speaks. To your surprise it is a woman's voice – that of Lynx, a Special Agent of TIME, like Bloodhound and yourself. The disguise is perfect. Her boyish features are smeared with mud from the battlefield. 'Falcon, Bloodhound, I have a Termination Order for you both from our leader, Agidy Yelov.' With that, she unleashes a hornet, a miniature guided missile, like an arrow with wings. It jets towards you. Do you:

| | |
|---|---|
| Try to blast the small and fast-moving hornet out of the air? | Turn to **47** |
| Run behind the ambulance which is drawing near? | Turn to **80** |

### 31

You both fire and twin streaks of white-hot lightning burn the Creche to a crisp before they reach the ground. You have defeated the renegade Lord. Turn to **188**.

## 32

The din of the battle is like a maelstrom around you. Swept on towards Alexander and Speke, you concentrate your mind. Speke, too, has mental powers and this will be a difficult struggle. Make a **Power of Will Roll.**

If you score 8-12, turn to **4**

If you score 2-6, turn to **13**

If you score 7, roll again.

## 33

As you take aim you are hit by the fragments of an energy grenade, fired by the weapon of the second guard, who has a launcher attached to his laser-rifle. You *lose 14 Endurance points.* If you are still alive you manage to blast. Make an **Attack Roll.**

If you score 6-12, turn to **57**

If you score 2-5, turn to **27**

## 34

While you are deciding what to do, next, blackness engulfs you. Someone has changed the timelines and one of your ancestors has been killed before his time. It is as if you had never existed. You have failed.

## 35

You bring the soldier under your control and force him to discharge his musket through a crack in the ambulance's side planking. Bloodhound suddenly tenses and, drawing his blaster, takes aim at you. You are about to dive onto the ground when the musket goes off and Bloodhound regains control of himself. You run up to the ambulance, but before you arrive the front explodes and a flyer accelerates out of it. Six giant ants, their red eyes glaring at you balefully, are clinging onto the honeycomb-like seats. One of them appears to have been killed by a musket ball. You realise it is the Hivers, Creche 82282. The Creche skim low through the smoke of the battlefield, almost faster than the eye can see, making a sonic boom like the explosion of a powder magazine, the ammunition stores for the cannon. As they go you catch the thought that they are heading for the planet Hel. You have succeeded in preserving the past and decide to follow the Creche to Hel.

Turn to **161.**

## 36

You give your Epsilon Security Code and the micro-display on your wrist lights up:

SECURITY CLEARANCE CODE INSUFFICIENT
ACCESS DENIED

Knowing that your Epsilon Security Code should be high enough to gain access, you request the level of Security Code necessary. CAIN responds with the information that this report has been reclassified: Access Code Theta. Theta is the level of Security Clearance held by Section Chiefs, and Special Agents cannot cause information to be classified at this level. The Service Computer intones softly: 'You have arrived at the Hall of Honours. Your graduation is about to commence.'

Turn to **110.**

## 37

The Emperor, bewildered by the mental attacks of the Creche, falls easily under your control. You force him to give the order that recalls the Imperial Guard and the attack does not take place. Deprived of reinforcements, Marshal Ney does not fling his men into another attack and both sides, exhausted, are reduced to the occasional cannonade. The French have won, but it is not a decisive victory. Thirty thousand Frenchmen are dead or wounded; the Russians have lost ten thousand more. The battlefield is strewn with the dead and dying and they are piled in mounds around the redoubts. You have made sure that history is not changed and you decide to return to Falcon's Wing and follow the Creche to the planet Hel.

Turn to **161.**

## 38

You draw the sabre which is part of your uniform and parry Bloodhound's thrust. You have trained a little with the sword and are able to frustrate most of Bloodhound's attacks as he forces you steadily backwards. Make an **Evasion Roll.**

If you score 7-12, turn to **74**

If you score 2-6, turn to **61**

## 39

Your mental barrier throws off the mind attack of the drummer boy, and you recognise Lynx, another Special Agent of TIME. The disguise is perfect, her boyish features smeared with mud from the battlefield. Like Bloodhound was, she may well be trying to kill you. Do you:

| | |
|---|---|
| Thinkstrike her back? | Turn to **6** |
| Use your Power of Will on her? | Turn to **25** |
| Use your blaster to kill her? | Turn to **59** |
| Explain to her that she must not attack you? | Turn to **96** |

## 40

The guards are already drunk on koumiss, fermented mare's milk, and slump to the floor. You slip into the courtyard beyond the gate and approach the palace itself but are faced with another group of guards, resplendent in red and white lacquered armour, who have seen their comrades fall. Seeing you appear suddenly through the gate they cry out and others come running towards you from a nearby barracks, some drawing swords, others readying their bows. Do you:

| | |
|---|---|
| Pull out your blaster and use it on them? | Turn to **139** |
| Run back out of the city, hoping to lose them? | Turn to **156** |

## 41

A white-hot bolt, like lightning, shoots from your blaster, felling Lord Speke. Alexander stares at you in shock, but some of the Macedonians behind you, thinking that you are an evil spirit trying to kill their king, bury their swords in your back. Alexander is slain while his attention is on you and you die together. You have failed.

## 42

You hurl a blast of mental energy at Clone, gesturing majestically as you do so, hoping to scare the low-life gang off. Clone collapses and his bike spins like a top. The others hesitate, astonished. Make a **Chance Roll**.

If you score 1-3, turn to **72**
If you score 4-6, turn to **91**

## 43

Ripping the ambulance doors open reveals a bizarre sight, six creatures like giant ants, mandibles clicking in agitation are backing into a honeycomb structure, their dull, red, compound eyes menacing. One shrivels as the white-hot plasma from your blaster hits home; they were concentrating on controlling Napoleon once more. The honeycomb is on top of a flyer similar in design to your own, and you both throw yourselves back to the ground outside to avoid the ion drive exhaust as the flyer explodes from the front of the ambulance. You sense that the six Hiver beings who together are Lord Creche, the renegade Lord, are flying back to their time machine, with one exception. The victim of your Thinkstrike had not reached his seat in the honeycomb. Toppling backwards as the flyer took off, it was vaporised by the ion drive. Quickly you search the ambulance and find a small capsule. It is an Interstellar Code, a message from Agidy Yelov to the Creche suggesting that if the mission is aborted, they should effect a rendezvous on planet Hel. As quickly as you can, after checking that the Emperor's Imperial Guard are not advancing, you decide to follow the Creche.

Turn to **161**.

## 44

You concentrate your mind but find no thought patterns to latch onto! Your pursuer is evidently either a cydroid or a robot of advanced design. Do you:

Duck into a doorway and wait to
    confront him at close quarters?                 Turn to **81**
Slip through the warehouse and
    lose your pursuer in the lowlife
    area, Old Geneva?                               Turn to **10**
Blast him?                                          Turn to **29**

## 45

Falcon's Wing rematerializes in the Eiger Vault and you
follow Bloodhound's hovrail car to TIME headquarters. You
are approaching the TIME building when you are suddenly
engulfed in blackness. Then you find yourself in a smoke-
filled shelter, a fugitive from an alien race on your own world.
The past has been changed and your memories with it. You
leap out of the shelter to hurl a grenade at a strange alien
aircraft on the street above you… As Falcon, Agent of TIME,
you have failed.

## 46

Without warning he levels his laser rifle at you as if to fire.
You have barely a second in which to save yourself. Make an
**Evasion Roll**.

If you score 7-12, turn to **192**
If you score 2-6, turn to **180**

## 47

The hornet quickly picks up speed as it jets towards you. This
a difficult test of your marksmanship. Make an **Attack Roll**.

If you score 8-12, turn to **65**
If you score 2-7, turn to **88**

## 48

You let loose a blast of mental energy, but to your
consternation, feel the interference effect of a psionic damper
circlet. These are a recent invention of the Hivers. You have no
option but to go for your blaster. As you draw your blaster the
energy weapon sensors trigger the sirens. If you can stay alive

a few moments longer, security droids will arrive. Make a **Chance Roll**.

If you score 1-4, turn to **208**
If you score 5 or 6, turn to **218**

### 49

The French have begun to launch an attack on the great earthen ramparts which the Russians are defending, and along the left-hand end of the Russian line. Great columns of blue-coated soldiers toil uphill towards their green-jacketed enemies. The guns roar and belch smoke and the crackle of musket fire begins. Both sides have magnificently dressed cavalry. Some of these, called Cuirassiers after the metal breastplates they wear, are big men mounted on what are almost cart-horses. Your own horses, bays, are much nimbler and more fleet of foot, and resemble those nearest to you, a battalion of Polish lancers under Prince Poniatowski's command. Their lance pennants, blue and white, flutter in the wind. Bloodhound asks whether you think it would be better to split up in order to search the battlefield more quickly or to stay together in case of danger. Do you:

Decide to split up?                      Turn to **408**
Stay together?                          Turn to **419**

### 50

You sense that your Thinkstrike has succeeded but still the mental power exists inside the ambulance, confirming that the renegade Lord is the Creche, the six Hiver beings that form one mind. You have knocked out one of them, weakening their power but they Thinkstrike back at you and you are unable to withstand the force of the mental blast even though it must be weakened. You sink unconscious to the ground. When you awake Bloodhound is lying next to you. You shake your heads to clear the pain and look up to see that the Imperial Guard are marching to the attack. The renegade Lord is changing history. You both begin to run up the hillside and the ambulance comes into view a hundred yards away from the Emperor. Turn to **344**.

## 51

You realise that controlling two others will be difficult, but bend your thoughts to the task. Luckily they are drunk on koumiss – fermented mare's milk. One of them removes a strip of raw meat from his sandal and begins to chew on it. The other laughs and says drunkenly: 'Now that you've pressed the blood out of it, can you not be bothered to dry it in the sun ?' Make a **Power of Will Roll**, as the smell of their unwashed bodies hits you.

If you score 7-12, turn to **257**
If you score 2-5, turn to **270**
If you score 6, roll again.

## 52

As you are drawn up into Falcon's Wing you are suddenly engulfed in blackness. Then you find yourself in a smoke-filled shelter, a fugitive from an alien race on your own world. The past has been changed and your memories with it. You leap out of the shelter to hurl a grenade at a strange alien craft on the street above you… You have failed in your mission.

## 53

As you approach the ambulance you both pick up another source of mental power, not so strong but even closer. Bloodhound says that he is going to investigate the newcomer before attacking. Do you:

Go with Bloodhound?                        Turn to **30**
Try to attack the renegade Lord alone?     Turn to **7**

## 54

You unleash a surge of mental energy at both of the Mongols. Make a **Thinkstrike Roll**.

If you score 7-12, turn to **103**
If you score 2-6, turn to **90**

## 55

Your blaster cuts down several of the bikers, including their leader, Clone, and more pile in to vehicles which career out of control, rocking on their cushions of air. But you don't have time to deal with them all.

Turn to **91**.

## 56

You call up the Free Fall Recreation Centre at Spiro's Ringworld, a massive wheel-like world-in-miniature orbiting the Earth. Their holo-coordinator seems to appear in your time machine. She is a striking girl, her skin tinted blue with orange flashes. She puts you through to Lord Pilota's personal assistant. He is a bony, hollow-cheeked man, showing signs of the Medawar Syndrome, the onset of rapid ageing. You identify yourself and ask for Her Lordship. The hologram winks out momentarily. When the holo-picture of the assistant reappears, he says: 'Lord Pilota is temporarily indisposed. Under no circumstances may she be contacted at the moment. If you would care to visit Spiro's Ringworld, however, she will be pleased to grant you immediate audience, as she believes she has some information which may interest you, as an Agent of the TIME Police.'

With that, he breaks contact and the blue-skinned coordinator informs you that the line has been closed to all callers. She asks: 'What is that weird spaceship you're in?' CAIN informs you that by requisitioning a shuttle from the Eiger Base you could dock at Spiro's Ringworld in eighteen minutes. Ignoring the holo-coordinator, you decide to set off for Spiro's Ringworld.

Turn to **335**

## 57

Your aim is true. A lancing white bolt of superheated plasma erupts against one of the guards. He is blown back against the end wall of the corridor and then slumps to the floor. The second guard runs off as two security droids arrive. You walk up to the fallen man after giving your Security Code to the hovering droids as they aim their stun-lasers at you. You identify yourself. Satisfied, they begin to hunt the second assassin. Your fallen assailant is dying, there is nothing you can do. You ask who sent him, and lean close to hear him gasp: 'Time Lord…', but the rest is lost in a spasm of coughing as he dies. You head back to the safety of Falcon's Wing.

Turn to **336**.

## 58

Suddenly an arrow glances from the shield which Alexander has taken from his fallen shield-bearer, and pierces his thigh. He stumbles and drops his sword. The archer rushes in to kill him but the King picks up his sword and, with a last great effort, runs the man through. Alexander is almost done for, but the Macedonians will reach him soon and Lord Speke is amongst the first of them. Do you:

| | |
|---|---|
| Use your Power of Will on Lord Speke? | Turn to **32** |
| Draw your blaster and kill Lord Speke? | Turn to **41** |
| Thinkstrike Lord Speke? | Turn to **23** |

## 59
### [score a D]

Lynx is well-trained in combat, but you pull out your blaster in a single blur of movement, knowing that she will attack your mind again if, in your haste, you miss. Make an **Attack Roll**.

If you score 7-12, turn to **168**
If you score 2-6, turn to **184**

## 60

You give your Epsilon Security Code and the micro-display on your wrist lights up: 'Section Chief Yelov unavailable at time of transmission. (Vacation.) Section Chief Jobanque (Head of TIM, Temporal Irregularity Monitoring), received last transmission of Agent Q, and passed to Section Chief Yelov on his return to active duty thirty-seven minutes before your meeting with Yelov.' Will you:

| | |
|---|---|
| Ask CAIN where Agidy Yelov spent his vacation? | Turn to **101** |
| Ask to see the last file which Special Agent Q transmitted to Agidy Yelov? | Turn to **36** |

Bloodhound is strong. The heavy butt of the musket narrowly misses your head, but smashes your collarbone and dislocates your shoulder. *Lose 8 Endurance points.* If you are still alive, your shoulder pops painfully back into its rightful place, you grab the musket and struggle with Bloodhound, rolling down the hillside together trying to wrench the musket from each other's grasp, Bloodhound tries to strangle and kick you and you are bruised and exhausted by the time you break the renegade Lord's control of his will. Bloodhound stops fighting and you both look up to see that the Imperial Guard are marching to the attack The renegade Lord is changing history. You begin to run up the hillside and the ambulance comes into view a hundred yards away from the Emperor.

Turn to **344.**

You wake up dazed in a detention cubicle at TIME headquarters. Your arms and legs are secured through holes in the couch upon which you are lying and you no longer have your helmet. You have been heavily sedated, but now you can see that the drummer boy was in fact Special Agent Lynx. She is still dressed in her drummer's uniform but her hair falls freely about her shoulders now that she has taken her shako-helmet off. She looks pleased with herself. Behind her, Yelov, amber eyes glinting, also looks satisfied. Suddenly all goes blank. Your last sight is of Yelov beginning to laugh as both you and Agent Lynx wink out. He has tricked her. It is as if you both had never existed. You have failed.

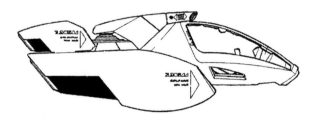

## 63

You cruise about the city, unseen in the darkness. Torches light some of the streets and there are fires at some of the crossroads around which people are dancing. Will you:

Hover above the pagoda-like roof of the
palace, which is well lit, and climb
down to the balcony where Ogedei
showed himself to the crowd?                   Turn to **28**

Hover above the gardens behind the
palace, which are large and unlit, and
climb down the flyer's rope ladder?       Turn to **16**

## 64

You drive your fist towards your pursuer's temple. Make an **Attack Roll.**

If you score 7-12, turn to **406**
If you score 2-6, turn to **233**

## 65

Your aim is true and the hornet explodes like a shell soon after it leaves Lynx's hands, startling her. You run in and aim a karate kick at her shins, while Bloodhound tries to wrestle her to the ground.

Turn to **339.**

## 66

The melee rages around you. The Macedonians, fighting with dreadful ferocity, are advancing towards Alexander, who is beset by soldiers, backed up against a tree, a ring of dead bodies surrounding him. The townspeople are hesitating before risking a cut from his sword, but the King is obviously tiring. Suddenly your Psi Sense tells you that Lord Speke is ahead of you, fighting his way towards Alexander.

Turn to **58**.

## 67

You force Napoleon to recall the Imperial Guard and Ney, deprived of his reinforcements, does not launch his men in another attack. Beside you, Bloodhound suddenly tenses and draws his blaster, as if to shoot you. Do you:

| | |
|---|---|
| Thinkstrike Bloodhound? | Turn to **292** |
| Use your blaster on him? | Turn to **248** |

## 68

Only one collapses, but the other clutches his head. He screams out: 'Evil spirits! Evil spirits! Help me!' Twenty or more guards come running from the building outside which the horses are tethered. Whispering together, they look out into the shadows fearfully. Strengthening their resolve, they fan out towards you in four groups, drawing their swords. You cannot use your blaster in the darkness. Do you:

| | |
|---|---|
| Run back to your flyer? | Turn to **401** |
| Hide in a stand of cherry trees? | Turn to **412** |

## 69

You pull out your blaster as the energy weapon sensors trigger the sirens. If you can stay alive a few moments longer security droids will arrive. Make a **Chance Roll.**

If you score 1-4, turn to **33**

If you score 5 or 6, turn to **158**

## 70

Your blast catches Bloodhound in the shoulder as he ducks, and spins him backwards towards the gas-tank that is in fact his time machine. He staggers inside the hologram and you hear the sound of the hatch opening. Do you:

| | |
|---|---|
| Rise up through the hatch, blasting? | Turn to **146** |
| Use your Power of Will to try to control him? | Turn to **95** |

## 71

You approach the second Phocian Corsair ship and notice a guard on watch. Your Psi Sense tells you nothing, but he is not alert. You decide to Thinkstrike him and the power of your mental attack makes the tired guard unconscious. You board the sleek, arrow-shaped ship, passing through the small hold and up the stairwell to the bridge and sleeping quarters. These small ships were built for a one- or two- man operation Their design is archaic to your eyes, but the ship computer assists you to pilot the vessel. The scanners show the other Phocian ship climbing into orbit, soon to leave the atmosphere Wasting no time, you secure yourself in the oddly-shaped, free fall couch, and gun the Phocian pirate ship into the sky, on the trail of her sister ship. As you clear the atmosphere, locked on to the other Phocian's course, its pilot hails you on the ship-to-ship lascom. Your ship computer picks up the coded bursts of low intensity laser light and converts them to speech. 'Why are you following me?' Do you:

| | |
|---|---|
| Ignore the laser communication? | Turn to **136** |
| Tell the Phocian that he is under mind control? | Turn to **155** |
| Open fire on the Phocian with the ship's pulse lasers? | Turn to **172** |

## 72

'A mental! A mutie mental!' shouts one of the gang, starting a hysterical screaming. Some drag Clone's hovbike to safety while others turn tail and scud into the maze of alleys crisscrossing the old city. Thankful that they are terrified of psionics, you find your way out of Old Geneva as quickly as possible and make your way to the hovrail embarkation point.

Turn to **169**.

## 73

While you dismount and look around, trying to locate the source of the mental powers which you sense, an infantry battalion passes you, marching to the attack. You are within a hundred yards of Marshal Poniatowski and his staff when the battalion's drummer boy, in the rear rank, stops drumming and turns towards you. You look at him suspiciously as he frowns in your direction. Before you can look into his mind you realise that he is attacking you with a blast of mental power, a Thinkstrike! You were half ready for this and you put up a mental barrier. Make an **Evasion Roll.**

If you score 4-12, turn to **39**

If you score 2-3, turn to **62**

## 74

Bloodhound is strong and when he misses you with the musket the force with which it hits the ground snaps it like a twig. You try to control his mind but he throws himself at you and you tumble down the hillside, locked together. Bloodhound tries to strangle and kick you. You are bruised and exhausted by the time you break the renegade Lord's control of his will. *Lose 3 Endurance points.* Bloodhound stops fighting and you both look up to see that the Imperial Guard are marching to the attack. The renegade Lord is changing history. You begin to run up the hillside and the ambulance comes into view a hundred yards away from the Emperor.

Turn to **344**.

## 75

You instruct CAIN to examine the Eiger Service Computer and type your Epsilon Security Clearance Code at the terminal, before asking for information relating to a cydroid, serial number SAT75YV. Moments later, CAIN responds. 'SAT Section Security Cydroid 75YV, built 3027, assigned to Section Chief Agidy Yelov. Reported missing 3031, prior to discontinuation of this model due to faults in CPU. Armed: particle disrupter, sensors: infra-red, ultra-violet and radar. Appearance: man-like. Intelligence unit: Fordec 5000. Power Plant – '

You interrupt his list of specifications. 'Reported missing?'

'Yes, Falcon. SAT Section Chief Agidy Yelov reported that it tried to kill him before escaping into Old Geneva. No witnesses. Some damage to Yelov's office, certainly caused by a particle disrupter. No further information.'

If you wish to call up Yelov's file, note the number **15** on your Agent Profile. Whenever you are in your time machine and wish to access Yelov's file from CAIN, turn to paragraph **15** after noting the paragraph you are already at, as no options will be given at the end of it.

When you are ready, turn to **243.**

## 76

You strap yourself into the crash couch, which at a command from CAIN, moves backwards and swivels upwards into your flyer and the flyer's cockpit canopy clicks into place. The launch doors at the top of Falcon's Wing slide apart and the flyer is catapulted into the outside air.

Turn to **400.**

## 77

Throwing up your shield arm you manage to deflect the arrow and jump down into the melee below you.

Turn to **66.**

## 78

The translucent ruby laser beam pierces clean through your left shoulder, almost cutting off your arm as you roll to the ground. At least the wound is cauterised, and there is not much blood. *Lose 10 Endurance points.* Still rolling, will you:

| | |
|---|---|
| Thinkstrike? | Turn to **48** |
| Pull out your blaster? | Turn to **69** |

## 79

Napoleon's will is too strong for you and you realise you cannot control him. In your efforts, you have failed to notice Bloodhound beside you, controlled by the renegade Lord, tense up and draw his blaster. As you turn towards him he pulls the trigger and you are vaporised. You have failed and the Space Federation will never be.

## 80

You drop into the long grass beside the ambulance and the hornet drops down towards you, shattering as it hits the side of the ambulance, which you placed between it and yourself. Unfortunately, it does not explode and damage the ambulance, perhaps because its microcomputer registers the fact that it has not found its target. Bloodhound moves in to attack Lynx hand-to-hand as she closes in on you, and at the same moment you sense that the renegade Lord is reaching out to control the Emperor's mind. Realising that using your mental powers will give your position away, will you:

Run to help Bloodhound against Lynx,
    who is a master at unarmed combat?     Turn to **102**
Use Power of Will on the renegade Lord?     Turn to **131**
Jump into the ambulance?     Turn to **362**

### 81

You flatten yourself in a doorway of the warehouse, listening to the measured tread of your pursuer. He appears before the doorway and swivels his head in your direction, a forgettable but immaculate face, not a hair out of place. Do you:

Thinkstrike your pursuer?     Turn to **217**
Punch to disable him?     Turn to **64**

### 82

For three hours you circle the hill near Shevardino on which Napoleon's command post is set up, but there is no sign of the renegade Lord. At one time, Napoleon is forced to receive the attentions of an army surgeon and you overhear a rumour that he may have had a minor stroke. He recovers, however, and you continue your vigil. Bloodhound looks at you and motions you to concentrate. Soon you can feel a presence approaching, a very strong mental presence. Your heads turn as one towards a strange contraption coming nearer Napoleon and his escort. Two horses, one behind the other, are harnessed to a wooden, covered wagon with two small holes high up on either side for windows and doors which open at the back. A medical orderly is riding the first of the horses. It is one of the first ambulances ever made of the pattern designed by Baron Larrey, a French army surgeon, in 1805. The strength of the mental presence within the ambulance leads you to believe that the renegade Lord must be inside, and you prepare to attack together.

    Turn to **53**.

## 83

The Creche tumble, stunned, onto the tree carpet and you move forward to make sure of your victory. Suddenly, Agidy Yelov, wearing a psionic damper circlet on his head, that gives protection from mental attacks, appears from behind the Creche's time machine and a bolt of white lightning leaps from his blaster, burning the Hivers to a crisp. You hesitate in surprise as he turns to you, his blaster pointing at the ground. 'Well done Falcon, Bloodhound. Of course you know that I had set up a trap for the renegade Lord, but I really must congratulate you for a truly outstanding performance against the Creche.' Bloodhound looks at you to see what you will do. Will you:

| | |
|---|---|
| Blast Yelov? | Turn to **259** |
| Await Yelov's orders? | Turn to **120** |

## 84

For ten minutes you race through the confusion of the battlefield towards your time machines as the Imperial Guard approach the Russians. It is too late to call off the attack now. Marshal Ney has flung his men at the Russians, confident of success now that he has reinforcements. Unfortunately, your ancestor, the young hussar, is killed leading the charge and all goes black. He will never have the son who would have carried on the bloodline which leads to you. It is as if you had never existed. You have failed.

## 85

Your Thinkstrike fails and you try to tell her that for the sake of the Space Federation she must listen to what you have to say.

Turn to **96**.

## 86

Before you can pull your arm down from your head to your blaster. Bloodhound's finger triggers a bolt of superheated plasma which catches you in the face. Death is instantaneous, you are completely unrecognisable. You have failed.

[score a C]

Pilota responds, her voice high-pitched in the thin air, 'I noticed yesterday that someone has spent much time researching the history of Earth around the timehole of 1241 AD. A very great deal of time, according to the Central Library Log. I suggest you make it your first mission to investigate that timehole, just in case someone is doing something they shouldn't be. I know that there isn't much to go on here; call it a hunch if you like, but I would appreciate it if you would move quickly and check that all is well.'

You decide to keep your real mission secret and return to Earth for further information. Saluting Pilota and taking your leave, you are back at the console of your time machine within thirty minutes. CAIN confirms that what Pilota says about the library is true and that Pilota herself is not the one who has researched this part of Earth history. If you have seen a man in golden armour called Iskander, turn to **114**. If you have seen a Phocian pirate, turn to **34**. If you have seen neither of these, will you:

| | |
|---|---|
| Try to follow Lord Speke into the past? | Turn to **220** |
| Follow Lord Kirik to Kelados in 3033 AD? | Turn to **284** |
| Move back into the timehole in 1241 AD, the time of the Mongols? | Turn to **414** |
| Spend some time in your autodoc before continuing? | Turn to **196** |

You miss the hornet and it finds its target. To your surprise it is not filled with explosive but with a drug which sends you quickly to sleep. You wake again some minutes later to find Lynx and Bloodhound struggling on the ground, locked in combat. Bloodhound is bleeding badly and Lynx is manoeuvring so that she can finish him off with the knife she is wielding. You move quietly over and chop her in the back of the neck, knocking her out cold. Bloodhound sighs with relief and thanks you. Looking around, you take stock of the situation. Everybody has moved off down the hill towards the line of battle. The Imperial Guard are marching to the attack and the ambulance, too, is trundling away down the hill. Napoleon has ordered the attack and the renegade Lord has changed the past.

Turn to **344**.

You were not fast enough. Two blasts of plasma at short range vaporise most of your body. You have confronted the renegade Lord but failed at the last moment.

They hold their heads in pain, but the Imperial guard recovers and attacks you ferociously. You manage to keep out of his way for a time, dodging and weaving, but cannot find a way past the swirling of his sword and soon others pour into the room from the banqueting hall below and you are taken. The fate of the Khan's assassin is not a pleasant one. They discuss your punishment, which will be to have molten silver poured into your eyes and ears before you are boiled alive, a death reserved for their respected enemies. You have failed and the Space Federation will never be.

Despite the fall of Clone, they come on, howling for revenge and you are faced with a solid wall of spiked steel. You are dashed backwards into Machine's bike and before you can pull yourself up, one of them turns off his hover rotor, allowing his bike to settle heavily on your legs. Several others dismount, laughing cruelly. You stare at the spiked metal-capped boots which soon start to kick you senseless. Grabbing your helmet, they leave you for dead. *Lose 16 Endurance points.* If you are still alive, you cannot use your mental powers until you have taken a new helmet from the equipment locker of your time machine.

You wake up in the Health Executive Hospital, a medtech orderly bending over you, saying, 'We've put you back together again. Rapid tissue regeneration. I'm afraid you may find a slight weakness in the right knee. *Subtract one from your Evasion Modifier but restore your Endurance to 18.* Declining further sedation you discharge yourself from the hospital and board a hovrail car in the Vault. Leaving the car at the Eiger Vault you walk to the checkpoint outside the enormous plasteel doors where your ID chip is checked and the mind scanner is used to verify that you are Falcon. You step through a small personnel door, past two security droids and into the cavern which houses the time machines and the Research Section of TIME. The area in which the machines are kept is partitioned at intervals and you head straight for your own bay. In the centre of the bay, which is lined on three sides with racks carrying maintenance equipment, spare parts, the Variac drive recharger and sundry other useful items, lies Falcon's Wing. You approach the access hatch and the mind scanner lights up red and then green and you are drawn up into the machine by invisible tractor beams, activated by CAIN. Soon you are standing on the glowing access disc and CAIN chimes, 'Welcome, Falcon.'

Turn to **210.**

You soon detect a hologram of trees at the forest's edge, further from the village. You approach it warily but are jarred backwards by an invisible force-field that glows orange as you touch it. *Lose 2 Endurance points.*

You are amazed that such a field can be generated from so

small an area as the inside of a time machine. This is beyond the technology of Earth. You cannot even approach closely enough to see through the hologram and confirm whose the time machine is. You have no choice but to follow the flyer to Karakorum.

Turn to **76**.

Turn to **76**.

## 93

You wend your way through the fog of battle but your horse catches its foot in a burrow and goes lame. You abandon it and continue on foot, but in the cannon smoke you lose your way. The sound of firing is all around you and you mistake some Russians for Frenchmen who are withdrawing for a new attack. When the smoke clears you realise you have wandered close to the Russians. Bugles sound behind you and a charge of French infantry is launched with Marshal Ney at their head. The Frenchmen, singing the Marseillaise, come on shoulder-to-shoulder, magnificent in their blue and white uniforms. You are swept up in the charge and carried forward, unable to do anything against the hundreds of men, exhilarated in the heat of battle. On the redoubt ahead of you, the Russian commander, Prince Bagration, rides out in front of his line of green jacketed men and salutes the French columns, crying in French, *'Bravo, messieurs, c'est superbe!'* As you approach Bagration's men they unleash a hail of musket fire and you take this opportunity to throw yourself to the ground as if dead, and let the charge pass over you.

Afterwards, battered and muddied, you pick yourself up. You have found no trace of the renegade Lord and you decide to return to Napoleon's command post at Shevardino in case Bloodhound needs help. You are approaching the command post when Bloodhound rides to greet you. You tell him of your experiences and decide to look for Murat, the King of Naples, when you both feel a presence approaching, a very strong mental presence. Your heads turn as one towards a strange contraption coming nearer Napoleon and his escort. Two horses, one behind the other, are harnessed to a wooden, covered wagon with two small holes high up on either side for windows and doors which open at the back. A medical orderly is riding the first of the horses. It is one of the first ambulances ever made of the pattern designed by Baron Larrey, a French Army Surgeon, in 1805. The strength of the mental presence within the ambulance leads you to believe that the renegade Lord must be inside, and you prepare to attack together.

Turn to **53**.

## 94

You cut him down and leap over the wall, closely followed by other Macedonians and Persians, one of whom shouts, 'Bravely done, man.' Your shield stops two arrows, but others behind you are not so lucky. Archers in the towers of the wall are finding their mark. Turn to **66**.

## 95

You reach out with your thoughts and contact Bloodhound's mind, inside his machine, in an attempt to control him. He is wounded so he will have less resistance, as his mind is distracted. However, he too has psi training. Make a **Power of Will Roll**.

If you score 7-12, turn to **126**
If you score 2-5, turn to **20**
If you score a 6, roll again.

## 96

As soon as you open your mouth to shout against the din of battle she hurls a throwing knife at you in one lithe, fluid movement. You try to throw yourself to the ground to avoid the spinning blade that is about to transfix you. Make an **Evasion Roll**.

If you score 6-12, turn to **184**
If you score 2-5, turn to **240**

## 97

With a great effort you manage to dominate their wills, holding them under control. You walk up to them and order them to take you to Ogedei Khan and to pretend you are a messenger. They walk through the door with a rolling, bandy-legged gait and you follow entering a store room lined with barrels of koumiss, fermented mare's milk. A row of carcasses hangs on hooks above a smoking fire. In the corner lies the huddled form of an unconscious Mongol, obviously drunk. The two guards lead you out of a door opposite into a banqueting hall whose walls are lined with gold, the plunder of half the world. It is full of Mongols, eating and drinking. To your surprise there are no tables, but a great fire has been lit in the centre of the hall. Musicians are playing fast rhythmic music and some of the Mongols strut around the fire, showing off the splendour of their leather coats, decorated and lined with fur. Others are still gorging themselves, tearing chunks of meat from whole carcasses with their hunting knives. As the music quickens some begin to whirl and leap around the fire, dancing wildly. Your guards lead you up a wooden stairway just to the left of the storeroom door.

Turn to **278**.


## 98

You roll to one side as a translucent beam of ruby light connects the tip of the laser-rifle to the end of the corridor. Still rolling do you:

Thinkstrike?                                    Turn to **48**
Pull out your blaster?                          Turn to **69**


## 99

You tell Bloodhound that the Phocian pirate guarding the nearest Corsair ship is under mind control. Bloodhound suggests that you look into this while he returns to Earth in 3033 AD, and reports to Yelov that he has successfully killed you, so that you can operate without fear of further trouble from your comrades. When he has done that, he will explore the timelines and help you with your mission. You thank him.

'Good luck and look after yourself, my friend,' he calls, and with that he returns to his machine, Hunter, which winks out suddenly. You look towards the sleek Phocian ships and

see the pirate enter one and seal the hatch. As you watch, the Corsair's fusion drive fires up and the ship hurtles out of the starport, breaking the noise and launch regulations as it does so.

If you wish to examine Yelov's file on CAIN's records, when you return to Falcon's Wing, turn to **15**. You can look at Yelov's file whenever you are in your machine, but don't forget to remember the paragraph you are at before going to **15**, as no further options are given there. When you are ready, do you:

Return to Falcon's Wing and follow
    Bloodhound in order to confront
      Agidy Yelov?                  Turn to **45**
Investigate the second Corsair ship?    Turn to **71**

## 100

As you approach the carriage, the mind inside senses you and you are locked in a battle of wills. It is a battle which you are bound to lose as the renegade Lord's mind is stronger than yours. All of your being is taken up with the struggle when, abruptly, the attack ceases. You shake your head dizzily, but it is only the lull before the storm. A wave of mental energy flows into you and your brain goes haywire. You seem to feel hot, cold, rain and fire all at once. It is as if you can see all colours at once and myriad voices speak in every language you have ever studied. Your brain overheats, literally burning itself out like a faulty electric motor. You are a zombie, incapable of thought, swaying on your horse and gurgling like a baby. You have failed.

## 101

The readout changes:

Agent Yelov was at the residence
of TIMELORD •••••

TIMELORD IDENTITY SECURITY
CLASSIFICATION OMEGA

NO FURTHER INFORMATION AVAILABLE

END OF EXCHANGE

Before you can ask for more information the service computer
intones softly, 'You have arrived at the Hall of Honours, your
graduation is about to commence.'

Turn to **110**.

## 102

Lynx has drawn a knife on Bloodhound and though he is very
strong, he is no match for her and is already bleeding badly.
They are locked together and you cannot use your blaster. Do
you:

Thinkstrike Lynx?                                    Turn to **164**

Join in the combat with a karate kick
    against Lynx?                                    Turn to **186**

## 103

They both slump to the floor, stunned, and you move quickly
to Ogedei's bedside. Knowing what must be done and hoping
to make his death look natural you place a silken cushion over
Ogedei's face and press down. His hands scrabble feebly at
yours but he is too weak to resist. Ogedei's face turns purple
as he dies. Suddenly, the door swings open and several
members of the Imperial Guard rush in and charge at you.
You try to dive through the awning to the balcony. Make an
**Evasion Roll**.

If you score 6-12, turn to **143**

If you score 2-5, turn to **8**

## 104

Suddenly the screen flares as the Phocian Corsair opens fire on the Keladi ship, its lasers piercing the hull of the larger ship which lurches sickeningly. You decide to open fire in order to prevent the death of the envoy, Korakiik, realising that whoever is controlling the Phocian desires war between the Keladi and Earth. You are too late. As your finger moves to the fire button the Corsair rakes the envoy's ship again with its pulse lasers. There is a brilliant explosion which fills the scanner screen with light and then you are suddenly engulfed in blackness. You find yourself in a smoke-filled shelter, a fugitive from an alien race on your own world. The past has been changed and your memories with it. You leap out of the shelter to hurl a grenade at a strange alien aircraft on the street above you… As Falcon, Agent of TIME, you have failed.

## 105

A brilliant white bolt of burning plasma takes your would-be assassin in the chest, knocking him backwards and taking his life as it melts through his armour. You kneel by him as a security droid arrives. Seeing signs of life in his eyes, though he is beyond help, you ask who sent him to kill you. 'One of the Lords…'

His words are choked off by a rattling cough as the blood from his lungs begins to spill from his mouth and death takes him. The security droid hovers towards you, its stun-lance aimed. You hand over your identification and report what happened. A message appears in red on the screen set in the droid's chest. 'ID: Passed. Your story coincides with videographic evidence. A report will be filed. Please continue your business.' And it begins to drag the body of your assailant out of the bay. Turn to **336**.

## 106

The outside camera begins to swivel, showing you the land all around. Behind you is a forest, shrouded in snow, and the hologram generator disguises Falcon's Wing as part of this forest. You are on high ground and to the right you can see a village with a pall of smoke rising above it. Outside the village is a mound of bodies, each missing both ears. The Mongols have been busy. Ahead, the frosted ground falls away into a wide river valley. The river is frozen over but you can plainly see its graceful curves stretching to a walled city a few miles away. Here and there on the plain you can see parties of horsemen riding swiftly. You ask CAIN for some historical information. CAIN responds. 'It is winter, 1241 AD. The city you see is Vienna and the river, the Danube. The Mongol horde led by the general, Subutai, has conquered Russia and Poland, and defeated a western army at Liegnitz, before overrunning Hungary. They are a few miles from Vienna, poised to ravage the rest of Europe. Their ruler is Ogedei, son of Ghenghis Khan. He will die within the next few days and when the news reaches the Golden Horde, they must, under Genghis Khan's code of law, the Yasa, return to the Mongol capital, Karakorum, to decide who will succeed him. Vienna will not fall and Europe will be saved.'

You break in, 'And if Ogedei should live?'

CAIN continues, 'The likelihood is that Europe would be overrun and the timelines changed beyond recognition. Civilisation would be set back a thousand years.'

As you reach for your holo-detector, a black disc-like shape crosses your path of vision, streaking skyward with a sound like a thunderclap. CAIN chimes, 'A small ion drive craft, probably a flyer, has taken off nearby.' You ask for an estimate of its destination and CAIN responds, 'I estimate China. The Mongol capital, Karakorum, is in China, Falcon.' Do you:

Leave Falcon's Wing and try to find the
time machine that launched the flyer?    Turn to **92**

Get into your own flyer and race to
Karakorum?    Turn to **76**

### 107

Bloodhound passes out, slumping to the floor of the refuelling bay. You drag him to Falcon's Wing and tie him up in front of CAIN, removing his psionic enhancer helmet as you do so.

When he comes round you show him CAIN's records. It soon becomes obvious to him that you are on a vitally important mission and that his mission to kill you must be abandoned. You untie him and return his helmet.

Bloodhound says, 'I'm sorry, Falcon, someone has used me. Someone who wants the timelines to be changed.'

'Who gave the order to kill me?'

'Our Section Chief, Agidy Yelov. He told me you had killed Lord Kirik.'

'But Kirik has only been dead a matter of minutes.'

Bloodhound pauses then says, 'Yes, of course, Falcon, how can he know of Kirik's death so soon? Either he was responsible or he is in league with the traitor that did it.'

Your Section Chief is working with the renegade Lord. Turn to **99**.

## 108

A lancing white bolt of superheated plasma strikes the cydroid which short-circuits in a flood of sparks and pitches forward, inert. A nearby plasma sensor begins to flash, signalling Citpol Enforcers, the civil police. A blue and gold Citpol jetcopter lands nearby as you examine the charred remains of the cydroid, but the damage is too severe for you to gain a clue as to its origins. Two Enforcers alight from their 'copter, pointing their stunlances at you. 'Let's see your ID.' You produce your ID chip and hand it to the one who spoke, still covered by the other. He clips it into his Remote Access Terminal (RAT) on his arm and a look of disappointment crosses his features, as he realises who you are. 'What's been going on here?' he says. You report exactly what happened and he returns your chip and turns to examine the cydroid.

Turn to **137**.

## 109

Ney nods and, wheeling his horse, canters back towards the battle lines with his staff and you set off towards the hill at Shevardino, where Bloodhound has gone to watch over Napoleon. Turn to **145**.

The silver doors hiss apart, affording you your first view of the Hall of Honours, which boasts a marble floor and colonnades. In the centre is a large oaken table, in the shape of a horseshoe, the only wood in the TIME building, around which sit the five Lords of TIME. Your universal translator synthesises an unusual watery gurgling into words of welcome that sound in your ear: Welcome, Agent Falcon, never has a candidate graduated from the Academy with so high a score.' Your self-control allows you to smother any outward betrayal of surprise at the sight of the being which greets you. Submerged in a huge tank, along with some small aquatic mammals, is what looks like a giant lobster with bloated bluish brain-sacs floating under its spiked carapace. It waves a fearsome purplish pincer and clicks and gurgles: 'I am Time Lord Kirik of the Keladi.'

You bow respectfully and turn to look at the other Lords. You recognise Lord Speke, a dapper little Earther in a Navy 'dress uniform'. On his left sits a squat, humanoid figure, with blue skin and a mane of bristling white hairs – Lord Silvermane of Rigel Prime. On the other side of the table sits Lord Pilota, a seven-foot tall Lastlander woman with the fragile build and sharp-boned features of all those who live on that low gravity world. She is supported in her chair by a hydraulic exoskeleton which gives her the appearance of a robot, but it is the fifth Lord of TIME sitting on her right who looks the strangest of them all. A network of silica, like an oversized honeycomb, rests on the floor. Inside each of the six cells of the honeycomb is what looks like a giant ant, swathed in silk, like a cocoon. Their front parts protrude from the silk, plainly showing dull-red, compound eyes and wicked looking mandibles which are in constant motion. Collectively, they are called The Creche 82282 and they are six parts of a communal mind, in constant mind-link with each other. They are Hivers, a separate part of the Hive.

The ceremony is brief. You swear an oath of allegiance to TIME and are duly commissioned as a Special Agent. Pilota rises and steps forward, uncomfortable in the relatively high

gravity of Earth, and pins your wings to your chest. Your universal translator renders a mixed babel of applause. The ceremony is drawing to a close and you still have little information on the Lords of TIME. You know that this will be your last chance to meet them together in the same room for some time, perhaps ever.

If you know why Section Chief Yelov did not contact you until the last minute about your mission, turn to **153**. If you do not, will you:

Use your Psi Sense to contact one of
 them mentally?                                    Turn to **121**
Ask if any of them have travelled in time
 since the death of Agent Q?                       Turn to **140**
Smile and make a short speech of thanks?           Turn to **167**

## 111

He steps back and a Macedonian behind shouts 'Move on!' and you are pushed onto the parapet from behind. The Indian jabs you in the thighs. *Lose 6 Endurance points.* He is soon overwhelmed, but a hail of arrows rains down from the towers of the wall, and you jump down to the ground inside the city. The arrows claim the Macedonian who shoved you and he falls dead at your feet.

Turn to **66**.

## 112

The bear is not much shorter than you, but must be twice as heavy and the prospect of wrestling with it is daunting. You leap and kick towards its snout. Make an **Attack Roll**.

If you score 6-12, turn to **3**
If you score 2-5, turn to **318**

## 113

You twist and side-kick the general in the throat, knocking him senseless. The Emperor's guard aims a vicious sword cut at your head, but you duck and, spinning quickly, sweep his legs from under him. He falls to the ground with a clatter of armour and you chop down hard onto the back of his neck with your elbow, and he slumps, unmoving. You move quickly to Ogedei's bedside. Knowing what must be done, and hoping to make his death look natural, you place a silken cushion over Ogedei's face and press down. His hands scrabble feebly at yours, but he is too weak to resist. Ogedei's face turns purple as he dies. Suddenly, the door swings open and several members of the Imperial Guard rush in and charge at you. You try to dive through the awning to the balcony. Make an **Evasion Roll**.

If you score 6-12, turn to **143**

If you score 2-5, turn to **8**

## 114

As the fading chimes of CAIN echo in your ears darkness engulfs you. You find yourself in a smoke-filled shelter, a fugitive from an alien race on your own world. The past has been changed and your memories with it. You leap out of the shelter to hurl a grenade at a strange alien craft on the street above you… As Falcon, Agent of TIME, you have failed.

## 115

They shake their heads and, making signs to ward off evil spirits, stare out into the darkness. Do you:

Try to Thinkstrike them?                Turn to **369**

Use your blaster to fry them?           Turn to **387**

## 116

A brilliant white bolt of burning plasma takes your would-be assassin in the chest, knocking him backwards and taking his life as it melts through his armour. You kneel by him as a security droid arrives. Seeing signs of life in his eyes, though he is beyond help, you ask who sent him to kill you. 'One of the Lords…' His words are choked off by a rattling cough as the blood from his lungs begins to spill from his mouth and death takes him. You can take his psionic damper circlet, if you wish. Add it to your Agent Profile.

The security droid comes towards you, its stun-lance aimed, and you hand over your identification and report what happened. A message appears in red on the screen set in the droid's chest. 'ID - Passed. Your story coincides with videographic evidence. A report will be filed. Please continue your business,' and it begins to drag the body of your assailant out of the bay.

Turn to **336**.

Turn to **336**.

## 117

Bloodhound's mental defences are enough to shrug off your Thinkstrike. While you pause to collect your thoughts after your effort, he blasts you once again. You double up as the plasma bolt hits your side; *lose 13 Endurance points.* If you are still alive, you find yourself too stunned to do anything. Bloodhound walks over to your stricken body and levels his weapon for the final blast. 'Wait, Bloodhound! Kill me and the population of all earth and the colonies may perish. I am helpless, but look at CAIN's memory banks before you void me.' He hesitates , then drags you into Falcon's Wing and ties you up. Examining CAIN's records, it soon becomes obvious to him that you are on a vitally important mission and that his mission to kill you must be abandoned. He unties you, but your wounds are so bad you must *subtract one from your Evasion Modifier.*

Bloodhound says, 'I'm sorry. Falcon, someone has used me, someone who wants the timelines to be changed.'

'Who gave the order to kill me?'

'Our Section Chief, Agidy Yelov. He told me you had killed Lord Kirik.'

'But Kirik has only been dead a matter of minutes.'

Bloodhound pauses then says, 'Yes, of course, Falcon. How can he know of Kirik's death so soon? Either he was responsible or he is in league with the traitor that did it.'

Your Section Chief is working with the renegade Lord. Turn to **99**.

## 118

Your blast of mental energy has overcome Lynx's defences and she slumps to the ground, inert. She comes round quickly. Holding her at blaster point, you open your mind to her as she recovers and she is able to see you are fighting for a just and important cause. She explains that she had been sent by Agidy Yelov to kill or capture you, believing you to be a highly dangerous traitor. You explain the current situation to her and she decides to help you with your mission.

Turn to **219**.

### 119

As you turn the corner into the corridor leading to the bay which houses Falcon's Wing, you see two security guards approaching. They are wearing power-armour and full-face helmets which are not standard issue. One of them raises his laser-rifle, aiming at you. Make an **Evasion Roll.**

If you score 6-12, turn to **98**

If you score 2-5, turn to **78**

### 120

Instead of asking you to help with the bodies of the Hivers, Yelov swings up his blaster and fires. He is very quick and his aim is true. You are hurled backwards and find yourself, badly wounded, falling through a gap in the foliage to the leaf mould which covers the ground below. Seconds later, Bloodhound falls a few yards away from you. He is unconscious. One of the trees seems to bend slightly above him. Suckers which sprout from its trunk begin to converge on him slowly. They wrap around him and he begins to dissolve. You too are caught by tentacles and you hear Yelov's laughter deadened by the foliage as you succumb to the man-eating tree. You have failed.

### 121

Who will you try to contact first:

| | |
|---|---|
| Silvermane? | Turn to **280** |
| Pilota? | Turn to **260** |
| Speke? | Turn to **241** |
| The Creche? | Turn to **223** |
| Kirik? | Turn to **209** |

## 122

### [score a G]

Once again you are at the forest's edge, overlooking the Danube and Vienna. The nearby village of Ramallo lies under a pall of smoke. The Mongols have finished their grisly work and a pile of corpses which lack ears lies near the edge of the village. You can see your own footsteps, muddled with hoof prints on the ground outside.

As you reach for your holo-detector, a black disc-like shape crosses your path of vision, streaking skyward with a sound like a thunderclap. CAIN chimes, 'A small ion drive craft, probably a flyer, has taken off nearby.' You ask for an assessment of its destination and CAIN responds, 'I estimate China. The Mongol capital, Karakorum, is in China, Falcon. Let me remind you that Ogedei Khan should be dying there even now. If he lives all Europe will be ravaged by the Golden Horde and civilisation will be set back a thousand years.' Do you:

| | |
|---|---|
| Leave Falcon's Wing and try to find the time machine that launched the flyer? | Turn to **92** |
| Get into your own flyer and race to Karakorum? | Turn to **76** |

### 123

You spur your horse forward towards Murat and his staff when the source of the mental power comes into view. Two horses, one behind the other, are harnessed to a wooden covered wagon with two small holes high up on either side for windows and doors which open at the back. A medical orderly is riding the first of the horses. It is one of the first ambulances ever made of the pattern designed by Baron Larrey, a French Army Surgeon, in 1805. You sense the strength of the mind within the strange carriage and its power seems awesome to you. As you watch, you can feel the mind reaching out to control Murat, King of Naples, Do you:

| | |
|---|---|
| Ride towards the carriage to foil the attempt to control Murat? | Turn to **100** |

Go back for Bloodhound so that you
can combine your powers?          Turn to **93**

## 124

You sense that your Thinkstrike has succeeded but still the mental power exists inside the ambulance, confirming that the renegade Lord is the Creche, the six Hiver beings that form one mind. You run up to the ambulance but before you arrive its front explodes and a flyer accelerates out of it, the Hivers clinging on inside the honeycomb-like seats. The Creche skim low through the smoke of the battlefield, almost faster than the eye can see, making a sonic boom like the explosion of a powder magazine, the ammunition stores for the cannon. As they go you catch the thought that they are heading for the planet Hel. Do you:

Try to control Napoleon's mind and use
him to call off the attack?          Turn to **37**
Return to Falcon's Wing and chase the
Creche to the planet Hel?          Turn to **84**

## 125

To your consternation you cannot reach through to his mind, instead you feel the interference effect of a psionic damper helmet. This is a recent invention of the Hivers. Do you:

Order him to stay where he is?          Turn to **177**
Wait for him to join you outside
Falcon's Wing?          Turn to **46**

## 126

You win the battle of wills but the mental strain saps you. *Lose 2 Endurance points.* You can control Agent Bloodhound. You take him to Falcon's Wing and instruct him to examine CAIN's records. It soon becomes obvious to him that you are on a vitally important mission and that his mission to kill you must be abandoned. You release him from your control and Bloodhound says, 'I'm sorry, Falcon, someone has used me, someone who wants the timelines to be changed.'

'Who gave you the order to kill me?'

'Our Section Chief, Agidy Yelov. He told me you had killed Lord Kirik.'

'But Kirik has only been dead a matter of minutes.'

Bloodhound pauses then says, 'Yes, of course, Falcon, how can he know of Kirik's death so soon? Either he was responsible or he is in league with the traitor that did it.'

Your Section Chief is working with the renegade Lord. Turn to **99**.

### 127

The drunken revelry continues and you manage to cross the banqueting hall and leave through the store room without trouble. The two guards outside are being cursed for falling asleep at their post by their noyan, or general. You stride past, looking the other way, and are soon lost in the darkness. You wade silently into the ornamental pond and, using the rope ladder, climb back into your flyer.

Turn to **254**.

### 128

You roll aside and come up ready to fire your blaster into the ambulance. The Hivers are scurrying backwards out of sight, but you send a bolt of plasma after them. One of them is too slow and it is torched to a frazzle by the white-hot beam. You are getting ready to leap into the ambulance when its front explodes and a flyer accelerates out of it, the Hivers clinging on inside the honeycomb-like seats. The Creche skim low through the smoke of the battlefield, almost faster than the eye can see, making a sonic boom like the explosion of a powder magazine, the ammunition stores for the cannon. As they go you catch the thought that they are heading for the planet Hel.

Turn to **161**.

### 129

Your shock wave of thought topples one of the lancers from the saddle and Bloodhound and Lynx have been similarly successful with two of the other lancers. The remaining one catches Lynx in the shoulder before she can topple him with the power of her thought, but she grabs the lance and swings herself up on it, kicking the lancer in the face. He tumbles, unconscious, from the saddle but Lynx falls beside him. She is badly wounded and has to return to her autodoc. She urges you to go on, saying: 'I'll see you at the Eiger Vault Rec Centre,' and wishes you luck before limping away. You run to catch up with the ambulance.

Turn to **251**.

## 130

You instruct CAIN to turn on the Variac drive to shift you into null-space and to re-engage the drive as soon as you have finished inputting the navigational co-ordinates for the timehole in the time of Alexander the Great. Your scalp tingles slightly as the time machine moves out of phase, and everything around you seems grey and insubstantial. You know that should you turn on the outside camera the screen would remain blank – not even blackness exists in Null-space. You cast your thought into the void and using your Psi Sense locate the timehole of Alexander the Great. When you have translated this location into co-ordinates for CAIN, the Variac drive engages once more. The process of re-emerging in real time is immediate, but seems to take around an hour for you. You can spend this time in the autodoc if you wish and *gain up to 12 Endurance points.*

You rematerialize and the holo-projector makes Falcon's Wing look like a bleak hillock. Your exterior camera shows a small range of desolate hills giving way to a dry plain crossed by a small river. You press 'hold' and the camera stops swivelling as a small city of mud-baked houses appears on the screen, surrounded by tall white stone walls and towers. It is what lies before the city which catches your eye. An entire army, perhaps forty thousand strong, is encamped before the city walls. The tattered tents are braced against the breeze and hundreds of wagons stand in a second camp further from the city, where gaggles of wagoners, camp followers and walking wounded seem to mock the orderly precision of the ranks of men, resplendent in their armour, the sun glinting from the tips of their sixteen-foot-long spears. They stand as if on parade. You ask CAIN what happened here, historically.

CAIN chimes: 'This city is the local capital. The people marched out two days ago to give battle to Alexander the Great and his army of Macedonians and troops from other conquered lands, but fled when they saw Alexander and his men. Alexander is returning from India to Babylon, the capital of his new empire, and has decided to take this city. His men do not want to risk their lives again and he will soon head the assault in an attempt to inspire them. Realising that he is going to risk his life, his men will throw themselves onto the siege ladders, but these will be broken in their eagerness. Two men only will be with Alexander when he jumps down into the city and he will be severely wounded before the Macedonians break down the gates and rescue him…'

'Thank you, CAIN. What action would change the timeline here?'

'The assassination of Alexander would seem the most likely option, but I cannot compute the effect this would have on the past. Alexander will die in only a few years from now at the age of-thirty-three and his empire will be divided up and fought over by his successors.'

CAIN programs the molecular converter to create the dress of a phalangite, a Macedonian warrior, and you step from Falcon's Wing wearing sandals, bronze greaves, a long heavy skirt of boiled leather strips, a breastplate, and a small round shield strapped to your left forearm. Your psionic enhancer becomes a crested helmet covering your face, with a Y-shaped slit for you to see through. Unable to wield a sixteen-foot-long sarissa you make do with a short sword. Your blaster and holo-detector are concealed under your red cloak. You search the hills for Lord Speke's machine.

Turn to **403**.

## 131

You concentrate your mind on whoever is inside the ambulance, knowing that the renegade Lord has a powerful will. As soon as you attack, the battle starts to go against you. The power of the will which counter-attacks is awesome and you can do nothing as you lose control of your mind. You can only watch as an outsider, as your hand pulls the blaster from your jacket. Sweating with effort you vainly try to resist as, shaking wildly, your arm takes aim at Bloodhound. He sees you and draws his own blaster. You are about to shoot him against your will when a blast of white-hot plasma rips into your shoulder. Lose *10 Endurance points.* At least no blood flows – the plasma from the blaster seals the wound like boiling tar. The shock to your system allows you to try and reassert your own will. Make a **Chance Roll.**

If you score 1-3, turn to **413**
If you score 4-6, turn to **234**

## 132
### [score an M]
The members of Napoleon's staff clear a way and one of the Chasseurs rides by your side as you approach the Emperor. Napoleon's Chief of Staff, Marshal Berthier, spurs his horse forward and takes the despatch from you. He reads it quickly and passes it to the Emperor who is now in front of you. Napoleon reads it and sighs, saying, 'I've no men to spare for your headstrong Marshal Ney.' He waves you aside and you are thankful to leave the group that surrounds him to go over to Bloodhound.

Turn to **82.**

## 133
The arrow buries itself into your neck. You clutch at it and stand motionless. Then your arms go back as you begin to topple from the wall. You are dead before you hit the ground. You have failed.

## 134
You are half in and half out of null-space. You are able to see through the walls of your time machine and even through your own flesh as if they did not exist. You try to switch the

Variac drive on again, but nothing happens. You are caught in a time flux. Unable to do anything else, you look around. You are hanging in the air above verdant pastures and a wide blue river Before you is a magnificent city, its houses, mosques and minarets surrounded by a high and well-defended wall. Gold and turquoise gleam below in the sun. The pastures and groves are deserted but around the walls is a horde of Mongols beyond count. There are more horses than men – each warrior has a remount. You ask CAIN for an update on the history of this time and place. CAIN chimes, The city before you is Baghdad, on the banks of the river Tigris, in Mesopotamia. The year is 1258 AD and the people of Baghdad have been under siege for some months by the Mongols, led by their general, Hulagu.'

The Mongols, dressed in furs and leather, look strangely out of place by the warm banks of the Tigris. They wear conical helmets topped with spikes and plumes of horsehair, and strips of boiled ox-hide laced together and painted brightly, affording them the protection of armour without weighing down their horses. They carry curved swords, hooked lances and short bows made of layers of horn and wood. As you watch, some of them show off their skill, standing in their stirrups, drawing arrows from their quivers and shooting them at the city walls, all in one swift, lithe movement. They cannot see you hanging frozen in the air. As you watch, they gather together and the Caliph of Baghdad, Mustasin, walks forward from the gates of his starving city, flanked by faithful retainers. He kneels before Hulagu in a gesture of surrender. Using the external microphone, you can hear what passes between them. Mustasin is clearly petrified and he begs for his life and the lives of his people. The cold, impassive Hulagu demands to know where his treasures are hidden. Mustasin, seeing a ray of hope, tells Hulagu of his hiding place. When satisfied, Hulagu signals to his men, who massacre the Caliph and his attendants. The horrified people of Baghdad make no attempt to close the gates and the Mongols sweep into the city like a tide of soldier ants.

You are held in the air above Baghdad for over a month,

and in all that time the slaying continues, the bestial ferocity of the Mongols remains unslaked. Only after forty days and the death of 800,000 people does the stench of rotting flesh force Hulagu to abandon the smouldering palaces, mosques and libraries of the dead city. After they have gone you cannot see even a dog or cat moving in the streets. All life has been wiped out. Shaken by the awful spectacle you have had to witness you are thankful when your Psi Sense registers a change in the flux of time You engage the Variac drive once more and this time rematerialize as planned. Because you were trapped in a time flux, when you materialise no time has passed between the moment you were caught and the moment you were released. Your digital clock shows that in 3033 AD it is still the same day on which you began your mission.

Turn to **122**.

## 135

Your will has overcome Lynx's and she is under your control. You open your mind to her and she is able to see you are fighting for a just and important cause. You release her from your control. She explains that she had been sent by Agidy Yelov to kill or capture you, believing you to be a highly dangerous traitor. You explain the current situation to her and she decides to help you with your mission.

Turn to **219**.

## 136

You don't reply to the message and, seconds later, the Phocian increases speed. A third, larger ship appears on the scanner beyond an asteroid belt, and the Corsair changes course to intercept. You match course and increase speed as a second message reaches you, this time from the larger ship: 'This is the clanship *Keladan III*; we are on a priority diplomatic mission. Do not attack. Repeat, do not attack. Change course. We are Keladi, do not attack.'

You realise that this is the envoy ship carrying Korakiik, and that they will soon be within the attack range of the

Phocian Corsair. Do you:

Open fire on the Phocian Corsair with
    your ship's pulse lasers?           Turn to **141**
Wait to see what happens?          Turn to **104**

### 137

'Looks like you've done some expensive damage here,' says one of the Enforcers. 'I think well have to take you in.' He points his stun-lance at you. 'Just what you'd expect from a SAT. They give them all these wonderful toys and helmets that let them look into honest men's minds and what do they do? Pop off their blasters, like they've just escaped from the incubator.'

The first motions you into the jetcopter with his lance.

'Hold on,' says the other, 'this tin-can carries a particle disruptor.' After further examination he consults his RAT. 'This is an ex-SAT security droid, a banned model. Apparently they were unpredictable. Funny that, you being a SAT agent, wouldn't you say? Anyway just our luck, you've won yourself 50 creds bounty for eliminating this junk here!'

The other Enforcer spits in disgust and they turn on their heels and climb in, bathing you with the 'copter's hot exhaust as they take off. You continue on your way to the hovrail.

Turn to **169**.

### 138

You float down from the access hatch, lowered by invisible tractor beams. You can smell ozone in the air of the Spaceport. Rounding a bulkhead you come across a refuelling bay and your holo-detector indicates that the Keladi scoutship in front of you is in fact a time machine. Judging by its size it could only be that of Lord Kirik. There is no trace of Lord Speke's machine. As you walk through the hologram you are surprised to see water underfoot. Kirik's machine is normally water-filled, a much larger model than your own. Clearly all is not well for, as you look up, you see that his access hatch is open and on automatic, for his mind scan is not operating and you are drawn up into his machine. The grotesque body of

Lord Kirik lies inert across his crash couch, the disc which is his psionic enhancer lies in a pool of water at his side. The usually bloated brain-sacs are flaccid and his jointed legs are curled unnaturally. Looking more closely you notice a neat circular wound in the middle of one of his brain sacs, still pouring purplish fluid. There is no sign of the weapon that was used to do this. He has been killed quite recently by someone whom he had allowed into his time machine. There is no helping Lord Kirik. Do you:

| | |
|---|---|
| Leave the scene of the crime before you can be discovered here? | Turn to **262** |
| Send Kirik's machine into null-space? | Turn to **382** |

### 139

The plasma from your blaster claims the lives of several of the guards and their clamour increases, believing you to be a spirit. Some overcome their fear, however, determined to protect their Khan, and you are peppered with arrows, some from an unseen vantage point above. Your heart is pierced and you die. You have failed and the Space Federation will never be.

### 140

You ask the Lords of Time whether any of them have travelled in time since the death of Agent Q and the response is immediate. You step back in surprise as Kirik's pincers thresh the waters of his tank. He is plainly outraged. The Creche scuttle into and out of their cocoons but your translator cannot guide you as to what this may mean. Pilota volunteers 'Yes I have…' with a nonchalant air but is interrupted by Speke's raised voice: 'Really! I feel it is hardly your business as to enquire into our daily affairs.' Silvermane adds, not unpleasantly, 'There is nothing wrong with curiosity, it will be an asset, but perhaps you should focus it elsewhere.'

Turn to **194**.

## 141

Realising that whoever is controlling the Phocian pilot, almost certainly the renegade Lord, is trying to kill the Keladi envoy, so that Kelados and Earth will be plunged into war, you target and fire the ship's bow lasers. The Phocian has started an attack pattern, weaving in space and you must pilot the craft manually trying to outguess his every move. Make an **Attack Roll** to lock on successfully with your lasers.

If you score 7-12, turn to **224**

If you score 2-6, turn to **178**

## 142

Cautiously you shadow Lord Silvermane from the Eiger Vault to the hovrail, summoning a hovcar with which to follow him, using your RAT. Silvermane also consults his RAT, but for longer than the time needed to summon a hovcar, even for an alien. Before he enters his hovcar, Agidy Yelov's call-sign flashes on your micro-display. You accept his transmission and he asks you how your investigation is progressing. You reply that it has not progressed far, but give a brief report. Yelov thanks you and breaks contact. You enter a hovcar and lock it onto the trail of Silvermane and follow him. An hour later he debarks at the Galactic Trade Centre. As your own hovcar glides to a halt, Yelov calls you to his office at TIME headquarters, a journey which takes a further fifty minutes. He cannot see you immediately and you wait for over an hour before deciding to return to the Eiger Vault. As you approach its gates you are suddenly engulfed in blackness. Then you find yourself in a smoke-filled shelter, a fugitive from an alien race on your own world. The past has been changed and your memories with it. You leap out of the shelter to hurl a grenade at a strange alien craft on the street above you… As Falcon, Agent of TIME, you have failed.

## 143

You roll onto the balcony as a hand-axe, thrown by one of the Imperial Guard, tangles itself in the silken awning behind you. You leap from the balcony to the edge of the palace roof, swinging by your arms and pulling your legs up over the edge as the guardsmen rush onto the balcony. You run to your flyer. Some of the Mongols, shouting ferociously, will be upon you before you can climb aboard. Balancing on the edge of the roof and mentally exhausted, you are forced to use your blaster. Make an **Attack Roll.**

If you score 5-12, turn to **157**

If you score 2-4, turn to **175**

### 144

The driver wavers but the renegade Lord feels your attack and tries to control your will. The power of the will which attacks is awesome and you can do nothing as you lose control of your mind. You can only watch, an outsider trapped inside your own skull, as your hand pulls the blaster from your jacket. Sweating with effort you vainly try to resist as, shaking wildly, your arm takes aim at Bloodhound. He sees you and draws his own blaster. You are about to shoot him against your will when a blast of white-hot plasma rips into your shoulder. *Lose 10 Endurance points.* If you are still alive, at least no blood flows – the plasma from the blaster seals the wound like boiling tar. The shock to your system allows you to regain control of your mind. Fighting the pain you must decide what to do next. Do you:

| | |
|---|---|
| Thinkstrike whoever is inside the ambulance? | Turn to **299** |
| Try to use your Power of Will on whoever is inside the ambulance? | Turn to **330** |

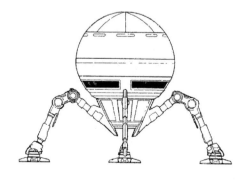

### 145

Picking your way through the fog of the battle you finally come across Bloodhound again, who is pretending to adjust the girth of his horse. Breathlessly, you tell him that you have detected the presence of a being with mental powers, probably the renegade Lord. He suggests that you both remain near Napoleon and wait to see what happens. Do you:

| | |
|---|---|
| Throw the despatch into the mud and agree to wait? | Turn to **82** |
| Deliver the despatch to Napoleon in case you risk changing history if you do not? | Turn to **132** |

### 146

Bloodhound is sprawled in his autodoc, ready for you. As you aim your blaster, lit in the glow of the access disc, so the superheated plasma from his weapon catches you in the belly, turning your guts to steam. Death is instantaneous. You have failed.

### 147

You follow several Macedonians up the ladder. They manage to clear a way and you reach the top of the wall as the screams of the dying begin. Below you a few Greeks and Persians are forcing their way through the townspeople towards Alexander, dealing death with the skilled precision of battle-hardened veterans. Before you can jump down, an archer in one of the towers lets loose an arrow. Your Psi Sense warns you Make an **Evasion Roll.**

If you score 6-12, turn to **77**
If you score 2-5, turn to **133**

### 148
### [score a G]

You seize control of Lord Silvermane's mind after a brief battle of wills. You send a question to him, demanding whether he is guilty of the tampering with Kelados' past, but his conscience is clean. It seems he is not your man. As you relinquish control you catch him thinking that, if anyone, it is likely to be Lord Speke. Lord Silvermane becomes outraged, but you quickly apologise and tell him of your mission. He grows alarmed, but compliments you, saying: 'Never have I striven with so strong a will. You may find that implanting the suggestion of extreme hunger in the mind of your victim will make domination even easier for you.' You thank him and take the advice to heart. *Add one to your Power of Will Modifier.* He says: 'I would help you further, but it is not my place to risk a diplomatic incident by compromising one of my fellow Lords. However, I shall report to Agidy Yelov.'

You bid him well and return to your time machine. Turn to **119**.

## 149

You are half in and half out of null-space. You are able to see through the walls of your time machine and even through your own flesh as if they did not exist. You try to switch the Variac drive on again but nothing happens. You are caught in a time flux. Unable to do anything else, you look around you. You are hanging in the air above verdant pastures and a wide, blue river, before you is a magnificent city, its houses, mosques and minarets surrounded by a high and well-defended wall. Gold and turquoise gleam below in the sun. The pastures and groves are deserted, but around the walls is a horde of Mongols beyond count. There are more horses than men – each warrior has a remount. You ask CAIN for an update on the history of this time and place. CAIN chimes, 'The city before you is Baghdad, on the banks of the river Tigris, in Mesopotamia. The year is 1258 AD and the people of Baghdad have been under siege for some months by the Mongols, led by their general, Hulagu.'

The Mongols, dressed in furs and leather, look strangely out of place by the warm banks of the Tigris. They wear conical helmets topped with spikes and plumes of horsehair, and strips of boiled ox-hide laced together and painted brightly, affording them the protection of armour without weighing down their horses. They carry curved swords,

hooked lances and short bows made of layers of horn and wood. As you watch, some of them show off their skill, standing in their stirrups, drawing arrows from their quivers and shooting them at the city walls, all in one swift, lithe movement. They cannot see you hanging frozen in the air. As you watch, they gather together and the Caliph of Baghdad, Mustasin, walks forward from the gates of his starving city, flanked by faithful retainers. He kneels before Hulagu in a gesture of surrender. Using the external microphone, you can hear what passes between them. Mustasin is clearly petrified and he begs for his life and the lives of his people. The cold, impassive Hulagu demands to know where his treasures are hidden. Mustasin, seeing a ray of hope, tells Hulagu of his hiding place. When satisfied, Hulagu signals to his men, who massacre the Caliph and his attendants. The horrified people of Baghdad make no attempt to close the gates and the Mongols sweep into the city like a tide of soldier ants.

You are held in the air above Baghdad for over a month, and in all that time the slaying continues, the bestial ferocity of the Mongols remains unslaked. Only after forty days and the death of 800,000 people does the stench of rotting flesh force Hulagu to abandon the smouldering palaces, mosques and libraries of the dead city. After they have gone you cannot see even a dog or cat moving in the streets. All life has been wiped out. Shaken by the awful spectacle you have had to witness you are thankful when your Psi Sense registers a change in the flux of time. You engage the Variac drive once more and this time rematerialize as planned. Because you were trapped in a time flux, when you materialise no time has passed between the moment you were caught and the moment you were released. Your digital clock shows that in 3033 AD it is still the same day on which you began your mission.

Turn to **106**.

## 150

The Mongols are clever hunters, used to the night and the smells of the wild. Before you realise it you are running into the midst of one of the groups tracking you, appearing like demons from the darkness. You are overwhelmed and carried helplessly to the ornamental pool. Laughing cruelly, they force your head beneath the water lilies until your lungs are bursting. You try to use your mental powers but realise, too late, that your helmet was knocked from your head in the struggle. Your whole life flashes before you in the slow seconds of your death. You have failed and the Space Federation will never be.

### 151

Taken by surprise they both fall, cut down by a blast of white-hot energy. You manage to keep the other guards under control and order them to lead the way through the door. Inside is a bedchamber, and sitting on a large litter, swaddled in silks and furs, is Ogedei Khan, still weak from his illness. He looks up, his narrow eyes questioning your purpose. Golden statues, chests of treasure, and tapestries line the walls. Silk awnings close off the balcony at the back of the room. Do you:

| | |
|---|---|
| Order the two guards under your control to kill Ogedei? | Turn to **341** |
| Order them to guard the door and kill Ogedei yourself? | Turn to **309** |

### 152

Your blast misses Bloodhound and loses itself somewhere in the recesses at the back of the bay. He returns your fire as the tang of ionized air fills your nostrils. You double up as the plasma bolt hits your side – *lose 13 Endurance points.* If you are still alive, you find yourself too stunned to do anything. Bloodhound walks over to your stricken body and levels his weapon for the final blast. 'Wait, Bloodhound! Kill me, and the population of all Earth and the colonies may perish. I am helpless, but look at CAIN's memory banks before you void me.' He hesitates, then drags you into Falcon's Wing and ties you up. Examining CAIN's records, it soon becomes obvious to him that you are on a vitally important mission and that his mission to kill you must be abandoned. He unties you, but your wounds are so bad you must *subtract one from your Evasion Modifier.*

Bloodhound says, 'I'm sorry, Falcon, someone has used me – someone who wants the timelines to be changed.'

'Who gave the order to kill me?'

'Our Section Chief, Agidy Yelov. He told me you had killed Lord Kirik.'

'But Kirik has only been dead a matter of minutes.'

Bloodhound pauses then says, 'Yes, of course, Falcon. How can he know of Kirik's death so soon? Either he was responsible or he is in league with the traitor that did it.'

So, it seems your Section Chief is working with the renegade Lord. Turn to **99**.

### 153

Do you:

| | |
|---|---|
| Ask with which of the Lords of TIME Section Chief Yelov spent his vacation? | Turn to **179** |
| Use your Psi Sense to contact one of them mentally? | Turn to **121** |
| Ask if any one of them has travelled in time since the death of Agent Q? | Turn to **140** |
| Smile and make a short speech of thanks? | Turn to **167** |

### 154

Without warning he levels his laser rifle at you as if to fire. You have a brief second in which to save yourself. Make an **Evasion Roll**.

If you score 7-12, turn to **222**

If you score 2-6, turn to **202**

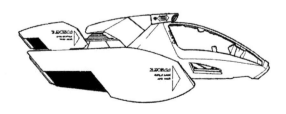

## 155

You send a lascom message to the Phocian, telling him that his mind is being controlled by another. Suddenly his ship begins to weave in space as if about to attack. You decide to take evasive action. Make an **Evasion Roll,** treating your Evasion Modifier as 0 for this roll only.

If you score 6-12, turn to **19**

If you score 2-5, turn to **190**

## 156

They are skilled with their shortbows and some loose arrows as you duck back through the gate. Make an **Evasion Roll.**

If you score 6-12, turn to **185**

If you score 2-5, turn to **171**

## 157

You score a hit and three of the Mongols are swept off the roof to the muddy street below, screaming as they fall. You climb aboard your flyer. The cockpit canopy clicks into place, deflecting Mongol arrows as it does so. You accelerate away into the night sky, engaging the ion drive.

Turn to **254**.

## 158

The second guard raises a laser rifle equipped with an energy grenade launcher but you manage to blast before he takes aim. Make an **Attack Roll.**

If you score 6-12, turn to **57**

If you score 2-5, turn to **27**

## 159

He leaps at you as you grab for your blaster and trigger it just in time. A lancing white bolt of superheated plasma eats into the cydroid's chest. Sparks fly and there is the unmistakeable tang of vaporised metals. A nearby plasma sensor begins to flash and the siren of a Citpol jetcopter wails as the cydroid buckles, short-circuiting in a sea of sparks, before falling inert. You have been fighting a machine. You examine it, but the damage is too severe for you to gain a clue as to its origins, before two Enforcers alight from their 'copter, pointing their stun-lances at you. 'Let's see your ID.' You produce your ID chip and hand it to the one who spoke, still covered by the other. He clips it into his Remote Access Terminal (RAT) on his arm and a look of disappointment crosses his features, as he realises who you are. 'What's been going on here?' he says. You report exactly what happened and he returns your chip and turns to examine the cydroid.

Turn to **137**.

## 160

You parry the spear-thrust with your sword and counter quickly, slashing across his midriff. Make an **Attack Roll.**

If you score 7-12, turn to **94**

If you score 2-6, turn to **111**

## 161
### [score a C]

Bloodhound hurries back with you to your time machines, Falcon's Wing and Hunter, and you both set out for the only timehole on planet Hel, 600 AD, hoping finally to corner the Creche. You may use your autodoc to *restore up to 12 Endurance points* on the way. While waiting to rematerialize, you ask CAIN about planet Hel. CAIN chimes: 'Planet Hel was discovered in 2978 AD by Skirrow, head of the Research Section of TIME, during the same voyage on which he discovered Skirrow's World. It is a tropical world with many dangerous predators, and plants which can trap and digest humans. There are no intelligent life forms. The air is breathable.' It seems that planet Hel was well named by its discoverer.

You rematerialize at the same instant as Bloodhound and Falcon's Wing settles slightly, as if on soft ground. You are resting on the top of a tropical rain forest. The tops of the trees are flattened by a mass of tangled creepers which form a carpet so dense that CAIN mistook it for the surface of the planet. Even the weight of Falcon's Wing has only bowed it

slightly. You meet outside on the tree carpet and move towards a time machine, undisguised by a hologram, which rests on the foliage a hundred metres away. Your Psi Sense tells you that the Creche are inside. As you watch, they begin to descend from the hatch of their machine. You must act quickly. What do you shout?

| | |
|---|---|
| 'Thinkstrike, Bloodhound!' | Turn to **12** |
| 'Power of Will, Bloodhound!' | Turn to **21** |
| 'Blast to kill, Bloodhound!' | Turn to **31** |

### 162

A lancing white bolt of superheated plasma shatters a floodlight behind your target. You have missed. A plasma sensor flashes blue, indicating that Citpol, the civil police, have been alerted. As you take aim again the cydroid points at you with its arm. The hand snaps upwards revealing a small nozzle which protrudes from its wrist. The red pulse of a particle disruptor streaks towards you. You have an instant to react; make an **Evasion Roll**.

If you score 7-12, turn to **191**

If you score 2-6, turn to **173**

### 163

You instruct CAIN to engage the Variac drive and using your Psi Sense, set coordinates for Earth, 1241 AD. During the journey, you can lie in your autodoc and *restore your Endurance points to 20.*

As you wait to rematerialize, you become aware of a flux in the psychic forces of the universe. You are forced out of null-space, but not at your destination. You look at the digital time read-out which tells you that you are in the year 1258 AD, seventeen years after the death of Ogedei Khan, Genghis's son. Turn to **149**.

### 164

Your mental attack is successful and Lynx slumps to the ground, dropping her knife. 'Come on, let's go,' shouts Bloodhound, running towards the ambulance. You run with him, but the renegade Lord senses your intention and tries to invade your mind. Make a **Chance Roll**.

If you score 1, 3, or 5, turn to **265**

If you score 2, 4, or 6, turn to **17**

### 165

At this close range it is difficult to miss completely and you shear the general in two with a blast of white-hot energy. You have missed the other, however, and he screams the alarm as he throws himself on you, willing to give his life to save his Khan. You have no choice but to order the guardsmen under your control to attack him. While they battle you slip through the door. Inside is a bedchamber, and sitting on a larger litter, swaddled in silks and furs, is Ogedei Khan, still weak from his illness. He looks up, his narrow eyes questioning your purpose, Golden statues, chests of treasure and tapestries line the walls. Silk awnings close off the balcony at the back of the room. You sense that your controlled guards will soon be defeated. You do not have much time. Knowing what must be done and hoping to make his death seem natural, you place a silken cushion over Ogedei's face and press down. His hands scrabble feebly at yours, but he is too weak to resist. His face turns blue as he dies. Suddenly the door swings open and several members of the Imperial Guard run in and charge at you. You try to dive through the awning to the balcony. Make an **Evasion Roll**.

If you score 6-12, turn to **189**

If you score 2-5, turn to **8**

### 166

Lord Silvermane's will shrugs off your attempt at mind control. He enters his time machine shouting, 'I'll have you decommissioned for this.' The time machine does not wink out, indeed Silvermane comes out a moment later bearing a message capsule. Do you:

| | |
|---|---|
| Return to Falcon's Wing? | Turn to **119** |
| Follow Silvermane to find out where he is going? | Turn to **142** |

### 167

You thank the Lords of TIME for attending your graduation ceremony, saying that you will repay their trust in you many times over. Lord Speke thanks you on behalf of the Lords of TIME and exhorts you to further the cause of harmony within the Space Federation while being vigilant against anyone so diabolical as to tamper with the past. After his speech you salute and are just leaving when Lord Kirik grabs one of the small seal-like creatures in his tank and thrusts it into his mouth with voracious ferocity. He is obscured by a cloud of blood as you finally leave.

Turn to **22**.

### 168

Lynx's training has left nothing to be desired. Her reactions are superb and even as your blaster leaves its place of concealment she has hurled herself behind a dead horse. The crackling plasma stabs above her head, lost in the rolling smoke of the guns, and she ducks out of sight. Unable to hit her with your blaster, do you:

| | |
|---|---|
| Thinkstrike her? | Turn to **268** |
| Use Power of Will to control her? | Turn to **286** |

### 169

You step into the small hovrail car, secure the bubble hatch, and type in your destination and clearance code as the car rises on its air buffer. The acceleration is steady but not uncomfortable and lasts for half the journey, before you decelerate to the Eiger Vault embarkation point. After many changes of direction, occasionally riding above slower moving cars, you leave the spectacular vista of the neon-clad city behind and plunge into the tunnel to the Eiger. Leaving the monorail you walk to the checkpoint outside the enormous plasteel doors, where your ID chip is checked and the mind scanner is used to verify that you may be allowed into the vault. You step through a small personnel door, past two security droids, and into the cavern which houses the time machines and the research section of TIME.

The area in which the machines are kept is partitioned at intervals and you head straight for your own bay. In the centre of the bay, which is lined on three sides with racks carrying maintenance equipment, spare parts, the Variac drive recharger and sundry other useful items, lies Falcon's Wing. You approach the access hatch and the mind scanner lights up red, then green. You are drawn up into the time machine by invisible tractor beams activated by CAIN. You are standing on the glowing access disc and CAIN chimes, 'Welcome, Falcon.'

Turn to **210**.

## 170

As you step over the prone bodies of the general and the guard, a group of Imperial Guards mounting the wooden stairs catch sight of you. You slam the door and run across Ogedei's room towards the balcony. The door swings open and several members of the Imperial Guard charge at you. You dive through the awning to the balcony. Make an **Evasion Roll**.

If you score 6-12, turn to **189**

II you score 2-5, turn to **8**

## 171

You are not quick enough. An arrow takes you in the back. You throw up your arms and collapse in a heap. You have failed and the Space Federation will never be.

## 172
### [score an M]

Guessing that whoever is controlling the Phocian, possibly the renegade Lord, is planning to destroy the Keladi envoy Korakiik and plunge Earth and Kelados into war, you attempt to target the ship's pulse lasers onto the Corsair craft and open fire. Make an **Attack Roll**.

If you score 6-12, turn to **224**

If you score 2-5, turn to **203**

**173**

You throw yourself behind a plasteel container but are too late. Unluckily for you, this is a very advanced model and the particle disrupter catches your side, and uniform and flesh fizz to nothing. The siren wail of an approaching Citpol jetcopter sounds more than pleasant as you wait for the cydroid to appear behind the container. Instead it makes a superhuman leap to the edge of the loading bay and drops fifty feet to the level below, cracking the streetmetal on impact. Unaffected by the cloud of sparks this causes, it disappears into the maze of the city's traffic lanes. You drag yourself to your feet in time to greet the two Enforcers who alight from the jetcopter. There are always two of the City Police, and they both cover you with their stunlances. 'Let's see your ID.' You produce your ID chip and hand it to the one who spoke, still covered by the other. He clips it into the Remote Access Terminal (RAT) on his arm and a look of disappointment crosses his features as he sees you are a genuine SAT. 'Fun and games on your first day, eh? What have you to say for yourself?' You report exactly what happened and the Enforcer hands back your ID chip, saying, 'A file of your statement will be flashed to your Section Chief.'

The second says, 'I have summoned an ambulance – they'll look after you.' He leaves a homing beacon for the ambulance and they take off. Soon, the Health Executive ambulance is hovering above you. Two medtechs jump down with a stretcher and you are soon within one of the autodocs, an outdated model. Your vaporised tissue is regenerated at an incredible rate, but a wound of this nature does not always heal perfectly. *Subtract one from your Attack Modifier* as your reactions are not what they were. *Restore your Endurance points to 18*. Refusing sedatives, you are soon ready to board the hovrail.

Turn to **169**.

**174**

You instruct CAIN to engage the Variac drive and, using your Psi Sense, set coordinates for Earth, 1241 AD. During the journey, you can lie in your autodoc and *restore your Endurance points to 20.* As you wait to rematerialize, you become aware of a flux in the psychic forces of the universe. You are forced out of null-space, but not at your destination. You look at the digital-time read-out which tells you that you are in the year 1258 AD, seventeen years after the death of Ogedei Khan, Genghis's son.

Turn to **134**.

### 175

You lose balance at the vital moment and miss. They pause uncertainly at the sight of your flyer, but one unleashes an arrow which finds its mark and you topple to the muddy street below, breaking your neck. You die instantly. You have failed; the Space Federation will never be.

### 176

You concentrate your mind on the driver of the ambulance. Hoping the Lord's attention is distracted, you make your effort. Make a **Power of Will Roll**.

If you score 8-12, turn to **258**
If you score 2-6, turn to **144**
If you score 7 roll again.

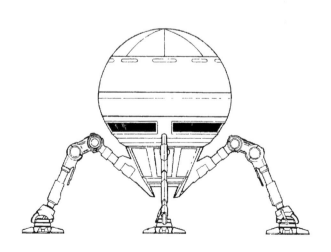

### [score a C]

He goes for his laser rifle, but with superb reactions and the skill of a trained combateer you draw your blaster and fire first. Make an **Attack Roll**.

If you score 6-12, turn to **116**

If you score 2-5, turn to **238**

The computer has been unable to keep your lasers targeted, owing to your failure to stay on the Phocian's tail. The lasers do not fire. As you wrestle with the controls to attempt another attack, suddenly the screen flares as the Phocian Corsair opens fire on the Keladi ship, its lasers piercing the hull of the larger ship which lurches sickeningly. You are too late. As your finger moves to the fire button the Corsair ship rakes the envoy's ship again with its pulse lasers. There is a brilliant explosion which fills the scanner screen with light and then you are suddenly engulfed in blackness. You find yourself in a smoke-filled shelter, a fugitive from an alien race on your own world. The past has been changed and your memories with it. You leap out of the shelter to hurl a grenade at a strange alien craft on the street above you… As Falcon, Agent of TIME, you have failed.

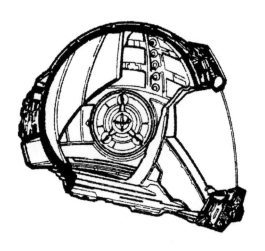

You ask the Lords of Time with which one of them Yelov spent his vacation. You step back in surprise as Kirik's pincers thresh the waters of his tank. He is plainly outraged. The Creche scuttle into and out of their cocoons but your translator cannot guide you as to what this may mean. Pilota raises her eyebrows and exchanges glances with Silvermane, before Speke demands: 'What do you want to know that for? It is none of your business.'

Turn to **194**.

## 180

Too late! A translucent beam of ruby light connects the tip of the laser rifle to your hip, shearing through skin and bone like a hot knife through fungspread. *Lose 10 Endurance points.* If you are still alive, as you fall to the ground you manage to ready your blaster. The Eiger Vault energy weapon detector sirens begin to **Attack Roll**.

If you score 8-12, turn to **116**
If you score 2-7, turn to **238**

## 181

Caught by surprise, Lord Silvermane's powerful body falls over your leg largely under his own momentum. With a shout of alarm he turns to look at you only to find your blaster inches from his face.

'With respect sir, I must again ask, where are you going?'

Barely controlling his rage he says: 'I have come for an important document, kept in the safest place I know of here on Earth, my time machine.' The hatch opens in response to his mind scanner and he directs you to a document holder. Looking inside you can see that it contains the blueprints of some of the most advanced Rigellian technology together with information which shows that Silvermane is carrying out a technology trade to the mutual benefit of both Earth and Rigel Prime. 'Thank you,' says Silvermane, taking the documents from you. 'I must be at the Galactic Trade Centre within the hour. Your career with TIME has been a short one has it not?' Realising that you will be powerless if your security code clearance with CAIN is revoked, you decide to take a risk and tell him of your mission. He listens, at first with impatience which changes to alarm. 'Then I shall defer court martial, but I expect a full report of the investigation which I am sure Agidy Yelov will commission.' He turns to leave, then pauses. 'Lord Speke bears investigation if I am not mistaken,' and with that he strides to the exit of the Vault.

You return to Falcon's Wing. Turn to **119**.

### 182

You protest your innocence and tell him he is a fool if he shoots you, but with a look of contempt Bloodhound triggers a bolt of superheated plasma that catches you in the head. Death is instantaneous; you are completely unrecognisable. You have failed.

### 183

Bloodhound is telling you that everything has been quiet, except that the Emperor has been attended by a doctor, when all three of you feel a very strong mental presence. Your heads turn as one towards a strange contraption coming nearer Napoleon and his escort. Two horses, one behind the other, are harnessed to a wooden, covered wagon with two small holes high up on either side for windows and doors which open at the back. A medical elderly is riding the first of the horses. It is one of the first ambulances ever made of the pattern designed by Baron Larrey, a French Army Surgeon, in 1805. The strength of the mental presence within the ambulance leads you to believe that the renegade Lord must be inside, and you prepare to attack together.

Turn to **304**.

### 184

Lynx attempts to Thinkstrike you again, but she is still not powerful enough to overcome your mental defences. Turn back to **39** and choose again.

## 185

You run through the gateway just in time and arrows whistle past you. They chase you through the streets as you dodge between drunken revellers. At last you sight the city gate and sprint towards it. Two more sentries see you fleeing from the palace guard and draw their bows. In desperation you fire your blaster. Make an **Attack Roll.**

If you score 7-12, turn to **199**
If you score 2-6, turn to **207**

## 186

You move behind Lynx but she watches out of the corner of her eye, waiting for you to make a move while she keeps Bloodhound at arm's length with the knife. Make an **Attack Roll**.

If you score 7-12, turn to **339**
If you score 2-5, turn to **352**
If you score 6, roll again.

## 187

You try to twist aside from the wicked thrust but are caught under the arm. Flailing wildly you fall backwards off the ladder to the ground below. *Lose 14 Endurance points.* If you are still alive, you bind your wound with a piece of your cloak to staunch the blood. Do you:

| | |
|---|---|
| Wait outside the city leaving Alexander to his fate? | Turn to **200** |
| Try again to scale the wall? | Turn to **147** |

## 188

The Creche fall onto the tree carpet and you move forward to make sure of your victory. Suddenly, Agidy Yelov, wearing a psionic damper circlet on his head that gives protection from mental attacks, appears from behind the Creche's time machine. You hesitate in surprise as he turns to you, his blaster pointing at the ground. 'Well done, Falcon, Bloodhound. Of course you know that I had set up a trap for the renegade Lord, but I really must congratulate you for a

truly outstanding performance against the Creche.' Bloodhound looks at you to see what you will do. Will you:

Blast Yelov? Turn to **259**

Await Yelov's orders? Turn to **120**

### 189

You roll onto the balcony as a hand-axe, thrown by one of the Imperial Guard, tangles itself in the silken awning behind you. You leap from the balcony to the edge of the palace roof, swinging your arms and pulling your legs up over the edge as the guardsmen rush onto the balcony behind you. Thinking quickly, you activate the flyer's homing beacon which you keep in your hand as you run round the edge of the roof, away from the guardsmen who are now helping each other onto the roof's lacquered wooden slats. The flyer approaches but you must stand still now, to avoid confusing the flyer's computer. Some of the Mongols, shouting ferociously, will be upon you before you can climb aboard. Balancing on the edge of the roof and mentally exhausted, you are forced to use your blaster. Make an **Attack Roll.**

If you score 5-12, turn to **296**

If you score 2-4, turn to **175**

### 190

Twin laser pulses from the Phocian ship strike your bows. The ship shudders and there is a thunderous report as the lights fail. The computer flashes up a damage report:

LIFE SUPPORT: BRIDGE ONLY
MAIN DRIVE: 10% EFFICIENCY
ENERGY: LOW
ATTACK LASERS: INTACT
CABIN PRESSURE: NORMAL
SCANNERS: FUNCTIONAL
LASCOM SYSTEM: RECEPTION ONLY

The scanner shows a second ship approaching from behind an asteroid belt and the Phocian changes course to intercept it. The large ship flashes a lascom message: 'This is the Clanship

*Keladan III*; we are on a priority diplomatic mission. Do not attack. Repeat, do not attack. Change course. We are Keladi, do not attack.'

You realise that whoever is controlling the Phocian pilot, almost certainly the renegade Lord, is trying to kill the Keladi envoy so that Kelados and Earth will be plunged into war. You have energy enough for one attack only and in a desperate attempt to save the envoy's life you try to target and fire your lasers. Make an **Attack Roll**.

If you score 8-12, turn to **213**

If you score 2-7, turn to **242**

### 191

You throw yourself behind a plasteel container and the particle disruptor dissolves part of a nearby stanchion with a fizzing sound. This cydroid is apparently a very advanced model. You hear the siren wail of an approaching Citpol jetcopter. The cydroid makes a superhuman leap to the edge of the loading bay and drops fifty feet to the level below, cracking the streetmetal on impact. Unaffected by the cloud of sparks this causes, it disappears into the maze of the city's traffic lanes. You are on your feet in time to greet the two Enforcers who alight from the jetcopter. There are always two of the City Police, and they both cover you with their stun-lances. 'Let's see your ID.'

You produce your ID chip and hand it to the one who spoke, still covered by the other. He clips it into the Remote Access Terminal (RAT) on his arm and a look of disappointment crosses his features as he sees you are a genuine SAT. 'Fun and games on your first day, eh? What have you to say for yourself?'

You report exactly what happened and the Enforcer hands back your ID chip, saying, 'A file of your statement will be flashed to your Section Chief.' With that they turn on their heels and take off, bathing you with the hot exhaust of their 'copter as they go.

Turn to **169.**

## 192

Acting with the instincts of a trained combateer, you throw yourself through the air, roll, and come up in a shooting position on one knee, both hands steadying your blaster. A translucent beam of ruby light connects the tip of the laser rifle to the wall of the bay behind your shoulder, severing a camera from its gimbals, and the Eiger Vault energy weapon siren begins to wail. You open fire. Make an **Attack Roll.**

If you score 6-12, turn to **116**

If you score 2-5, turn to **238**

## 193

Ripping the ambulance doors open reveals a bizarre sight. Six creatures like giant ants, mandibles clicking in agitation, are backing into a honeycomb structure, their red, compound eyes menacing. The honeycomb is on top of a flyer, similar in design to your own. The six beings, together known as Lord Creche 82282, the renegade Lord, are unaffected by the combined Thinkstrike. Bloodhound suddenly grabs you and throws you out of the ambulance, leaping down after you and drawing his sabre. He is being controlled by the Creche! A long battle follows during which time you both struggle to find an opening. Although entranced, Bloodhound is a fine swordsman and you begin to bleed heavily from several cuts. *Lose 8 Endurance points.* If you are still alive, your battle continues and the ambulance rolls on. Nobody intervenes in your fight because Napoleon has given the order for his Imperial Guard to advance and everybody moves off down the hill. At last you break the control over Bloodhound's mind and, dropping his sabre, he mumbles an apology.

Turn to **344.**

## 194
### [score a B]

Speke says, 'Discretion is important to an Agent of the Time Police. If you are to prove that you can further the cause of peace within the Space Federation while being vigilant against anyone so diabolical as to tamper with the past, you must learn this quickly. I trust you will show more respect for your superiors from now on.' Feeling that your graduation ceremony has not been a complete success, you salute and are about to leave when Lord Kirik grabs one of the small seal-like creatures in his tank and thrusts it into his mouth with voracious ferocity. He is obscured by a cloud of blood as you finally leave.

Turn to **22**.

## 195

The crackling bolt of lightning from your blaster pierces through the hussar's body and he falls back into the brook with a splash. You are turning to ride out of the hollow when all goes black around you. You have killed your ancestor and neither you, your father, nor your father's father have ever existed. You have changed the course of history and failed in your mission.

## 196

You lie down in the autodoc and the anaesthetising pad which rests over a small vein in your neck sends you into unconsciousness. You never come round again. The course of the past will be changed too soon after you would have left the autodoc for you to prevent it. While Falcon's Wing lies idle at the Eiger Vault an evil intelligence has been at work. You have failed.

## 197

The cydroid's mechanical reactions are even faster than yours. It catches your leg in its hand and then, with amazing strength, begins to crush it slowly. Pain overcomes you as you dangle helpless, before it places its foot on your head, and pulverises it as if it were an over-ripe melon. You have failed.

## 198

You concentrate your mind in an attempt to control Bloodhound's mind. Bloodhound also has powers of the mind and it will be no easy task. Make a **Power of Will Roll.**

If you score 7-12, turn to **126**
If you score 2-5, turn to **20**
If you score a 6, roll again.

## 199

One is vaporised by the superheated blast of plasma and the other immediately throws himself to the ground. You jump over him and out of the city. Your pursuers have stopped at the gate looking in sheer disbelief for the remains of the warrior you have killed. Hoping your actions have not seriously changed the timelines, you arrive back at the cave mouth in time to see a large bear poking at the flyer. If you blast it you will damage the flyer. Do you:

Try to Thinkstrike the bear?                    Turn to **216**
Move in to attack the bear using
    unarmed combat?                          Turn to **112**

## 200

You wait outside, pretending to be wounded as the clamour inside the city increases. New siege ladders are brought up and a phalanx of men smashes through the city gates. Soon the clash of arms gives way to the screams of the townspeople as the Macedonians massacre them in the frenzy that has seized them when Alexander was lost to sight. Minutes later, Alexander, badly wounded, is carried by several soldiers from the gate to his great white tent. Your Psi Sense tells you that one of the nearby soldiers is Lord Speke, and he has also noticed you. He pauses, then approaches you. He is carrying a sword but he gives himself up.

You walk up into the hills, and he explains that for some time he has been breaking the First Law of TIME and living as an ancient Greek. He has always been careful not to upset the timelines seriously, but he knows he has been acting wrongly. His collection of ancient Greek weapons in his time machine is authentic and he has even buried ancient artifacts in places where he could 'discover' them as archaeological finds in the 31st century.

You look into his mind, with his consent, and see that it is all true. Speke is not the renegade Lord. Tears run down his face as he realises his hobby is over. 'At least,' he says, 'I can say I saw the man whose people thought he was a god.' He asks you how you discovered him and you tell him about your mission. He is shocked by the news of a traitor Lord but offers a few words of advice. 'It is not likely to be either Pilota or myself – we are both Earther stock and interference with Earth's past might mean that we had never existed.' You thank Speke, but feel obliged to order him to return to 3033 AD and give himself up. Downcast, he assents and returns to his time machine while you continue with your mission.

Turn to **272**.

## 201

Turning left you move towards a junction only to find that the exits are blocked by barricades made of smashed hovmobiles and game-booths. You hear the unmistakable whine of hovbikes behind and, turning, are dazzled by ten or more floodlights, which flare suddenly. 'Well, well, an upper in the Morgue – hey, those epaulettes have real warp!' says a guttural voice, menacingly. 'What shall we do with the upper, Street'roids?'.

Then a woman's voice: 'I need that pacy helmet, Clone. Get it for me?' The whine of the hovbikes increases as their lights are turned off in unison. Your eyes became accustomed to the gloom in time to see twenty or more members of a hovbike gang. Their archaic machines are loaded with rams, sharpened flanges and spikes. The riders' faces are painted silver and gunmetal, their clothes adorned with parts of the casing of various types of robot, hair spiked silver and gold.

'Get the exec, Machine,' says Clone, their leader. A man wearing a tattered hydraulic suit, covered in spikes, races his bike at you. You dodge and he piles into the barricade, impaling himself on a snapped driveshaft. Clone signals and they all start towards you. Do you:

| | |
|---|---|
| Open fire with your blaster? | Turn to **55** |
| Thinkstrike Clone? | Turn to **42** |
| Use your Power of Will to control Clone? | Turn to **24** |

## 202

Too late! A translucent beam of ruby light connects the tip of the laser rifle to your hip, shearing through skin and bone like a hot knife through fungspread. *Lose 10 Endurance points.* If you are still alive, as you fall to the ground you manage to ready your blaster. The Eiger Vault energy weapon detector sirens begin to wail. Overcoming the pain you fire your blaster. Make an **Attack Roll**.

If you score 8-12, turn to **105**

If you score 2-7, turn to **238**

## 203

Twin laser pulses dart from your ship but your aim was off. They miss the Phocian ship and are lost in blackest space. As you lock on for a second shot you see your target darting and weaving. He is a skilful pilot, used to combat in these craft, and he will soon have you in his laser's sights. You decide to take evasive action. Make an **Evasion Roll,** but count your Evasion Modifier as 0 for this roll only.

If you score 7-12, turn to **253**

If you score 2-6, turn to **190**

## 204

To your horror you see that the Creche are unaffected by your Thinkstrike and you feel a powerful wave of irresistible mental energy beginning to hit you. Suddenly Agidy Yelov, wearing a psionic damper circlet on his head that gives protection from mental attacks, appears from behind the Creche's time machine and a bolt of white lightning leaps from his blaster, burning the Hivers to a crisp. You hesitate in surprise as he turns to you, his blaster pointing at the ground. 'Well done Falcon, Bloodhound. Of course you know that I had set up a trap for the renegade Lord, but I really must congratulate you for a truly outstanding performance against the Creche.' Bloodhound looks at you to see what you will do. Will you:

| | |
|---|---|
| Blast Yelov? | Turn to **259** |
| Await Yelov's orders? | Turn to **120** |

The two guards collapse against each other, propping each other up like dolls for a moment, before sliding to the ground. You slip past them to the door which opens into a store-room lined with barrels of koumiss, fermented mare's milk. A row of carcasses hangs on hooks above a smoking fire. In the corner lies the huddled form of an unconscious Mongol, obviously drunk. You open another door opposite into a banqueting hall, the walls of which are lined with gold, the plunder of half the world. It is full of Mongols, eating and drinking. To your surprise there are no tables, but a great fire has been lit in the centre of the hall. Musicians are playing fast rhythmic music and some of the Mongols strut around the fire, showing off the splendour of their leather coats, decorated and lined with fur. Others are still gorging themselves, tearing chunks of meat from whole carcasses with their hunting knives. As the music quickens some begin to whirl and leap around the fire, dancing wildly. Opposite you is a door leading outside to the palace courtyard. There is a wooden stairway just to the left of the store-room door and you decide to climb it, as you guess it leads towards the rooms behind the balcony.

Turn to **247**.

You wheel your horse about and wishing Bloodhound *bonne chance* head back towards the battle line. You veer right, deciding to begin near Poniatowski and then work your way along to the great redoubt. You crouch low as a cannon ball whistles overhead, bouncing along for three hundred yards before coming to rest against a tree stump. Every now and then you see a small gap appear in the French columns where a cannon ball has mown down as many as ten men before losing momentum. But each time they close ranks and charge on. You are approaching Poniatowski's wing when suddenly your Psi Sense tells you that a being with mental powers is nearby.

Turn to **73**.

## 207

The guards gape at you, as the plasma burns a hole in the ground before them. Their bows go slack. You leap over the hole and decide to charge one of the guards and force your way by. Make an **Attack Roll**.

If you score 6-12, turn to **246**
If you score 2-5, turn to **255**

## 208

The second guard raises a laser rifle equipped with an energy grenade launcher but you manage to blast before he takes aim Make an **Attack Roll**.

If you score 6-12, turn to **232**
If you score 2-5, turn to **27**

## 209

You reach into the mind of the huge crustacean, Lord Kirik, using your power of Psi Sense. With a shock you realise his overpowering thought is one of hunger, but that this is linked to the small seal-like beings captive in his tank. When he realises that you are probing his mind, the waters of his tank start to boil as his pincers thresh in anger. He is outraged; imbued with the deference for authority of the caste society of Kelados he appears appalled at your cheek. Your universal translator changes the bubbles issuing from his mouth into the words: 'You inedible prawn!'

He surges above the surface of his tank, water rushing in rivulets from his purple carapace but, containing his anger, subsides once more, pincers snapping, as he informs the other Lords what you have done.

Pilota smothers a smile, the Creche crawl deep into their cocoons, Silvermane shakes his head in seeming disappointment, but Speke shouts angrily: 'I must apologise for the action of this undoubtedly foul-tasting Earther. How dare you? You are risking an interstellar incident.'

Turn to **194**.

The hatch seals as you settle into your crash-couch and run routine system checks. Noting that all is in order you decide to ask CAIN for some information.

If you have recorded the serial number of a cydroid and wish to investigate its origin, turn to the number contained within the serial code.

Otherwise, turn to **243**.

## 211

You hurl a blast of mental energy at Bloodhound. But he himself is trained in this art and has his own defences. Make a **Thinkstrike Roll**.

If you score 8-12, turn to **107**

If you score 2-6, turn to **117**

If you score 7, roll again.

## 212

You concentrate on trying to control the mind of the Emperor Napoleon, one of the greatest leaders in Earth's history! He is an exceptionally strong-willed man, but the mental attack of the renegade Lord and his illness have left him weakened in spirit. Make a **Power of Will Roll**.

If you score 8-12, turn to **67**

If you score 2-6, turn to **79**

If you score a 7 roll again.

## 213

Twin laser pulses cut through space from your ship to the Phocian's. You can see parts breaking away from the hull in the dazzling red light of your lasers.

Suddenly the scanner screen lights up fiercely. You have scored a direct hit on his power plant and the Phocian has been vaporised with his ship. You can only hope that his descendants were not to be shapers of history and that changes in the timelines will be small.

You have, however, saved Korakiik, the Keladi envoy, and thwarted the renegade Lord. You try to turn your ship back to the starport but she is badly damaged. Make a **Chance Roll**.

If you score 3-6, turn to **231**

If you score 1-2, turn to **242**

### 214

You try to throw him over your hip but he is solid and immovable. His race evolved on a high-gravity world and his powerful blue-skinned frame is many times more powerful than yours. He grunts in indignation and cuffs you to the ground. *Lose 2 Endurance points.*

'I am in a hurry,' he says, controlling his anger, 'on important diplomatic business, but I will make sure you are demoted for this outrageous assault.' He enters his time machine, and then storms back past you with a message capsule which he has retrieved from inside, and strides bullishly towards the exit of the Eiger Vault. Will you:

| Follow Lord Silvermane to find out | |
|---|---|
| where he is going? | Turn to **142** |
| Return to Falcon's Wing? | Turn to **119** |

### 215

You have taken them by surprise and they both slump to the floor. You step over them and go through the door. Inside is a bedchamber, and sitting on a large litter, swaddled in silks and furs, is Ogedei Khan, still weak from his illness. He looks up, his narrow eyes questioning your purpose. Golden statues, chests of treasure and tapestries line the walls. Silk awnings close off the balcony at the back of the room. Knowing what must be done and hoping to make his death look natural, you place a silken cushion over Ogedei's face and press down. His hands scrabble feebly at yours, but he is too weak to resist. His face turns blue as he dies. You leave the room, hoping to slip back out to the flyer without being seen. Make a **Chance Roll**.

If you score 1-3, turn to **170**

If you score 4-6, turn to **127**

The bear is not clever enough to be affected. It just snarls and rushes at you. You have no time to do anything other than meet it in unarmed combat.

Turn to **112**.

You hurl a blast of thought at your pursuer, but too late realise that he has no mind, is in fact a cydroid. The cydroid lifts you easily above its head and throws you against a wall. *Lose 6 Endurance points.* Do you:

| | |
|---|---|
| Reach for your blaster? | Turn to **159** |
| Attempt a flying kick to its head? | Turn to **197** |

As you take aim you are hit by the fragments of an energy grenade fired by the weapon of the second guard, who has a launcher attached to his laser-rifle. You *lose 14 Endurance points.* If you are still alive you manage to blast. Make an **Attack Roll**.

If you score 6-12, turn to **232**

If you score 2-5, turn to **27**

You describe the situation to Lynx and tell her that Bloodhound had also been sent by Yelov to kill you and that he is now watching over Napoleon at the hamlet of Shevardino. Your horse has been frightened away and you set out on foot to explore the battle line nearer the redoubts.

As you approach, bugles sound behind you and a great charge of French infantry is launched with Marshal Ney at their head. The Frenchmen, singing the Marseillaise, come on shoulder to shoulder, magnificent in their blue and white uniforms. You are swept up in the charge and carried forward, unable to do anything against the hundreds of men, exhilarated in the heat of battle. On the redoubt ahead of you, the Russian commander, Prince Bagration, rides out in front of his line of green-jacketed men and salutes the French columns, crying in French, *'Bravo, messieurs, c'est superbe!'* As you approach Bagration's men they unleash a hail of musket fire and you take this opportunity to throw yourself to the ground as if dead, and let the charge pass over you.

Afterwards, battered and muddied, you pick yourselves up. You have found no trace of the renegade Lord and Lynx suggests you return to Napoleon's command post at Shevardino in case Bloodhound needs help. You agree and after a short time lost in the fog of battle, you approach the Emperor and his staff. Bloodhound rides to greet you and you tell him what has passed between you and Lynx.

Turn to **183**.

### 220

Where will you search for Lord Speke?

| | |
|---|---|
| In the time of Alexander the Great. | Turn to **303** |
| Earth 2700 AD at the time of the great interstellar colonial expansion. | Turn to **249** |
| The planet Kelados in 2710 AD, where Q found a Lord of Time tampering with the past. | Turn to **138** |
| The planet Dyskra, home of the Repnids, in 1985 AD. | Turn to **373** |

### 221

You draw and fire with the speed of a striking cobra. Make an **Attack Roll**.

If you score 7-12, turn to **70**

If you score 2-6, turn to **152**

### 222

Acting with the instincts of a trained combateer, you throw yourself through the air, roll, and come up in a shooting position on one knee, both hands steadying your blaster. A translucent beam of ruby light connects the tip of the laser rifle to the wall of the bay, behind your shoulder, severing a camera from its gimbals, and the Eiger Vault energy weapon siren begins to wail. You open fire. Make an **Attack Roll**.

If you score 6-12, turn to **105**
If you score 2-5, turn to **238**

## 223

You use your power of Psi Sense to enter the communal mind of the Creche. Their alien thought patterns are disturbing but your initial impression is one of group harmony. They think a message back to you which seems devoid of emotion: *We note your thought probe. Under TIME regulations you are beyond the parameters of permitted activity. We must inform the other Lords, those who are not we, myself.*

Their mandibles click and via your universal translator you understand that they are informing the other Lords that you have tried to read their minds. Lord Pilota smothers a smile, but the waters of Kirik's tank boil as his pincers thresh angrily. Silvermane shakes his head in seeming disappointment whilst Speke shouts angrily, 'How dare you? You are risking an interstellar incident.'

Turn to **194**.

## 224

Twin pulses from your lasers light up the back of the Phocian's ship. You have hit part of the main drive reactor and the Corsair hangs in space, drifting. Small puffs of flame at one side of its hull show you that the pilot is using the weak retro rockets in an attempt to angle his ship towards that of the Keladi envoy. It will be a few minutes, you estimate, before he is able to target his lasers. Do you:

| | |
|---|---|
| Match velocity with the stricken hulk and board her? | Turn to **263** |
| Finish her off with your ship's pulse lasers? | Turn to **276** |

## 225

You arrive back at Falcon's Wing and the red light of the brain scanner comes on. As you wait for the green, a security guard approaches, wearing a full-face helmet and power-armour, which is not standard issue. He carries a laser-rifle. 'Excuse

me sir,' his voice hisses through the air-escape ducts of his armour. Turning to meet him, do you:

Wait for him to come closer?                Turn to **154**

Use your power of Psi Sense to
    find out his intentions?                Turn to **125**

## 226

The two Mongols step back, feeling the force of your Thinkstrike, but are not stunned. Seeing you, they draw their swords and charge. You have no option but to use your blaster. Make an **Attack Roll**.

If you score 5-12, turn to **311**

If you score 2-4, turn to **239**

## 227

Your Thinkstrike works. The hussar clutches his forehead and then tumbles gracefully from the saddle into the brook with a splash. As he lies there, spluttering, you seem to see an uncanny resemblance to the portraits of your early ancestors. An uneasy feeling comes over you as you spur your horse on, out of the hollow. Looking back you see the hussar emptying water out of his shako. Turn to **145**.

## 228

You set your two controlled Mongols against the Imperial Guardsman and the general who cry the alarm. You take advantage of the struggle to slip through the door and into the room beyond. Inside is a bedchamber, and sitting on a large litter, swaddled in silks and furs, is Ogedei Khan, still weak from his illness. He looks up, his narrow eyes questioning your purpose. Golden statues, chests of treasure and tapestries line the walls. Silk awnings close off the balcony at the back of the room. You sense that your controlled guards will soon be defeated. You do not have much time. Knowing what must be done and hoping to make his death seem natural, you place a silken cushion over Ogedei's face and press down. His hands scrabble feebly at yours, but he is too weak to resist. His face turns blue as he dies. Suddenly the door swings open and several members of the Imperial Guard run in and charge at you. You dive through the awning to the balcony. Make an **Evasion Roll**.

If you score 6-12, turn to **189**

If you score 2-5, turn to **8**

## 229

Back in your time machine you catch your breath and decide where in time to travel to next. Will you:

Try to track down Lord Speke?                    Turn to **220**

Follow Lord Kirik to Kelados in

3033 AD?                                         Turn to **284**

## 230

Lord Silvermane seems a little alarmed but he says, 'I am on important diplomatic business which cannot wait. Besides, it is not for me to cause an incident by compromising one of my fellow Lords. I will, however, give a report to Agidy Yelov and I will be available to meet you at 12:00 tomorrow.' With that he turns on his heel and strides bullishly towards the exit of the Eiger Vault. Do you:

Return to Falcon's Wing?                         Turn to **119**

Follow Silvermane to find out

where he is going?                               Turn to **142**

## 231

You manage to turn the stricken ship back towards the starport. As you do so you notice on the rear scanner an asteroid mining ship appear from behind the Asteroid Belt, and your Psi Sense registers the presence of a being with great powers of the mind, probably the renegade Lord. You catch a thought, *Golden Horde* and then *self destruct.* To your surprise the mining ship blossoms into a flowering white light, like a star gone nova, as it explodes. Is the renegade Lord dead, you wonder?

It takes all of your skill to land the under-powered Corsair ship which groans and shudders during re-entry but, thankfully, gains the safety of the starport after a very hard landing. Wasting no time, you run to Falcon's Wing before starport security come to question you. CAIN tells you that he registered a Variac drive emission from the centre of the asteroid mining ship just before it blew up. Whoever it was used their time machine to wink out to safety.

Do you have a nuclear bomb? If you do, turn to **415**. If you do not, turn to **306**.

## 232
### [score a G]
Your aim is true. A lancing white bolt of superheated plasma erupts against one of the guards. He is blown back against the end wall of the corridor and then slumps to the floor. The second guard runs off as two security droids arrive. You walk up to the fallen man after giving your Security Code to the hovering droids as they aim their stun-lances at you. You identify yourself. Satisfied, they begin to hunt the second assassin. Your fallen assailant is dying, there is nothing you can do to save him. You ask him who sent him and lean close to hear him gasp: 'TIME Lord…' but the rest is lost in a spasm of coughing as he dies. You can keep his psionic damping circlet. This would impede your own powers of the mind but may be useful. Note it on your Agent Profile, if you wish to keep it. You head back to the safety of Falcon's Wing.

Turn to **336**.

## 233
Your blow is blocked with surprising speed. Before you can dodge, his forearm catches you in the stomach, throwing you back against a wall. *Lose 4 Endurance points.* You are amazed at his speed and strength. Will you:

| | |
|---|---|
| Go for your blaster? | Turn to **5** |
| Aim a flying kick at his head? | Turn to **18** |

## 234
You regain control for a moment but the renegade Lord tries to subdue your will once again. Do you have a psionic damper? If you do, turn to **288**. If you do not, turn to **282**.

Cautiously you descend onto the ooze of the forest floor which is covered with rolling ferns. You cast around with your holodetector for some time, picking your way across the treacherous ground. Within minutes you have scanned the area of the timehole without finding anything more than a few giant black centipedes, a metre long or more. As you return to Falcon's Wing your attention is caught when the surface of the swamp ripples slightly. You cannot see beneath the floating green scum, but decide to hurry the last few steps to the access hatch. Suddenly, the surface parts and huge jaws surge towards you. A fifty-foot prehistoric crocodile is lumbering towards you with startling pace. Will you:

| | |
|---|---|
| Use your Power of Will to stop it attacking? | Turn to **379** |
| Use your blaster on the monster? | Turn to **326** |

You put your hands on your head and tell Bloodhound that if he kills you, all on Earth will perish, imploring him to consult CAIN's memory banks. 'Stop playing for time, Falcon,' he barks, readying his blaster. Do you:

| | |
|---|---|
| Insist that you are not just playing for time? | Turn to **182** |
| Try to control Bloodhound with your Power of Will? | Turn to **198** |
| Go for your blaster? | Turn to **86** |

A nearby outcrop of rock proves to be a hologram. Lord Speke or another traveller in time is here. You walk through the hologram and see a Model B time machine, that of one of the human or humanoid Lords of TIME. From the markings you guess it to be that of Lord Speke and, surprisingly, he has left the access hatch on automatic, an extraordinarily careless mistake. You are drawn up into the machine and come to rest on the access disc. Lord Speke, dressed as a Macedonian soldier, is sitting in his crash couch examining a Macedonian sword of unusually fine craftsmanship. He has not noticed you. The floor of his machine is strewn with maps, charts and texts in the languages of the period. There is a beautiful wooden display cabinet full of ancient Greek weapons, including a fine collection of swords which appear to be originals, showing no sign of age, as if they had been cast quite recently. His molecular converter has not been used recently, despite Speke's clothes. Then he looks up and sees you. You remove your helmet and he recognises you.

'Falcon, you have caught me in the act,' he says despondently. He says he will give himself up and he explains that for some time he has been breaking the First Law of TIME and living as an ancient Greek. He has always been careful not to upset the timelines seriously, but he knows he has been acting wrongly. His collection of ancient Greek weapons is authentic and he has even buried ancient artifacts in places where he could 'discover' them as archaeological finds in the 31st century. You look into his mind, with his consent, and see that it is all true – Speke is not the renegade Lord. Tears run down his face as he realises his hobby is over. 'At least,' he says, 'I can say I saw the man whose people thought he was a god.' He asks you how you discovered him and you tell him about your mission. He is shocked by the news of a traitor Lord but offers a few words of advice. 'It is not likely to be either Pilota or myself – we are both Earther stock and interference with Earth's past might mean that we had never existed.' You thank Speke, but feel obliged to order him to return to 3033 AD and give himself up. Downcast, he assents.

You leave and return to Falcon's Wing to continue with your mission. Have you spoken with Special Agent Bloodhound since your mission began? If you have, turn to **338**. If you have not, turn to **52**.

### 238

He ducks and the white-hot bolt of plasma scores a furrow in the shoulder of his power armour without penetrating. He fires another cutting streak from his laser rifle but his aim is slightly off, and he only catches you in the leg, though this

almost parts company with your body: *lose 8 Endurance points.*
You collapse to the floor. If you are still alive, turn to **277**.

239

Your aim is off and although the general is thrown backwards
by a bolt of lightning from your blaster the Emperor's guard
survives and gives the alarm before charging at you. You have
time to use your blaster once more before you are impaled
upon his curved sword. Make an **Attack Roll**.

If you score 5-12, turn to **311**

If you score 2-4, turn to **305**

240

You are not fast enough and the knife lodges in your chest, up
to the hilt. Before you can recover from the pain, Lynx follows
up with a tremendous blast of mental energy, a Thinkstrike.
Its power bursts against your unprepared mind and you lose
consciousness.

Turn to **62**.

241

Using your power of Psi Sense you explore the mind of Lord
Speke. He is currently trying to visualise you dressed in the
garb of an ancient Greek. Upon realising that you are probing
his mind he suffers a flash of guilt and anxiety but then,
strangely, calms his thoughts and sends a message: *I put it
down to youthful exuberance, but you should not be behaving in this
way.* You decide to break thought contact. Speke looks at you
disapprovingly. Will you:

| | |
|---|---|
| Give a speech of thanks to bring the ceremony to a close? | Turn to **167** |
| Continue to probe the mind of another Lord? If you wish to probe: | |
| Silvermane | Turn to **280** |
| The Creche | Turn to **223** |
| Kirik | Turn to **209** |
| Pilota | Turn to **319** |

The computer flashes up a revised damage report:

| | |
|---|---|
| LIFE SUPPORT | INOPERATIVE |
| MAIN DRIVE | INOPERATIVE |
| ATTACK LASERS | INOPERATIVE |
| CABIN PRESSURE | DROPPING |
| SCANNERS | INOPERATIVE |
| LASCOM SYSTEM | INOPERATIVE |

The ship has taken too much damage and is breaking up. Your body explodes as the air is sucked out into space. You have failed.

If you wish to do so you can use CAIN to look at the files on each of the Lords of TIME. Each file has a number corresponding to a paragraph in this book. You should note these down in the boxes provided on your Agent Profile. You may turn to these whenever you are in your time machine, but always note the number of the paragraph you are already at, as no paragraph numbers to turn to will be given in the files. The file paragraph numbers are as follows: Lord Speke: **381**, Lord Silvermane: **399**, Lord Kirik: **395**, Lord Creche 82282: **398**, Lord Pilota: **397**.

When you are ready you can either ask CAIN the current whereabouts of the Lords of TIME (turn to **295**), or ask if there have been any expeditions into the past since the death of Agent Q, (turn to **307**).

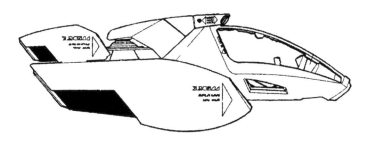

### 244

Your voice sounds flat and mechanical, unlike anything they have ever heard, as it comes via your translator. Shocked, they exchange glances. You have the chance to take them by surprise. Do you:

| | |
|---|---|
| Use your blaster on both of them? | Turn to **287** |
| Force your controlled guards to attack them? | Turn to **298** |

### 245

You exert your will to dominate the strong mind of Silvermane, Lord of TIME. Make a **Power of Will Roll**.

If you score 8-12, turn to **148**

If you score 2-6, turn to **166**

If you score 7, roll again.

### 246

You shoulder charge one of the astonished Mongols and sprint away from the city before the others can act. Your pursuers halt to examine in disbelief the hole you blasted. You hope your actions have not seriously changed the timelines. Arriving back at the cave mouth you see a large bear poking at the flyer. If you blast it you will damage the flyer. Do you:

| | |
|---|---|
| Try to Thinkstrike the bear? | Turn to **216** |
| Move in to attack the bear using unarmed combat? | Turn to **112** |

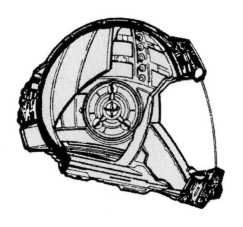

## 247

At the top of the stairs is a landing leading to a door with gold panels. A blackened staff with a tuft of horsehair hanging down from its top has been driven into the floor before it. A member of the Imperial Guard, dressed immaculately in gold and black lacquered armour is talking to an older man he refers to as 'Noyan' or general, who wears the long wraparound cloak of leather lined with fur, called a del, that the Mongols wear when not at war or if they cannot afford armour. You guess that this must be Ogedei's room, as the balcony must be just beyond it. You decide to Thinkstrike them both in quick succession. Make a **Thinkstrike Roll**.

If you score 6-12, turn to **215**
If you score 2-5, turn to **226**

## 248

Your blaster emits its lightning bolt of white-hot plasma and Bloodhound dies. Suddenly, you feel the attack of the renegade Lord, concentrating everything in a Thinkstrike against you. A wave of mental energy flows into you and your brain goes haywire. You seem to feel hot, cold, rain and fire all at once. It is as if you can see all colours at once and myriad voices speak every word in every language you have ever studied. Your brain overheats, literally burning itself out like a faulty electric motor. You are a zombie, incapable of thought, swaying on your horse and gurgling like a baby. You have failed.

## 249

You instruct CAIN to turn on the Variac drive to shift you into null-space and to re-engage the drive as soon as you have finished inputting the navigational co-ordinates for the timehole on Earth, 2700 AD. Your scalp tingles slightly as the time machine moves out of phase, and everything around you seems grey and insubstantial. You know that should you turn on the outside camera the screen would remain blank. Not even blackness exists in null-space. You cast your thoughts into the void and, using your Psi Sense, locate the timehole of

Earth 2700 AD. When you have translated this location into coordinates for CAIN, the Variac drive engages once more. The process of re-emerging in real time is immediate, but seems to take about an hour for you. You can spend this time in the autodoc, if you wish, and *gain up to 12 Endurance points.*

Your external camera pivots, showing a large starport loading hangar which appears to be completely automated. An Andromeda class star freighter of the series commissioned in 2692 AD to supply the outer colonies rests nearby, its immense cargo doors open for the robot cranes and packers. A line of the robot packers is quite close to Falcon's Wing which is disguised by hologram to resemble a large cold store. CAIN tells you that you are in Calgary Starport and that the star freighter is the Earth Federation ship *Frank Whittle*, named after the inventor of the jet engine used in aeroplanes of the 20th century. It is being loaded with supplies for the new colony world of Ascension, in particular the serum which will save almost the entire population from the deadly viral infection which broke out about ten days ago and is ravaging the colony. You can see no sign of Speke or his machine, but it could easily be beyond the freighter. You decide to check the hangar with your holodetector and CAIN prepares the uniform of a maintenance technician of 2700 AD in the molecular converter. You put on the boiler suit with its markings proclaiming you a grade 3 robotech attached to Calgary Starport. You are walking towards the freighter when, with a hiss and a screech, the boom of a packing robot descends upon you as if you were a piece of cargo. Its huge grab opens – evidently it intends to pack you! Make an **Evasion Roll**.

If you score 6-12, turn to **250**

If you score 2-5, turn to **353**

## 250

You jump aside just in time and the packer swings away once more. You are not disturbed again while checking the hangar, but find no trace of a time machine or Lord Speke. You return to Falcon's Wing, take off the boiler suit and feed it back into the converter. Where will you search for Lord Speke next?

| | |
|---|---|
| In the time of Alexander the Great (if you have not done so already). | Turn to **303** |
| The planet Kelados in 2710 AD, where Q found a Lord of Time tampering with the past (if you have not done so already). | Turn to **418** |
| The planet Dsykra, home of the Repnids, in 1985 AD (if you have not done so already). | Turn to **373** |

## 251

A soldier is stumbling towards the ambulance asking for a surgeon and one of Napoleon's Chasseurs has turned to see what is happening. The wounded soldier begins to clamber up to the doors at the back of the carriage. The eyes of the Chasseur, watching you, seem to glaze over and he turns away, as if unconcerned. The ambulance turns down the hill towards a hollow in the hillside and you run towards it. As the wounded soldier reaches for the handle he falls back, screaming, and lies limp on the turf. Do you:

| | |
|---|---|
| Use your Power of Will on whoever is inside? | Turn to **330** |
| Thinkstrike whoever is inside? | Turn to **229** |
| Use your Power of Will to control the driver and try to cause the ambulance to tip over? | Turn to **176** |

## 252

You are wiping the sweat from your brow when, suddenly, with bloodcurdling cries, a mass of horsemen burst from the trees behind you. They are armed with shortbows, hooked lances and curved swords. Their weathered yellow faces with oriental eyes and black moustaches are creased with the joy of slaughter. Many have conical helmets, spiked with a plume of horsehair at their centre. They wear painted strips of oxhide, laced together for armour over leather jackets and breeches. There seem to be hundreds of them boiling from the cover of

the trees, too many for you to use your mental powers. Will you:

Run for the shelter of the village?      Turn to **355**
Run the longer distance back to
    Falcon's Wing?      Turn to **368**
Use your blaster on them?      Turn to **343**

### 253

You bank and dive as twin laser pulses from the Phocian flash past your ship into the blackness of space. Then the Phocian increases speed. A third, larger ship appears on the scanner beyond an asteroid belt, and the Corsair changes course to intercept. You match course and increase speed as a second message reaches you, this time from the larger ship: 'This is the clanship *Keladan III*. We are on a priority diplomatic mission. Do not attack. Repeat, do not attack. Change course. We are Keladi; do not attack.'

You realise that this is the envoy ship carrying Korakiik, and that they will soon be within the attack range of the Phocian Corsair. You try desperately to target your lasers for another shot. Make an **Attack Roll**.

If you score 8-12, turn to **224**
If you score 2-7, turn to **178**

### 254

You hurtle away from Karakorum and soon see a greyness on the horizon ahead of you. When the flyer slows down near Vienna you are in daylight once more, but the sun is low in the sky. The flyer descends gently into Falcon's Wing, the launch doors open automatically, and the crash couch swivels and slides down into position before the instrument console. CAIN greets you with the information that the flyer you sensed leaving Karakorum as you arrived there returned to the time machine that you located near to your own. This machine then winked out, but another has recently arrived. Next CAIN flashes up a camera shot of the ground outside Falcon's Wing and you see Special Agent Bloodhound focussing his holo-detector.

You descend to the frost-rimed ground, greeting him. Bloodhound's news is that Yelov summoned him after he had returned to the Eiger Vault and reported you dead. When Bloodhound arrived, Yelov was deep in thought, studying a map of Borodino, a battle that took place on Earth in the year 1812 AD. As the doors slid open to allow Bloodhound in, Yelov had covered the map over, but not before the agent had caught sight of it. He entrusted Bloodhound with a message capsule, instructing him to open it in the hovrail on his way back to the Eiger Vault and then asked him how it was, if he had killed you, that Falcon had been reported as being alive in Earth's past at the time of the Golden Horde. Bloodhound feigned innocence and threw the message capsule away, after checking it and finding that it was a bomb designed to kill him. He travelled straight to the time of the Golden Horde in the hope of meeting you and suggests you both travel to Earth, 1812 AD, where there is a timehole situated conveniently close to Borodino, making it easy for the renegade Lord to change the past. Do you:

Do as he suggests and go forward to
    Borodino?                         Turn to **416**

Counter his suggestion and persuade him
    to come back to Earth in 3033 AD with
    you to confront Yelov?           Turn to **261**

### 255

You try to barge one of the Mongols out of the way, but fail to knock the stocky man over. He dives at you and the other guard strikes you across the back of the head with his sabre hilt. By the time you recover you have been bound hand and foot and they are examining your blaster and helmet. Powerless without the helmet, you are aghast to hear, as they carry you to the palace, that they regard you as a witch spirit of the Everlasting Blue Sky and will sew up your mouth and nostrils before killing you, lest your spirit escape to haunt them. You struggle but cannot get free. You have failed and the Space Federation will never be.

You believe you have been overlooked as the slaughter and pillage subsides, until you hear them deciding to cut the ears from each of the dead and throw them into sacks. You decide to slink out of the village while the Mongols are intent on their grisly ear count.

Turn to **229**.

## 257

With a great effort you manage to dominate their wills, holding them under control. You walk up to them and order them to take you to Ogedei Khan and to pretend you are a messenger. They walk across the Palace courtyard with a rolling, bandy-legged gait and you follow. At the palace door, two more guards stare at you impassively. One of the guards, controlled by you, speaks listlessly at your command. 'We bring a messenger whose message is for the ears of Ogedei Khan and no other.'

The door-guards step aside and usher you in. The doors open into a banqueting hall, the walls of which are lined with gold, the plunder of half the world. It is full of Mongols, eating and drinking. To your surprise there are no tables, but a great fire has been lit in the centre of the hall. Musicians are playing fast, rhythmic music and some of the Mongols strut around the fire, showing off the splendour of their leather coats, decorated and lined with fur. Others are still gorging themselves, tearing chunks of meat from whole carcasses with their hunting knives. As the music quickens some begin to whirl and leap around the fire, dancing wildly. Your guards lead you up a wooden stairway just to the left of a store-room door.

Turn to **278**.

## 258

You manage to wrest control of the ambulance driver's mind from the renegade Lord and he sets the carriage in motion. One of the wheels strikes a boulder and the ambulance tips over onto its side, and almost rolls down the hillside. The doors at the back open and you see six creatures, like giant ants. Their mandibles click in agitation and their dull, red, compound eyes stare at you. They are the six Hiver beings who together are Lord Creche the renegade Lord. Two are carrying small blasters in the mouthparts and you throw yourself aside in case they blast you. Make an **Evasion Roll**.

If you score 6-12, turn to **128**

If you score 2-5, turn to **89**

### 259

With the lightning reactions and skill of a trained combateer you draw your blaster and fire just as Yelov was preparing in blast you. You hit him and he is thrown backwards, one arm and leg burnt horribly. He falls down through a gap in the tree carpet and you run to the hole and peer down. His body is pillowed on an eerily glowing mass of jelly, like a giant amoeba As you watch he moves feebly and rolls off onto the leaf mould that covers the ground. As you peer through the hole the darkness below is lit by a faint blue light. Something much larger than Yelov is slithering slowly towards him. Yelov cannot move! Bloodhound cuts a rope from the creepers and you blast the fungoid mass that is moving towards him. It shudders and retracts and Bloodhound risks his life going down to save Yelov. He ties him up and you both haul him up to the tree carpet. You carry him to Falcon's Wing and, placing him in the autodoc, sedate him heavily, before returning to the Eiger Vault.

Turn to **420**.

### 260

You contact the mind of Pilota using your power of Psi Sense. She is far away, dwelling on her chances in the next solar yacht race. When she realises what you are up to her reaction is one of pleased surprise. She thinks a message to you: *I like a lot of warp, why don't you try the same thing on the others?* She is amused at the possibility but thinks a warning to you that they are: *a bunch of empty cargo pods.* Evidently she is impressed with your audacity. Will you:

| Give a speech of thanks to end the ceremony? | Turn to **167** |
| Probe the mind of another Lord? You can try: | |
| Silvermane | Turn to **280** |
| Speke | Turn to **301** |
| The Creche | Turn to **223** |
| Kirik | Turn to **209** |

## 261

You catch the hovrail to the TIME building. After about an hour, blackness engulfs you suddenly, just as the car is sliding to a halt. Someone has changed the timelines and one of your ancestors has been killed before his time. It is as if you had never existed. You have failed.

## 262

Before returning to Falcon's Wing you look around the rest of the refuelling bay. Two Phocian Corsair ships, sleek attack craft, have completed refuelling. A Phocian guard stands by the personnel ramp of the nearest ship, a squat humanoid with a brilliantly coloured head, like a macaw without a beak. To your surprise, your Psi Sense tells you that his mind is being dominated by another. Since Korakiik is the only known psionically aware Keladi at this time and he is in space orbit, a non-Keladi must be controlling him, possibly Kirik's killer and maybe the renegade Lord. Before you can investigate, your holo-detector begins to bleep continuously. A time machine has materialised behind you. Spinning round, you see a figure seeming to appear from the side of a gas tank that did not exist a few moments earlier. He looks like a Phocian pirate, but on seeing you he tips back his helmet to reveal the face of TIME Special Agent Bloodhound. Like you, he has a model A3 time machine, now disguised as the gas tank. His thoughts brush yours and he speaks before you can greet him, his blue eyes hard, 'I'm sorry, Falcon, I have a Termination Order for you.' You realise he has been ordered to kill you, just as he draws his blaster with the lightning reactions of an elite combateer. You dive to the floor, but are

wounded slightly as the lancing white bolt of plasma sears your neck. *Lose 4 Endurance points.* Will you:

| | |
|---|---|
| Attempt to use your Power of Will to control Bloodhound? | Turn to **198** |
| Try to Thinkstrike him? | Turn to **211** |
| Surrender and ask him to check CAIN's records before he kills you? | Turn to **236** |
| Draw your blaster and fire? | Turn to **221** |

### 263

You manage to dock with the stricken hulk and, unstrapping yourself from the free-fall harness, propel your weightless body through the air-lock. Using your blaster, you break through the airlock of the other ship. The metal melts and cracks as the plasma hits it and you thrust yourself quickly up the stairwell into the bridge. As your head clears the stairwell rim, the Phocian is about to fire his ship's lasers at the Keladi envoy vessel. You have only moments before the envoy is destroyed. Do you:

| | |
|---|---|
| Thinkstrike the Phocian? | Turn to **312** |
| Use your Power of Will to control the Phocian? | Turn to **325** |
| Use your blaster? | Turn to **333** |

### 264
#### [score a K]

Falcon's Wing reaches the surface and bobs gently. Your external camera revolves slowly until a floating platform comes into sight. A hideous apparition of jointed legs and bloated brain sacs slithers over its edge and is lost to the deep. Your exterior microphone amplifies a strange clicking which your translator reads as, '… unforgivable interruption of Kelcrrrrck'ick by a non-clan member…' Apparently there is no universal equivalent for Kelcrrrrck'ick. Puzzling as to what you may have interrupted, your attention is suddenly drawn to the screen as the camera tilts down towards the surface, picking up some movement. Through the reflected glare of the Keladi sun you see what looks like a hundred-metre long sea monster with six luminous eyes about to engulf you.

Falcon's Wing lurches violently as it erupts from the water and you realise it is a Keladi spaceboat with its floodlights on, a rakish space ship shaped like a manta ray. CAIN chimes, 'They are requesting holophone contact,' and you open a channel. You strain back in your crash couch as Falcon's Wing fills suddenly with water and a cruel looking Keladi appears before your eyes, claws waving. Remembering it is only a holo-projection, you relax and identify yourself as a member of TIME, codename Falcon.

The Keladi replies, 'It is well I arrived quickly. I am Rrillk, Argon of the TIME research station, here in the Biruk shallows. Had not I, a member of the bond-clan of TIME, arrived first you might have been treated with hostility, even attacked.' You ask where Lord Kirik is, and Rrillk informs you that he is at the research station on the sea floor.

You are towed slowly to the floating platform where you leave Falcon's Wing and descend to the bottom in a lift which travels down a long transparent shaft. As you descend you see various unusual and colourful sights. A coral-cloud, flapping its way through the sea like a scarlet underwater fern, and then a shoal of gorblefish, rainbow-hued aquatic creatures with anemone heads.

At the foot of the shaft, a man, Garren, is waiting, one of the consultants at the research station. He welcomes you to the air breathing section, a large transparent dome around which several Keladi gather to stare at you. Garren informs you that Lord Kirik recently travelled into Kelados' past, to the timehole in 2710 AD. You tell Garren that you must follow him immediately and he accompanies you to the surface in the elevator.

As you take your leave, Garren hands you a small container of pills, which he tells you are synthesised from the gills of Skorarli, the sleek predator of the depths of Kelados. They stimulate the reflexes. You thank him and take one before entering your time machine. *Add one to your Evasion Modifier* and note on your Agent Profile that you have a supply of these pills. You quickly instruct CAIN to switch on the Variac drive and, using your Psi Sense, plot your course through null space to the timehole in Kelados' past.

Turn to **281**.

## 265

You manage to close your mind to the renegade Lord and tell Bloodhound what has happened. You prepare to rip open the doors of the ambulance. What do you shout to Bloodhound?

| | |
|---|---|
| 'Thinkstrike now!' | Turn to **315** |
| 'Power of Will now!' | Turn to **330** |
| 'Blast to kill!' | Turn to **348** |

## 266

You try to trip the powerful Lord to the ground. Make an **Attack Roll**.

If you score 2-10, turn to **214**

If you score 11-12, turn to **181**

## 267

You are acting against the First Law of TIME, but as you step towards the village well, resplendent in your silver uniform with your helmet's reflecting plate pulled down like a mirror in front of your face, the slaughter stops, quite suddenly. They whisper in awe. You point at one of the Mongols and Thinkstrike him. He slumps to the ground. Next, you use the mechanical sounding voice box of your translator to order the Mongols to leave the village.

Their leader kneels before you and offers homage and the rest follow suit. 'We obey, O spirit of the Everlasting Blue Sky,' he says, and they mount up and ride quickly away.

The villagers gaze at you in fear and astonishment. Wasting no time, you gather up the clothes and the nuclear bomb and return to the safety of Falcon's Wing, hoping your actions have not seriously damaged the timelines.

You ask CAIN to what extent you have changed the past, and, to your relief, he responds, 'There is no significant change, Falcon. My files do carry a tale, however, about a sorcerer who saved the village of Ramallo from the Mongol

Horde, for a little while. Congratulations, Falcon, you are the sorcerer of Ramallo.'

Turn to **229**.

## 268

As she peeps out above the soiled saddle of the dead horse you concentrate and hurl a blast of mental energy at her, catching her somewhat by surprise since she expects you to try to blast her again. Make a **Thinkstrike Roll**.

If you score 6-12, turn to **118**

If you score 2-5, turn to **322**

## 269

### [score a C]

At this range you cannot miss and your blast overloads the cydroid's infra-red sensory circuits, leaving it temporarily inert. You step behind it and find the removable disc below which lies the deactivation switch. When you have thrown the switch you examine the cydroid carefully. It appears to be a very advanced model, equipped with a particle disrupter. Of particular interest is the serial number above the deactivation switch, SAT 75YV. Record this serial number on your Agent Profile sheet. Leaving the cydroid, you move on to the hovrail embarkation point.

Turn to **169**.

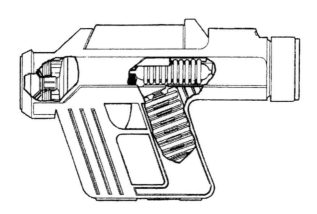

## 270

Your attempt fails. They look at each other and both cry, 'An evil spirit!' You have a chance to react before they cry for help Do you:

| | |
|---|---|
| Thinkstrike the guards? | Turn to **40** |
| Return to your flyer and use it to hover above the palace? | Turn to **63** |

## 271

As you ride up to him, Marshal Ney is scribbling hastily on a piece of paper, using the shoulder of one of his staff to rest on. He shakes sand from a silver pot onto the despatch to dry the ink and, rolling it up, hands it to you. 'To the Emperor – I need reinforcements,' he says. As you take the despatch he asks you which general you are assigned to. What do you say?

| | |
|---|---|
| 'Davout, *mon general*.' | Turn to **109** |
| 'Ledru, *les Cuirassiers*.' | Turn to **332** |

## 272

Before Speke enters his machine he turns to you and says, 'Falcon, if I were you I would investigate Kirik and Silvermane. It could be the Creche, but I think the Hivers have learnt their lesson. The Creche have no individuality, they do only what the Hive tells them.' With that he enters his machine and you enter Falcon's Wing. Do you:

| | |
|---|---|
| Travel to find Kirik on Kelados in 3033 AD? | Turn to **284** |
| Return to the Eiger Vault? | Turn to **334** |

## 273

Your phalanx hurls itself as one against the city gates, the men shouting in a frenzy, 'Iskander! Iskander!' The gates buckle under their ferocious assault and you are carried forward by the press of men into the city. The fighting is fierce and the screams of the dying are terrifying as the Greeks force their way towards the spot where Alexander jumped down from the wall.

Turn to **66**.

You find yourself unable to make your steed obey you, and are left staring sheepishly down the muzzle of the hussar's pistol as the hammer clicks shut and the round ball explodes into your forehead. You fall senseless to the ground, never to move again, you have failed.

You control the leader's mind and he calls his men back just before they strike you with swords and lances. They look at him in surprise as he orders them to return to loot the village, but they are well disciplined and obey. He rides with them and you, still carrying the nuclear bomb, manage to regain the safety of Falcon's Wing.

Turn to **229**.

The stricken hulk is a sitting duck, your computer is able to target your lasers automatically and you open fire. Twin laser pulses cut through space from your ship to the Phocian's. You can see parts breaking away from the hull in the dazzling red light of your lasers. Suddenly, the scanner screen lights up fiercely; you have scored a direct hit on his power plant and the Phocian has been vaporised with his ship. You can only hope that his descendants were not to be shapers of history and that changes in the timelines will be small. You have, however, saved Korakiik, the Keladi envoy, *and* thwarted the renegade Lord.

You turn your ship back to the starport. As you do so you notice on the rear scanner an asteroid mining ship appear from behind the Asteroid Belt, and your Psi Sense registers the presence of a being with great powers of the mind, probably the renegade Lord. You catch a thought: *Golden Horde* and then *self destruct*. To your surprise the mining ship blossoms into a flowering white light, like a star gone nova, as it explodes. Is the renegade Lord dead, you wonder? You manage to land the Corsair back at the starport without too much trouble. Wasting no time, you run to Falcon's Wing before starport security come to question you. CAIN tells you that he registered a Variac drive emission from the centre of the asteroid mining ship, just before it blew up. Whoever it was used their time machine to wink out to safety.

Do you have a thermo-nuclear device? If you do, turn to **415**. If you do not, turn to **306**.

The assassin walks calmly towards you, his voice hissing through the air escape ducts in his armour, 'What a pity, Falcon you seem to have dropped your blaster.' You are in too much pain to concentrate your mental powers, and you realise as he places his laser-rifle in front of your face that he is going to finish the job. This is the first time I've completed a commission given to me by a Lord of TIME,' he hisses. As he gloats a security droid appears, hovering soundlessly behind him, and discharges its stun-lance. The assassin is bathed in blue light and jerks back suddenly as the circuits in his power armour begin to short out. Unable to control the armour, which is too heavy to be moved without the assistance of its power pack, he falls on the floor, body arched like a crab, as the armour begins to steam. Sparks fly, and the power pack explodes, ripping his body apart. You may never find out who sent him to kill you. The security droid checks your ID and you drag yourself to Falcon's Wing before it can summon a medtech.

Turn to **336**.

At the top of the stairs is a landing leading to a door with gold panels. A blackened staff with a tuft of horsehair hanging down from its top has been driven into the floor before it. A member of the Imperial Guard, dressed immaculately in gold and black lacquered armour is talking to an older man he refers to as 'Noyan' or general, who wears the long wraparound cloak of leather lined with fur, called a del, that the Mongols wear when not at war or if they cannot afford armour. Your guards repeat their words, but the general

insists that he must hear what you have to say to the Khan of Khans. You know your voice will sound like a robot voice if you speak through the translator. What will you do?

Speak, saying 'I am a demon from the
ice-wastes'                                          Turn to **244**
Use your blaster on them.                            Turn to **165**
Force your controlled guards to attack
them.                                               Turn to **228**

279

You rematerialize in the Eiger Vault. All is as you left it. CAIN informs you that the machines of Lords Silvermane and Pilota are in their bays. Lord Pilota is still on Spiro's Ringworld and Lord Silvermane is in a meeting at the Galactic Trade Centre Will you:

Travel to TIME headquarters to
confront Agidy Yelov?                               Turn to **261**
Try to track down Lord Speke?                       Turn to **407**
Go back to the time of the Mongols,
Earth 1241 AD?                                      Turn to **174**

280

Using your power of Psi Sense, you reach out telepathically to the mind of Silvermane. His current train of thought is one of curiosity about you, but this changes to surprise as he realises that you are probing his mind. He thinks a message to you, the tone of which is condescending but tolerant: *You are exceeding your authority – I don't mind but others would,* and you realise he is thinking of Kirik. *I suggest you cease this probing of my mind immediately.* You decide to break off mind contact. Do you:

Go on to contact Kirik?                             Turn to **209**
Give a short speech of thanks to
conclude the ceremony?                              Turn to **167**

281

You emerge from the greyness of null-space into a huge spaceport on an artificial island, built so that the Keladi could trade with other spacefaring races without forcing them to adapt to an undersea environment. The huge, vaulted starport stretches for miles on each side; you can count more than forty different types of spacefaring vessels. The holo-generator throws the image of a large aluglass container around Falcon's Wing and the camera shows that nobody has noticed its sudden appearance. You ask CAIN for historical details of Kelados in 2710 AD. It chimes, 'At this moment in time the Keladi are on the brink of war with the Earth Federation. Reason: border incidents misinterpreted by Keladi as being a way of probing their defence systems. The Keladi, at this time, do not realise that many humans break the Earth Federation's laws and suppose that if one human kills a Keladi, his "clan", or all Earthers, approve his action. Phocian pirates are being encouraged to use Keladi starports as bases from which to prey on Earth Federation shipping.'

'What could be done to change the timeline here?' you interrupt.

CAIN waits for some seconds before replying: 'I can see one method of changing the timeline which would be both easy to do and disastrous in effect. The Keladi envoy, Korakiik, a telepath, regarded as insane and "clanless" by the Keladi but the only one who, through his psionic power, understands the Earth Federation and humans, is shortly due to leave Kelados orbit to meet an Earth envoy. Historically, he was responsible for preventing a war which would probably destroy both civilisations. To prevent this meeting would change the timeline to a greater degree than I can compute.'

You find yourself thanking CAIN as you pull on the uniform of a Phocian pirate which CAIN has already instructed the molecular convertor to prepare. Your psionic enhancer helmet now resembles the helmet of a Phocian laser-turret operator, disguising your features. Taking your holo-detector, you set out in search of Lord Kirik. Turn to **360**.

## 282

There is nothing you can do as the renegade Lord's mind bends its full power against you. A wave of mental energy flows into you and your brain goes haywire. You seem to feel heat, cold, rain and fire all at once. It is as if you can see all colours at once and myriad voices speak in every language you have ever studied. Your brain overheats, literally burning itself out like a faulty electric motor. You are a zombie, incapable of thought, gurgling like a baby. You have failed.

### 283

Your attempt to control his will fails and you are cut down by sword and lance. They leave you to die in a pool of blood, disappointed that you didn't offer better sport. As Falcon, you have failed.

### 284

You instruct CAIN to turn on the Variac drive to shift you into null-space and to re-engage the drive as soon as you have finished inputting the navigational co-ordinates for the timehole on present day Kelados (3033 AD). Your scalp tingles slightly as the time machine moves out of phase, and everything around you seems grey and insubstantial. You know that should you turn on the outside camera the screen would remain blank, not even blackness exists in null-space. You cast your thoughts into the void and, using your Psi Sense, locate the timehole of present day Kelados. When you have translated this location into co-ordinates for CAIN, the Variac drive engages once more. The process of re-emerging in real time is immediate, but seems to take about an hour for you. You may spend this time in the autodoc, if you wish and *gain up to 12 Endurance points.*

The feeling of disorientation when you rematerialize persists longer than is usual. Flipping the switch for the outside camera you are dismayed to see nothing in the floodlight but green fog. The machine rocks gently as if the stabilising legs were malfunctioning. With a start you remember that the surface of Kelados is one great ocean. Your altimeter tells you that the machine is floating to the surface, the hull can easily withstand the pressure of water at your depth of fifty metres. CAIN sends a TIME recognition signal to a nearby research station.

If you have seen a nuclear bomb, a man in golden armour named Iskander, or visited Spiro's Ringworld, turn to **300**.

If you have encountered none of these, turn to **264**.

### 285

Your Thinkstrike works. The hussar clutches his forehead and then tumbles gracefully from the saddle into the brook with a splash. As he lies there, spluttering, you seem to see an uncanny resemblance to the portraits of your early ancestors. An uneasy feeling comes over you as you spur your horse on, out of the hollow. Looking back you see the hussar emptying water out of his shako. Picking your way through the fog of battle you finally come across Bloodhound again, who is pretending to fix the girth of his horse. Breathlessly, you tell him that you have detected the presence of a being with mental powers, probably the renegade Lord. He suggests that you remain near Napoleon together and wait to see what happens.

Turn to **82**.

### 286

As she peeps out above the soiled saddle of the dead horse you concentrate your will in an effort to overcome strong-minded Agent Lynx, but she is still recovering from the near miss of your blaster's plasma and is taken somewhat by surprise. Make a **Power of Will Roll**.

If you score 6-12, turn to **135**

If you score 2-4, turn to **322**

If you score a 5, roll again.

### 287

Frawing and firing your blaster is difficult while holding two men under the control of your mind. *Lose 2 Endurance points* for the effort, but make an **Attack Roll.**

If you score 6-12, turn to **151**

If you score 2-5, turn to **165**

You place the circlet on your head, under your bearskin, and are able to withstand the mental might of the renegade Lord. In the meantime, Lynx has attacked Bloodhound and wounded him. Do you:

Go to help Bloodhound?           Turn to **417**

Rip open the doors and jump inside
    the ambulance?           Turn to **376**

The hussar loses his aim and has to reset the charge in his pistol. This does not take long, however, and you have only galloped a few paces when you are almost jolted from the saddle when the pistol ball buries itself in your left arm. *Lose 6 Endurance points.* Ney orders three of his officers to arrest you and they charge after you. You urge your mount on through the smoke of the French cannon. One of the officers, a young hussar, whose grey and red pelisse streams out behind him in the wind, has a good mount and is gaining on you. You ride down into a small dip, jumping a brook out of sight of the rest of the army and he follows. Do you:

Thinkstrike the hussar?           Turn to **227**

Rein in and blast him when he is
    near enough so you cannot miss?           Turn to **195**

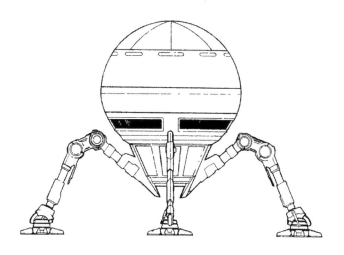

The superheated plasma from your blaster catches the monstrous crocodile in its opened jaws. It screams in pain and, threshing madly, retreats into the swamp. You float up into Falcon's Wing, intent on leaving this time as fast as you can. Will you:

| | |
|---|---|
| Travel to Earth in 2700 AD (if you have not done so already)? | Turn to **409** |
| Travel to Earth in the time of Alexander the Great (if you have not done so already)? | Turn to **303** |
| Travel to the alien world of the Repnids, Dyskra, 1985 AD (if you have not done so already)? | Turn to **375** |
| The planet Kelados in 2710 AD, where Q found a Lord of TIME tampering with the past? | Turn to **418** |

The nearest Mongol slides from his horse, but the others are upon you before you can do anything. A viciously hooked lance embeds itself in your chest and you cannot dodge their swords. They make your death as slow as possible, but you are already losing blood fast from several wounds. You are thankful when death takes you, but, as Falcon, you have failed.

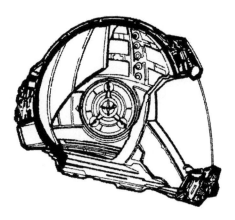

Bloodhound, controlled by the renegade Lord, cannot defend himself with a mental barrier and he slumps to the ground. You kneel down and revive him quickly. He is holding his head in pain, but thanks you for releasing him from the control of the renegade Lord. Do you:

| | |
|---|---|
| Try to control a nearby soldier and force him to shoot his gun into the ambulance? | Turn to **26** |
| Run to the ambulance and blast after ripping the doors open? | Turn to **43** |

You don your environmental suit as CAIN informs you that the atmosphere contains a great deal of methane gas and will not sustain human life. You descend to the floor of Dyskra. As you approach the nearest of the dark red outcroppings, the ground suddenly gives way beneath you. Repnids have tunnelled to within an inch of the surface and you fall into a boiling mass of hundreds of Repnid bodies in the cavern below. The end is swift, as several pairs of fangs inject their deadly venom and the deadly air of Dyskra contaminates your lungs. You have failed.

You leave the Eiger Vault and board the hovrail, *en route* for the Galactic Trade Centre. As you approach its gates you are suddenly engulfed in blackness. Then you find yourself in a smoke-filled shelter, a fugitive from an alien race on your own world. The past has been changed and your memories with it. You leap out of the shelter to hurl a grenade at a strange alien aircraft on the street above you… As Falcon, Agent of TIME, you have failed.

'Where are the Lords of TIME at this moment?' you ask CAIN. He chooses a visual display for this information from the files of the service computer.

| NAME | LOCATION | TIME NOW |
|------|----------|----------|
| Pilota | Freefall Recreation Centre, Spiro's Ringworld | 12:41 |
| Silvermane | Eiger Vault | |
| Kirik | Timehole trip, destination: Kelados 3033 AD | |
| Creche 82282 | EPSILON SECURITY CODE INSUFFICIENT | |
| Speke | EPSILON SECURITY CODE INSUFFICIENT | |

CAIN says, 'It is unusual that access to this kind of information should be denied to your level of security clearance. I have taken the precaution of linking with the service computer and I can tell you that Lord Kirik entered the Eiger Vault and left in his time machine. Lord Silvermane has just arrived here, at 12:40, as have two others with Omega security clearance – at 12:33 and 12:37. Only Lords have this code. The conclusion must be obvious even to a human, Falcon.'

You decide to act on CAIN's information after telling him to shut up, and hurry out to meet the recent arrivals.

Turn to **349**.

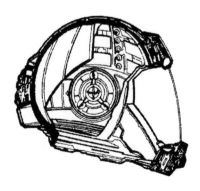

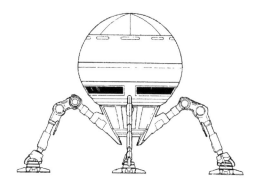

### 296

You score a hit and three of the Mongols are swept off the roof to the muddy street below, screaming as they fall. The flyer arrives, hovering next to you and you climb aboard. The cockpit canopy clicks into place, deflecting Mongol arrows as it does so and you accelerate away into the night sky, engaging the ion drive.

Turn to **254**.

### 297

You approach the time machine cautiously, but before you are close enough to see through the hologram which surrounds it a shock jars you. *Lose 5 Endurance points.* You have brushed against a force field which protects the machine. Since you cannot penetrate this shield you decide to search the battlefield for the renegade Lord.

Turn to **49**.

### 298

Taken by surprise, the general and the Imperial Guardsman are swiftly cut down. You manage to keep your guards under control and order them to lead the way through the door. Inside is a bedchamber, and sitting on a large litter, swaddled in silks and furs, is Ogedei Khan, still weak from his illness. He looks up, his narrow eyes questioning your purpose.

Golden statues, chests of treasure and tapestries line the walls. Silken awnings close off the balcony at the back of the room. Do you:

Order the two guards under your
control to kill Ogedei?                    Turn to **341**
Order them to guard the door and kill
Ogedei yourself?                           Turn to **309**

### 299

Fear and desperation spur you to superhuman efforts as you concentrate your mind and Thinkstrike the renegade Lord, but you are fighting against a strong mental barrier. Make an **Attack Roll**.

If you score 9-12, turn to **50**
If you score 2-8, turn to **9**

### 300

Falcon's Wing reaches the surface and bobs gently. Your external camera revolves slowly until a floating platform comes into sight. Two hideous apparitions of jointed legs and bloated brain sacs slither over its edge and are lost to the deep. Your exterior microphone amplifies a strange clicking which your Translator reads as, '… unforgivable interruption of Kelcrrrrck'ick by a non-clan member…' Apparently there is no universal equivalent for Kelcrrrrck'ick. Puzzling as to what you may have interrupted, your attention is suddenly drawn to the screen as the camera tilts down towards the surface, picking up some movement. Through the reflected glare of the Keladi sun you see what looks like a hundred-metre long sea monster with six luminous eyes about to engulf you.

Falcon's Wing lurches violently as it erupts from the water and you realise it is a Keladi spaceboat with its floodlights on, a rakish space ship shaped like a manta ray. CAIN chimes, 'They are requesting holophone contact,' and you open a channel. You strain back in your crash couch as Falcon's Wing fills suddenly with water and a cruel looking Keladi appears before your eyes, claws waving. Remembering it is only a holo-projection you relax and identify yourself as a member of TIME, codename Falcon. The Keladi replies, 'It is well I arrived quickly. I am Rrillk, Argon of the TIME research station, here in the Biruk shallows. Had not I, a member of the bond-clan of TIME, arrived first, you might have been treated with hostility, even attacked.' You ask where Lord Kirik is, and Rrillk informs you that he has just used his time machine to go back to the timehole in Kelados' past, 2710 AD. You decide to follow him immediately, and thanking Rrillk for his help, disengage the holophone connection and ask CAIN to engage the Variac drive.

Turn to **281**.

### 301

Using your power of Psi Sense you explore the mind of Lord Speke. He is currently trying to visualise you dressed in the garb of an ancient Greek. Upon realising that you are probing his mind he suffers a flash of guilt and anxiety, but then, strangely, calms his thoughts and sends a message: *I put it down to youthful exuberance, but you should not be behaving in this way.* You decide to break thought contact. Speke looks at you disapprovingly. Will you:

| | |
|---|---|
| Give a speech of thanks to bring the ceremony to a close? | Turn to **167** |
| Continue to probe the mind of another Lord? If you wish to probe | |
| Silvermane | Turn to **280** |
| The Creche | Turn to **223** |
| Kirik | Turn to **209** |

### 302

Your blaster spouts white-hot bolts of plasma, cutting a swathe through the horsemen. Ten or more perish and the squealing of their horses rings in your ears. Seeing what they take to be evil monk, they turn tail and flee. They are followed by the rest of the horsemen in the village as the word of your evil magic is shouted one to another.

Still carrying the nuclear bomb, you go back to Falcon's Wing, hoping your actions have not seriously changed the timelines. You ask CAIN to what extent you have changed the past and to your relief, he responds, 'There is no significant change, Falcon. My files do carry a tale, however, about a sorcerer who saved the village of Ramallo from the Mongol horde for a brief time. Congratulations, Falcon, you are the sorcerer of Ramallo,' CAIN then adds, 'Lucky to be alive.'

You tell CAIN to shut up. Turn to **229**.

### 303

You instruct CAIN to turn on the Variac drive to shift you into null-space and to re-engage the drive as soon as you have finished inputting the navigational co-ordinates for the timehole in the time of Alexander the Great. Your scalp tingles slightly as the time machine moves out of phase, and everything around you seems grey and insubstantial. You know that should you turn on the outside camera the screen would remain blank, not even blackness exists in null-space. You cast your thoughts into the void and, using your Psi Sense, locate the timehole of Alexander the Great. When you have translated this location into co-ordinates for CAIN, the Variac drive engages once more. The process of re-emerging in real time is immediate, but seems to take about an hour for you. You can spend this time in the autodoc, if you wish and *gain up to 12 Endurance points.*

You rematerialize and the holo-projector makes Falcon's Wing look like a bleak hillock. Your exterior camera shows a small range of desolate hills giving way to a dry plain crossed by a small river. You press hold and the camera stops swivelling as a small city appears of mud-baked houses surrounded by tall white stone walls and towers. A pall of smoke hangs above it and the gates have been flattened. Before the city is an army, celebrating victory amidst piles of booty in their camp. A stricken figure in golden armour is lying on a litter outside a great white tent, tended by doctors in grey robes. Others, soldiers and officers, stand about him, anxiously.

You ask CAIN what happened here, historically. He chimes, 'This city is the local capital. The people marched out to give battle to Alexander the Great and his army of Macedonians and troops from other conquered lands, but fled when they saw Alexander and his men. Alexander is returning from India to Babylon, the capital of his new empire and decided to take this city. His men did not want to risk their lives again and he led the assault in an attempt to inspire them. Realising that he was risking his life, his men threw themselves onto the siege ladders, but these broke in their eagerness. Two men only were with Alexander when he jumped down into the city and he was severely wounded before the Macedonians broke down the gates and rescued him, massacring the townspeople in their frenzy.'

'Thank you CAIN,' you interrupt. 'What action would change the timeline here?'

'The assassination of Alexander would seem the most likely option, but I cannot compute the effect this would have on the past. Alexander will die in only a few years from now at the age of thirty-three and his empire will be divided up and fought over by his successors.'

CAIN programs the molecular converter to create the dress of a phalangite, a Macedonian warrior, and you step from Falcon's Wing wearing sandals, bronze greaves, a long heavy skirt of boiled leather strips, a breastplate, a small round shield strapped to your left forearm, and your psionic enhancer becomes a crested helmet covering your face with a Y-shaped slit for you to see through. Unable to wield a sixteen-foot-long 'sarissa' you make do with a shortsword. Your blaster and holo-detector are concealed under your red cloak. You search the hills for Lord Speke's machine.

Turn to **237**.

## 304

The ambulance rattles up the hill towards the Emperor and his staff, the horses straining, and you all run to intercept it. As you approach it, four Polish lancers, attached to Napoleon's escort, wheel their horses towards you. They look magnificent in their maroon and navy uniforms but their eyes are oddly glazed as if entranced. Their hostile intentions are

all too clear, however, as they lower their long lances and charge at you, red and white lance pennons fluttering in the breeze. You haven't much time. Do you:

Throw yourself to the ground so that
the horses pass over you knowing
that they will try to avoid trampling
you?                                            Turn to **410**
Thinkstrike one of the Lancers?               Turn to **129**
Pull out your blaster and shoot one of
their horses?                                 Turn to **389**

### 305

You are too slow. The Emperor's guard lunges swiftly as your finger closes on the trigger. His sword buries itself in your heart a moment before the white-hot plasma of your blaster causes his own body to explode. You die together and the Space Federation will never be. You have failed.

### 306

You ask CAIN for information on the Golden Horde. The computer responds: 'The Golden Horde was a name given to Mongol tribesmen of the 12th and 13th century on Earth.' Looking at your timehole map you can see that there is a timehole on Earth in that period. Do you:

Travel back to 1241 AD, to the time of
the Golden Horde?                             Turn to **163**
Try to track down Lord Speke?                 Turn to **407**
Return to the Eiger Vault?                     Turn to **388**

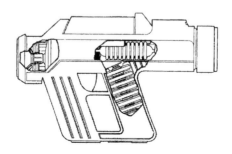

As a matter of course, all time trips into and out of the Eiger Vault timehole are logged by the Monitoring Section. You ask CAIN to provide you with the log of movements since the death of Agent Q, typing your Security Clearance Code at the terminal in front of you. The screen flashes up the following information.

| CURRENT EARTH DATE | TIME | NAME | DESTINATION |
|---|---|---|---|
| 15/10/33 | 04:15 | Q | Kelados 2710 AD |
| 15/10/33 | 08:04 | EPSILON SECURITY CODE INSUFFICIENT | |
| 15/10/33 | 09:22 | Q | Eiger Vault |
| 15/10/33 | 09:45 | Kirik | Kelados 2710 AD |
| 15/10/33 | 12:13 | Kirik | Eiger Vault |
| 16/10/33 | 01:10 | Pilota | Eiger Vault 3117 AD [ABORTED] |
| 16/10/33 | 06:01 | EPSILON SECURITY CODE INSUFFICIENT | |
| 16/10/33 | 08:20 | EPSILON SECURITY CODE INSUFFICIENT | |
| 16/10/33 | 12:03 | Kirik | Kelados 3033 AD |

TIME NOW: 12:40
DATE NOW: 16/10/33

It is evident that the Eiger Vault timehole has been busy but for some reason the information has largely been classified at Theta or Omega, the only Security Clearance Codes higher than yours, held by Section Chiefs and Lords. You decide to ask CAIN for the current whereabouts of the five Lords.

Turn to **295**.

## 308

As unobtrusively as you can you wander through the camp, casting around with your Psi Sense. You pick up a variety of the soldiers' thoughts. Some are full of fear at the thought of assaulting the city, others are casting their minds back to their homes in Macedon, more are simply bored, a few look forward to pillage and plunder. Suddenly the mood changes. Alexander has had a priest take the omens and they are not good, but Alexander decides to attack in any case. Anxiety spreads and most are unwilling to attack. The king orders his men to prepare to storm the city and the army organises as if by magic. Siege ladders are brought forward on carts. There is still no sign of Speke and you are curtly ordered to join a phalanx of men near the city gates. Hoping not to be noticed, you take your place in one of the columns. Sensing that his men, war weary and far from home, are reluctant to storm another city after the bad omens, Alexander exhorts them to attack. They hesitate and he grabs a ladder and thrusts it against the wall. He scales it quickly, followed by his shield-bearer and a member of his bodyguard, and is soon atop the wall. Seeing this, the Macedonians bring up the ladders and crying, 'Iskander, Iskander!' for that is how they say his name, they rush up the ladders, which break in their eagerness. Alexander, an obvious target, is pelted with missiles and jumps down inside the city, almost alone. Turn to **273**.

### 309
#### [score a T]
Knowing what must be done and hoping to make his death seem natural, you place a silken cushion over Ogedei's face and press down. His hands scrabble feebly at yours, but he is too weak to resist. The guards' wills seem to grow stronger, battling with yours, at the sight of you murdering their Khan. You must make another **Power of Will Roll** to see if you can maintain your control.

If you score 7-12, turn to **329**
If you score 2-6, turn to **317**

### 310
You concentrate on the Mongol wearing the most armour. Make a **Power of Will Roll.**

If you score 6-12, turn to **275**
If you score 2-5, turn to **283**

The white lightning of your blaster throws them backwards in a cloud of blood-red vapour, but the Khan's guard screams loudly as he dies. You move swiftly through the doorway. Inside is a bedchamber and, sitting on a large litter, swaddled in silks and furs, is Ogedei Khan still weak from his illness. He looks up, his narrow eyes questioning your purpose. Golden statues, chests of treasure and tapestries line the walls. Silk awnings close off the balcony at the back of the room. Knowing what must be done and hoping to make his death look natural, you place a silken cushion over Ogedei's face and press down. His hands scrabble feebly at yours, but he is too weak to resist. His face turns blue as he dies. You leave the room, hoping to slip back out to the flyer without being seen. Make a **Chance Roll.**

If you score 1-3, turn to **170**

If you score 4-6, turn to **127**

## 312
### [score a C]

Since the Phocian is not in control of his own mind he is defenceless against your Thinkstrike and he starts to float unconscious in his free-fall harness. You free him from the couch and tie him up with the harness before pushing his weightless body back into your ship. By the time he comes round you are on your way back to the starport. As you head back you notice, on the rear scanner, an asteroid mining ship appear from behind the Asteroid Belt, and your Psi Sense registers the presence of a being with great powers of the mind, probably the renegade Lord. You catch a thought: *Golden Horde* and then, *self destruct.* To your surprise the mining ship blossoms into a flowering white light, like a star gone nova, as it explodes. Is the renegade Lord dead, you wonder? Then you notice the Phocian coming round and you interrogate him. Your voice is mechanical, using the universal translator, and he readily informs you that his mind was taken over by a very alien and powerful mind, obviously neither Keladi, Phocian nor Earther. He had been instructed to destroy the envoy's vessel. He asks what is happening, but following the First Law of TIME, you ignore him.

You land safely and leave the pirate Phocian tied up in the ship. Wasting no time, you run to Falcon's Wing before starport security come to question you. CAIN tells you that he registered a Variac drive emission from the centre of the asteroid mining ship just before it blew up. Whoever it was used their time machine to wink out to safety. CAIN informs you that you have made history here, but that his memory banks remain essentially unchanged.

Do you have a nuclear bomb? If you do, turn to **415.** If you do not, turn to **306**.

## 313

You throw yourself towards Falcon's Wing. Luckily the fern before you is a hologram. Turning, you pull out your blaster, as the jaws snap shut inches from you.

Turn to **326**.

## 314

You press the button and the red star clicks forward onto the DISARMED line. You breathe a sigh of relief.

Turn to **252.**

## 315

Knowing the renegade Lord commands a strong mental barrier, you concentrate your minds together as you rip open the doors to the ambulance. Make an **Attack Roll** and add two points to the dice for Bloodhound's attack.

If you score 9-12, turn to **328**
If you score 2-8, turn to **193**

## 316

You jump aside just in time and the packer swings away once more. You are not disturbed again while checking the hangar, but find no trace of a time machine or Lord Speke. You return to Falcon's Wing, take off the boiler suit and feed it back into the converter. Where will you search for Lord Speke next?

In the time of Alexander the Great (if
you have not done so already)?          Turn to **303**
The planet Kelados in 2710 AD, where
Q found a Lord of TIME tampering
with the past (if you have not done
so already)?                            Turn to **418**
The planet Dyskra, home of the
Repnids, in 1985 AD (if you have not
done so already)?                       Turn to **375**
Earth in the Jurassic Period, the age
of dinosaurs (if you have not done so
already)?                               Turn to **394**

### 317

The mental effort makes you *lose 4 Endurance points.* If you are
still alive, you fail to keep them under control. One draws his
sword and runs at you, his face a mask of rage, whilst the
other rushes to the door and gives the alarm. You release
Ogedei, who gasps for air, and turn to meet your attacker.
There is no time to draw your blaster, and you must use
unarmed combat. Make an **Attack Roll.**

If you score 7-12, turn to **367**

If you score 2-6, turn to **356**

### 318

The bear, used to the wild, has naturally quick reactions and
it pulls back. Your kick lands on its shoulder, but it cuffs you
to the ground with stunning force. Before you can get up it
claws and bites you, eventually gripping you in a hug which
breaks your ribs. You die next to your flyer and the Space
Federation will never be. You have failed.

### 319

You contact the mind of Pilota, using your power of Psi Sense.
She is far away, dwelling on her chances in the next solar
yacht race. When she realises what you are up to her reaction
is one of pleased surprise. She thinks a message to you: *I like a
lot of warp, why don't you try the same thing on the others?* She is

amused at the possibility but thinks a warning to you that they are *a bunch of empty cargo pods.* Evidently she is impressed with your audacity. Will you:

| | |
|---|---|
| Give a speech of thanks to end the ceremony? | Turn to **167** |
| Probe the mind of another Lord? | |
| Silvermane | Turn to **280** |
| the Creche | Turn to **223** |
| Kirik | Turn to **209** |

320

CAIN links to the Eiger Vault Service Computer and reports that Lord Silvermane is leaving the Vault and heading for the hovrail embarkation point.

Will you leave your time machine and follow Lord Silvermane (turn to **142**)? Or, if you prefer not to follow him, return to **336** and choose again.

321

You pick your way through the mass of soldiery towards the large white tent, and are tall enough to crane your neck and see the figure of Alexander, resplendent in golden armour with a battered helmet which sports a white crest. He is a short man, but very athletic, his curly reddish-blond hair framing a determined face with piercing blue eyes. Nearby, a white-robed priest is fiddling with the entrails of a sheep. He looks towards Alexander whom he calls King Iskander and strongly advises him not to attack the town, saying that the omens are bad. The soldiers mutter, but Alexander replies, 'My business is to conquer cities. I do not have time to study the entrails of sheep. Leave me alone to finish my business.' Turning to his advisers he gives the word to prepare to storm the city. The army organises as if by magic, and siege ladders are brought forward on carts. There is still no sign of Speke and you are curtly ordered to join a phalanx of men near the city gates. Hoping not to be noticed, you take your place in one of the columns. Sensing that his men, war weary and far from home, are reluctant to storm another city after the bad omens, Alexander exhorts them to attack. They hesitate and he grabs a ladder and thrusts it against the wall. He scales it quickly, followed by his shieldbearer and a member of his bodyguard, and is soon atop the wall. Seeing this, the Macedonians bring up ladders and crying, 'Iskander, Iskander!' they rush up the ladders, breaking them in their eagerness. Alexander, an obvious target, is pelted with missiles and jumps down inside the city, almost alone. Do you:

Run up one of the few surviving ladders
   in case you can prevent him being
   assassinated?                                Turn to **405**
Wait and leave Alexander to his fate?    Turn to **200**

#### 322

Lynx's mental defences are too strong and she has made good use of the time since flinging herself behind the dead horse. You notice the muzzle of the blaster resting on the ground, under the horse's broken neck, just as a white bolt of plasma erupts from it. You are hurled backwards through the air, dead before you hit the ground. Lynx has fulfilled her mission and you have failed.

#### 323

An arrow catches you in the small of the back and you stagger. *Lose 6 Endurance points.* They will be upon you at any moment. What will you do:

Use your blaster on them?             Turn to **302**
Thinkstrike the nearest Mongol?     Turn to **291**
Use your Power of Will on the one
   you think is their leader?             Turn to **310**

#### 324

You blast the doors of the ambulance away, but whoever was inside was ready for you. Two blasters open fire and you are hit and killed instantly. You may have no idea whether you have killed the renegade Lord or not, but history has been changed and you have failed.

You suddenly find yourself locked in mental battle with a powerful alien will, the controller of the Phocian. It is too much for you to resist and you will be completely under its influence within seconds. Do you have a psionic damper? If you do, turn to **363**. If you do not, turn to **371**.

**326**

At this range you can hardly miss the huge monster that is lunging at you. Make an **Attack Roll.**

If you score 5-12, turn to **290**
If you score 2-4, turn to **345**

**327**

You press the button and the red star clicks forward one line. The dials look like this:

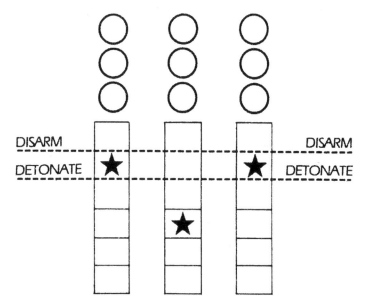

Which button do you press next?

| | |
|---|---|
| The top button. | Turn to **402** |
| The centre button. | Turn to **358** |
| The bottom button. | Turn to **342** |

Ripping the ambulance doors open reveals a bizarre sight. Six creatures like giant ants, mandibles clicking in agitation, are backing into a honeycomb structure, their dull, red, compound eyes menacing. One collapses as the combined force of your Thinkstrike hits home. The honeycomb is on top of a flyer, similar in design to your own, and you both throw yourselves back to the ground outside to avoid the ion drive exhaust as the flyer explodes from the front of the ambulance. You sense that the six Hiver beings who together are Lord Creche, the renegade Lord, are flying back to their time machine, with one exception. The victim of your Thinkstrike had not reached his seat in the honeycomb. Toppling backward as the flyer took off, he was vaporised by the ion drive. Quickly you search the ambulance and find a small capsule. It is in Interstellar Code – a message from Agidy Yelov to the Creche suggesting that if the mission is aborted, they should effect a rendezvous on planet Hel. As quickly as you can, after checking that the Emperor's Imperial Guard are not advancing, you return to your time machine.

Turn to **161**.

The mental effort has made you *lose 3 Endurance points,* but you manage to keep them under control. You continue until you arc sure Ogedei is dead, and then you order the Mongol guards to lead you back through the banqueting hall to the palace gate. In the hall the dancing goes on and you slip unnoticed out into the night. Outside the city gates you tell them to kneel and then knock them out with a couple of deft blows to the neck before returning to your flyer, amazed at your good fortune at killing the Khan of the Mongol horde and living to tell the tale.

Turn to **254**.

Ripping the ambulance doors open reveals a bizarre sight – six creatures like giant ants, mandibles clicking in agitation, are backing into a honeycomb structure, their dull, red, compound eyes menacing. The honeycomb is on top of a flyer, similar in design to your own. The six beings, together known as Lord Creche 82282, the renegade Lord, are unaffected by the combined Power of Will attack. Bloodhound suddenly grabs you and throws you out of the ambulance, leaping down after you and picking up a fallen musket. He is being controlled by the Creche! He aims a savage swipe with his musket.

Turn to **38**.

## 331

You call up the Free Fall Recreation Centre at Spiro's Ringworld, a massive wheel-like world-in-miniature, orbiting Earth. Their holo-coordinator seems to appear in your time machine. She is a striking girl, her skin tinted blue with orange flashes. She puts you through to Lord Pilota's personal assistant. He is a bony, hollow-cheeked man, showing signs of the Medawar Syndrome, the onset of rapid ageing. You identify yourself and ask for Her Lordship and the hologram winks out momentarily When the holo-picture of the assistant reappears, he says, 'Lord Pilota is temporarily indisposed. Under no circumstances may she be contacted at the moment. If you would care to visit Spiro's Ringworld, however, she will be pleased to grant you immediate audience, as she. believes she has some information which may interest you, as an Agent of the TIME Police.' With that, he breaks contact and the blue-skinned coordinator informs you that the line has been closed to all callers and asks, 'What is that weird space ship you're in?' CAIN informs you that by requisitioning a shuttle from the Eiger Base you could dock at Spiro's Ringworld in eighteen minutes. Ignoring the holo-coordinator, do you:

| | |
|---|---|
| Set off for Spiro's Ringworld? | Turn to **335** |
| Choose another course? | Return to **336** and choose again. |

As soon as you have said it you sense that you made a mistake. Marshal Ney looks at you, piercingly, and says, 'The Cuirassiers are commanded by Murat. Ledru commands infantry. What is this? Arrest this spy!' A young hussar officer who has been assigned to Ney's staff takes out a pistol and orders you to dismount. Thinking quickly, you decide there is no time to lose and, ducking, you drive your horse into his before galloping away. Make an **Evasion Roll**.

If you score 6-12, turn to **289**

If you score 2-4, turn to **274**

If you score a 5, roll again.

### 333

It is difficult to take aim in free fall, but your target has his back to you and is not moving. Make an **Attack Roll.**

If you score 5-12, turn to **380**

If you score 2-4, turn to **392**

### 334

You rematerialize at the Eiger Vault. All is as you left it. CAIN informs you that the machines of Speke, Silvermane and Pilota are in their bays. Speke is on his way to TIME headquarters, presumably to give himself up. Pilota is still on Spiro's Ringworld and Silvermane is at the Galactic Trade Centre. Do you:

Phone to arrange a meeting with Lord
   Pilota?                                   Turn to **56**

Go to the Galactic Trade Centre to find
   Lord Silvermane?              Turn to **294**

Follow Lord Kirik to Kelados, 3033 AD?    Turn to **284**

### 335

Through CAIN you order that a shuttle be prepared for your trip to Spiro's Ringworld and waste no time. You run from the doors of the Vault across the launch bay to the small, dart-shaped shuttle with its huge, ungainly drive vents, each as large as the cabin. The navigational computer is already set as

you strap into the acceleration web behind the pilot. With a flash of light the ion drive fires and you are accelerated sickeningly quickly. This is a Navy pilot – she has never flown civilian craft. Minutes later the docking computer locks onto the Ringworld, a glittering disc twenty miles across, turning silently in space, and the deceleration is equally unpleasant. As you step out into the air-lock, the pilot turns and smiles, 'You stood that well. You must be fit.' You ask her to stand by for your return journey and enter the Ringworld.

Lord Pilota's assistant meets you as you emerge from the airlock and, helping you into a jet pack, points up into the empty centre of the so-called Ringworld. You are standing on the inside rim of the disc which is rotating quickly enough to produce a gravity not far below that of Earth's. Looking up, you see the tops of the buildings, twenty miles away on the opposite side of the Rim. The assistant explains that Lord Pilota is in the gravity free zone, or free fall area, in the centre of the disc, half way to the other rim. You blast off with him confidently enough, and head for the centre of the rimworld. As you approach you see Lord Pilota, spinning slowly, head over heels, apparently at ease without the hydraulic exoskeleton she uses in Earth gravity. With a shock you realise that you cannot adapt easily to free fall and accidentally cannon into her, sending you both towards the other rim. She steadies you easily and with two deft jet-pack blasts returns you to a stationary position in free fall. She speaks, her voice high-pitched in the thin air. 'Falcon, you've come all this way to see me. Why? What is so important?' Will you:

| | |
|---|---|
| Accuse her of trying to change the past? | Turn to **340** |
| Tell her that a Lord of TIME has been interfering with the timelines and ask for help? | Turn to **391** |
| Ask if she has information for you? | Turn to **87** |

## 336

The scanner light above your head is now green and you are drawn up by invisible tractor beams into the relative safety of Falcon's Wing. Sitting in the crash couch you consider what to do next. You have no information as to the whereabouts of Creche 82282 but some about the other Lords. What will you do?

Try to follow Lord Speke into the past.　　Turn to **357**
Follow Lord Kirik to Kelados, 3033 AD.　　Turn to **284**
Ask CAIN where Silvermane is.　　Turn to **320**
Quickly contact Lord Pilota by
　　holophone.　　Turn to **331**

Or, if you are wounded and would rather spend two hours in your autodoc now then carry on later, turn to **196**.

## 337

You concentrate on an infantry man who has just reloaded his musket and is passing nearby, and try to control him. Make a **Power of Will Roll**.

If you score 5-12, turn to **385**
If you score 2-4, turn to **411**

## 338

Inside Falcon's Wing you sit in the crash couch and instruct CAIN to engage the Variac drive. Do you:

Go back to Earth in the time of the
　　Mongol hordes?　　Turn to **374**
Return to the Eiger Vault?　　Turn to **359**

## 339

You kick with the speed of a black belt and even Lynx is taken by surprise. She sprawls unconscious on the floor. Bloodhound suggests you run to the ambulance and attack, and you agree. As you approach, you feel the will within becoming aware of you. What do you shout to Bloodhound?

'Thinkstrike now!'　　Turn to **315**
'Power of Will, now!'　　Turn to **330**
'Blast to kill!'　　Turn to **348**

She laughs, 'That's ridiculous, are you insane? I asked you here to tell you that someone had been using the Central Library to investigate Earth history in 1241 AD, the time of the Mongol hordes. Think again, Falcon. If Earth's past were changed, we Lastlanders would never have existed, or had you forgotten that we are Earther colonials? I don't know how you ever managed to pass the tests of the Academy. Escort Falcon back to the shuttle please, Remo.'

Her assistant switches on his jet-pack and crashes into you while Pilota moves to the other rim. Two red dots appear ahead of you, growing in size until you recognise their security uniforms. The guards obey Remo's instructions to return you to your shuttle or terminate you if you resist, and you decide to obey since you are at a severe disadvantage in free fall. Minutes later you are in the shuttle *en route* for the Eiger Vault once more and soon back in your time machine.

If you have seen a man in golden armour called Iskander, turn to **114**. If you have seen a Phocian pirate, turn to **34**. If you have seen neither of these, do you:

| | |
|---|---|
| Try to follow Lord Speke into the past? | Turn to **220** |
| Follow Lord Kirik to Kelados in 3033 AD? | Turn to **284** |
| Move back into the timehole that exists in 1241 AD, the time of the Mongols? | Turn to **414** |
| Spend some time in your autodoc? | Turn to **196** |

You order the guards to slit Ogedei's throat. He is too weak to resist but, faced with the prospect of murdering their Khan, their wills revolt against yours and your control is thrown off. One of the guards draws his sword and runs at you, his face a mask of rage, whilst the other rushes to the door and gives the alarm. You turn to meet your attacker. There is no time to draw your blaster, and you must use unarmed combat. Make an **Attack Roll**.

If you score 7-12, turn to **367**
If you score 2-6, turn to **356**

You press the button and the red star clicks forward onto the line before the DETONATE line. The dials look like this:

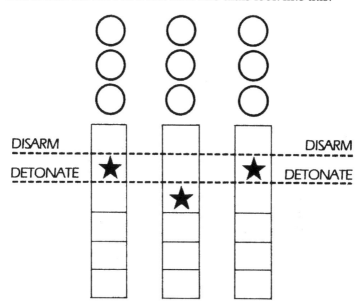

Which button do you press next?

The top button.                    Turn to **314**
The centre button.                 Turn to **402**
The bottom button.                 Turn to **358**

343

Your blaster spouts white-hot bolts of plasma, cutting a swathe through the horsemen. Ten or more perish and the squealing of their horses rings in your ears. Seeing what they take to be evil magic, they turn tail and flee, leaving the village alone. Still carrying the nuclear bomb, you go back to Falcon's Wing, hoping your actions have not seriously changed the timelines.

You ask CAIN to what extent you have changed the past and, to your relief, it responds, 'There is no significant change, Falcon. My files do carry a tale, however, about a sorcerer who saved the village of Ramallo from the Mongol horde for a brief time. Congratulations, Falcon, you are the sorcerer of Ramallo.' CAIN then adds, 'You are lucky to be alive.'

You tell CAIN to shut up. Turn to **229**.

### 344

You haven't long in which to stop the attack. The finest troops alive at this time, Napoleon's Imperial Guard, fresh and eager, will decisively change the course of the battle. The earlier French attacks by Marshals Ney and Davout were repulsed and the valiant Russian commander, Prince Bagration, counter-attacked, but was unsuccessful. His troops were flung back and he himself has been mortally wounded. If the Imperial Guard attack, the Russians will be routed and Murat's cavalry will cut them down in their thousands. The Russians will have lost this war and Europe will be plunged into bloody conflict against Napoleon for decades. The guards will meet the Russian line in minutes. Do you:

| | |
|---|---|
| Run towards the ambulance and Thinkstrike the renegade Lord? | Turn to **354** |
| Use your Power of Will to try to force a soldier to fire at the ambulance? | Turn to **337** |
| Try to control Napoleon so that he calls off the attack? | Turn to **212** |
| Run towards the ambulance and blast at the back doors? | Turn to **324** |

### 345

You throw yourself into the mud and fire your blaster at the giant crocodile which is lunging at you. In your haste you hit only its leg and the monster's jaws have closed around you before the sensation of pain reaches its sluggish brain. Powerless to resist, you are pulled below the surface of the swamp, threshing madly. Your ribs crack and you are soon too weak to struggle, drowned in the primeval swamp. You have failed.

You lose your grip on the blaster in your haste and before you can recover a lance is buried deep in your chest, the pennant hanging down against your stomach. Blood fills your lungs and you die before the other agents can come to your aid. At least you have led Bloodhound and Lynx to the renegade Lord, but you have failed.

As you gallop away. Marshal Ney orders you to stop and then, realising you are ignoring him, orders three of the young officers on his staff to arrest you. They charge after you and you urge your mount on through the smoke of the French cannon.

One of the officers, a young hussar, whose grey and red pelisse streams out behind him in the wind, has a good mount and is gaining on you. You ride down into a small dip, jumping a brook out of sight of the rest of the army and he follows. Do you:

| | |
|---|---|
| Thinkstrike the hussar? | Turn to **285** |
| Rein in and blast him when he is close enough so that you cannot miss him? | Turn to **195** |

Ripping the ambulance doors open reveals a bizarre sight – six creatures like giant ants, mandibles clicking in agitation, are backing into a honeycomb structure, their dull, red, compound eyes menacing. One shrivels as the white-hot plasma from your blaster hits home. The honeycomb is on top of a flyer, similar in design to your own and you both throw yourselves to the ground outside to avoid the Ion Drive exhaust as the flyer explodes from the front of the ambulance. You sense that the six Hiver beings who together are Lord Creche, the renegade Lord, are flying back to their time machine, with one exception. The victim of your shot had not reached his seat in the honeycomb. Toppling backward, he was vaporised by the plasma. Quickly you search the ambulance and find a small capsule. It is in Interstellar Code

– a message from Agidy Yelov to the Creche suggesting that if the mission is aborted, they should effect a rendezvous on planet Hel. As quickly as you can, after checking that the Emperor's Imperial Guard are not advancing, you decide to follow the Creche.

Turn to **161**.

### 349

You float down out of Falcon's Wing and walk quickly to the adjacent bays. You pass the bay used for the Creche machine first – it is empty. Then you see the powerful, squat form of Lord Silvermane striding towards his machine just as that of Lord Speke winks out of its bay, back into the past. Catching up with Lord Silvermane you ask him where he intends to go. He replies brusquely, 'I'm on important official business. You need not concern yourself with it. Speke has just left, however, and you may well be able to guess where he has gone if you examine his file. Goodbye, Falcon.' And he hurries towards his time machine. Do you:

| | |
|---|---|
| Stop Lord Silvermane and insist he tells you where he is going? | Turn to **383** |
| Return to your time machine and try to go after one of the other Lords? | Turn to **225** |

### 350

You instruct CAIN to turn on the Variac drive to shift you into null-space and to re-engage the drive as soon as you have finished inputting the navigational co-ordinates for the timehole on Earth, 2700 AD. Your scalp tingles slightly as the time machine moves out of phase, and everything around you seems grey and insubstantial. You know that should you turn on the outside camera the screen would remain blank, not even blackness exists in null-space. You cast your thoughts into the void and, using your Psi Sense, locate the timehole of Earth 2700 AD. When you have translated this location into coordinates for CAIN, the Variac drive engages once more. The process of re-emerging in real time is immediate, but seems to take about an hour for you. You can spend this time in the autodoc, if you wish, and *gain up to 12 Endurance points.*

Your external camera pivots, showing a large starport loading hangar which appears to be completely automated. An Andromeda class star freighter of the series commissioned in 2692 AD to supply the outer colonies, rests nearby, its immense cargo doors open for the robot cranes and packers. A line of the robot packers is quite close to Falcon's Wing which is disguised by hologram to resemble a large cold store. CAIN tells you that you are in Calgary Starport and the freighter is the Earth Federation ship *Frank Whittle*, named after the inventor of the jet engine used in aeroplanes of the 20th century. It is being loaded with supplies for the new colony world of Ascension, in particular, the serum which will save almost the entire population from the deadly viral infection which broke out about ten days ago and is ravaging the colony.

You can see no sign of Speke or his machine but it could easily be beyond the freighter. You decide to check the hangar with your holodetector and CAIN prepares the uniform of a maintenance technician of 2700 AD in the molecular converter. You put on the boiler suit with its markings proclaiming you a grade 3 robotech, attached to Calgary Starport. You are walking towards the freighter when, with a hiss and a screech, the boom of a packing robot descends upon you as if you were a piece of cargo. Its huge grab opens – evidently it intends to pack you! Make an **Evasion Roll**.

If you score 6-12, turn to **316**

If you score 2-5, turn to **353**

## 351

You duck, but a cannonball, whizzing through the air, hits your horse, which topples to the ground before falling on top of you. The horse dies and you are left to pull yourself from underneath it having suffered several broken ribs and other injuries. *Lose 11 Endurance points.*

If you are still alive, you force yourself on despite the pain. The cannon continue to roar on both sides, but you arc confident the renegade Lord is not nearby. Do you:

Veer right to explore the wing of the
   battle where Prince Poniatowski is
   trying to outflank the Russians?            Turn to **361**
Drop back to where the French heavy
   cavalry wait for Murat, King of Naples,
   to unleash them against the enemy?          Turn to **372**

### 352

Lynx crouches, cat-like, and grabs your leg as your boot
flashes past her shoulder. She heaves upward and you fall
backwards heavily. Bloodhound attacks her again, but she is
able to hold you off for some time. Eventually you overcome
Lynx, but not before she gashes your hip with her knife. *Lose
5 Endurance points.*

   If you are still alive, you take stock of your surroundings.
Lynx is out cold and, while you were struggling, everybody
has moved down the hill towards the battle line. The Imperial
Guard are marching to the attack and the ambulance, too, is
trundling away down the hill. Napoleon has ordered the
attack and the renegade Lord has changed the past.

   Turn to **344**.

### 353

The mechanical packer grabs you. You swing up into the air
towards an aluminium cylinder. The machine is apparently
going to bottle you, but the cylinder is smaller than you are
and you suppose that both packer and cylinder are stronger
than you are. You are held fast, but at the last moment you
manage to free your blaster and pull the trigger. The white hot
streak of superheated plasma hits the mechanical brain of the
packer which seizes up, leaving you dangling helpless in
midair. The plasma sets fire to the machine and this fire
spreads rapidly to a container nearby. To your horror, you see
that it is the container holding the vat of serum for the people
of Ascension. Your great-grandfather was born on Ascension.
The fire spreads, causing some damage to the freighter. The
delivery of serum will now be delayed by a week. Many
thousands will die, including the young woman who is

carrying the baby that would have been your great-grandfather. You have never existed. You have failed.

## 354

You run up to the ambulance together and, focusing your minds, at a word from Bloodhound you hurl a blast of thought at the mind within. The renegade Lord has a strong mental power, but at least you have combined your minds. Make a **Thinkstrike Roll** and add 2 to the dice score for Bloodhound's help.

If you score 8-12, turn to **124**

If you score 2-7, turn to **100**

## 355

You manage to reach the village before the Mongols and hide yourself in an empty hut. They fall upon the village in their hundreds and their bestial cries mixed with the screams of the peasants sound like those of fiends and victims in hell. It seems the Mongols kill for sport and you are certain you will soon be discovered. Will you:

| | |
|---|---|
| Tear off your peasant's clothes and step out in your uniform? | Turn to **267** |
| Wait to be discovered and pretend that you are already dead? | Turn to **256** |
| Make a run for your time machine? | Turn to **368** |

## 356

You twist and try to side kick your attacker in the throat, but he is too quick for you and slashes your calf with his sword. The second guard rushes at you from the other door as you sink to one knee, hamstrung. You hold them off for a time, but soon others pour into the room from the banqueting hall below and you are taken. The punishment of the Khan's would-be assassin is not a pleasant one. They discuss your fate, which will be to have molten silver poured into your eyes and ears before you are boiled alive – a death reserved for their respected enemies. You have failed and the Space Federation will never be.

Which timehole will you travel to in search of Lord Speke?

| | |
|---|---|
| The planet Kelados in 2710 AD, where Q found a Lord of TIME tampering with the past. | Turn to **418** |
| Earth in the Jurassic Period. | Turn to **394** |
| Earth at the time of Alexander the Great. | Turn to **130** |
| The planet Dyskra, home of the Repnids, in 1985 AD. | Turn to **375** |
| Earth in 2700 AD, at the time of great colonial expansion. | Turn to **350** |

## 358

You press the button and, to your horror, the dial clicks forward, moving the star onto the DETONATE line. The stars are lined up and the nuclear device explodes. You and everyone else within twenty miles of the spot are killed. Your failure is spectacular.

## 350

You rematerialize in the Eiger Vault and CAIN tells you that the machines of Speke, Silvermane and Pilota are also in the Vault. While you are deciding what to do next, blackness engulfs you suddenly. Someone has changed the timelines and one of your ancestors has been killed before his time. It is as if you had never existed. You have failed.

## 360

You float down from the access hatch, lowered by invisible tractor beams. You can smell ozone in the air of the spaceport. Rounding a bulkhead you come across a refuelling bay and your holo-detector indicates that the Keladi scoutship in front of you is in fact a time machine. Judging by its size it could only be that of Lord Kirik. As you walk through the hologram you are surprised to see water underfoot. Kirik's machine is normally water-filled, a much larger model than your own. Clearly all is not well for, as you look up, you see that his

access hatch is open and on automatic. His mind scan is not operating and you are drawn up into his machine. The grotesque body of Lord Kirik lies inert across his crash couch. The disc which is his psionic enhancer lies in a pool of water at his side. The usually bloated brain sacs are flaccid and his jointed legs are curled unnaturally. Looking more closely you notice a neat circular wound in the middle of one of his brain sacs, still pouring purplish fluid. There is no sign of the weapon that was used to do this. He has been killed quite recently by someone whom he had allowed into his time machine. There is no helping Lord Kirik. Do you:

Leave the scene of the crime before you
    can be discovered here?             Turn to **262**
Send Kirik's machine into null-space?    Turn to **382**

### 361

As you approach the magnificent Polish lancers in their white lance caps, or czapstas, blue jackets and red-striped trousers, you catch sight of the wavy dark hair and trim moustache of dashing Prince Poniatowski, who is urging his men to the attack. Then your Psi Sense warns you that a person with mental powers is somewhere nearby. Do you:

Investigate alone?             Turn to **73**
Go back to find Bloodhound so you can
    tackle the danger together?        Turn to **404**

### 362

You run for the ambulance but Lynx sidesteps Bloodhound and knocks you sideways. Bloodhound recovers and you both attack Lynx as she stands ready for you, knife poised. Make an **Attack Roll**.

If you score 7-12, turn to **339**
If you score 2-6, turn to **352**

### 363

Sweating with the effort you place the damper circlet upon your head using your last trace of free will. The mental attack on your mind is broken and you start moving backwards, accidentally throwing your weightless body into the wall of the bridge. The Phocian, who had turned to stare, is now controlled once more and he will soon be in a position to destroy the envoy's vessel again. You cannot use your mental powers while wearing the psionic damper, so you decide to blast him.

Turn to **333**.

### 364

Your horse shies suddenly and a cannonball whizzes past your ear. Looking back you see a French artillery man looking down in amazement at where his right leg used to be. It now lies behind him and the cannonball which removed it bounces onward, its momentum barely checked. There is nothing you can do for the man and feeling slightly sickened, you ride on as he starts to moan. The cannon roar on both sides but you are confident that the renegade Lord is not nearby. Do you:

| | |
|---|---|
| Veer right to explore the wing of the battle where Prince Poniatowski is attempting to outflank the Russians? | Turn to **361** |
| Drop back to where the French heavy cavalry wait for Murat, King of Naples, to unleash them against the enemy? | Turn to **372** |

### 365

The horse dies and its rider is pitched headlong onto the turf. Bloodhound and Lynx Thinkstrike two more. The remaining lancer catches Lynx in the shoulder but she grabs the lance and swings herself up on it, kicking the lancer in the face. He tumbles unconscious from the saddle, but she falls beside him. She is badly wounded and has to return to her autodoc. She urges you to go on, saying, 'I'll see you at the Eiger Vault Rec Centre,' and wishes you luck before she limps away. You run to catch up the ambulance.

Turn to **251**.

The floor of the machine is strewn with maps, charts and texts in the language of the period. There is a beautiful wooden display cabinet full of ancient Greek weapons including a fine collection of swords which appear to be originals, showing no sign of age, as if they had been cast quite recently; but a sword and shield and some armour appear to be missing from the numbered collection. You attempt to access his computer but it flashes up

OMEGA CLEARANCE CODE REQUIRED.
INCORRECT INPUT LOGGED

You decide to leave and follow Lord Speke to find out what he is doing here. Turn to **409**.

You twist and side-kick your attacker in the throat, and he collapses, unconscious, his head striking the floor with a thump. The second guard runs at you from the door and Ogedei, recovering, shouts for help. In desperation you draw your blaster and fire at the guard before he runs you through with his sword. Make an **Attack Roll**.

If you score 5-12, turn to **390**
If you score 2-4, turn to **378**

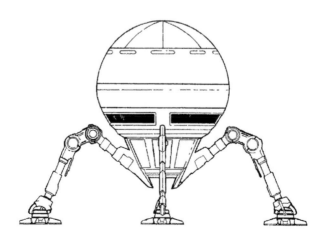

## 368

You sprint as fast as you can towards the group of trees which are in fact Falcon's Wing. A group of horsemen, seeing you, wheel their mounts and charge after you. They shoot their bows from horseback. You try to zig-zag as you run, to spoil their aim. Make an **Evasion Roll**.

If you score 7-12, turn to **370**

If you score 2-6, turn to **323**

## 369

Knowing this will be difficult, you try to blast them both with mental energy, one after the other. Make a **Thinkstrike Roll**.

If you score 7-12, turn to **205**

If you score 2-5, turn to **68**

If you score 6, roll again.

## 370

Arrows fly all around you, but you make it back to Falcon's Wing still carrying the nuclear bomb. You are drawn up just in time. The Mongols are close behind you, but you see on your camera screen that they are puzzled by your sudden disappearance. Some are making signs to ward off evil spirits.

Turn to **229**.

## 371

Powerless to resist, you come under the sway of the alien mind. You find yourself opening the Phocian's medicine cabinet and taking out a syringe. Dripping with sweat you try to resist but you place the needle into a vein at your wrist and inject yourself with air. Your death is agonising. You have failed.

## 372

As you ride along the battle line, the tide of battle seems to be ebbing and flowing. The first attack of the French columns, under Marshals Ney and Davout have been repulsed, but they are preparing to attack again. Behind Ney's position Murat's cavalry are drawn up. You soon catch sight of Murat,

the King of Naples himself, the most extravagantly dressed man on the battlefield, great cockades of white feathers adorning his busby. He looks every inch a cavalry general, dashing and stylish with long hair and a sleek look, but he is a veteran of many campaigns. He and his staff are before a thousand French heavy cavalry, the Cuirassiers with their steel breastplates and crested helmets each with its scarlet plume. Before you come close to him your Psi Sense alerts you to a very powerful mental presence nearby. Do you:

Continue and find out who it is coming
    from? Turn to **123**
Go to find Bloodhound? Turn to **404**

### 373

You instruct CAIN to turn on the Variac drive to shift you into null-space and to re-engage the drive as soon as you have finished inputting the navigational co-ordinates for the timehole on Dyskra, 1985 AD. Your scalp tingles slightly as the time machine moves out of phase, and everything around you seems grey and insubstantial. You know that should you turn on the outside camera the screen would remain blank. Not even blackness exists in null-space. You cast your thoughts into the void and, using your Psi Sense, locate the timehole on Dyskra. When you have translated this location into coordinates for CAIN, the Variac drive engages once more. The process of re-emerging in real time is immediate, but seems to take about an hour for you. You may spend this time in the autodoc, if you wish and *gain up to 12 Endurance points.*

The outside camera scans the terrain. It appears as a featureless red expanse of desert apparently devoid of life, but with the occasional unusually-shaped outcropping of rock against which dunes of reddish sand are piled. CAIN chimes in with a brief report on the world of Dyskra. The dominant life forms are the Repnids, intelligent beings, a strange fusion of lizard-like skin, tongue and body with a wolf-spider's legs, compound eyes and poisonous fangs, weighing about half a ton each. They burrow through the soft red rock, inhabiting cities and tunnels underground, heated by the winds of Dyskra, a warm world with few seas. CAIN warns that the predatory Repnids are uncivilised in this era and that he believes there is a high density of life forms nearby. You estimate that it will take five minutes to check the nearby rock outcroppings with your holo-detector to see if any of them are Speke's disguised time machine. Do you:

| | |
|---|---|
| Leave the machine to check the rocks? | Turn to **293** |
| Go to the planet Kelados in 2710 AD, where Q found a Lord of Time tampering with the past? | Turn to **418** |
| Travel to Earth in 2700 AD (if you have not done so already)? | Turn to **249** |
| Travel to Earth in the time of Alexander the Great (if you have not done so already)? | Turn to **303** |

### 374

Falcon's Wing rematerializes at the edge of a forest near hills. It is dark outside but you can see the lights of thousands of camp fires. Switching the camera to night vision you make out an enormous army of Mongols, their horses tethered near them, outside a large town. There is a river running through the town. You ask CAIN for historical data. Before CAIN responds, blackness engulfs you suddenly. Someone has changed the timelines and one of your ancestors has been killed before his time. It is as if you had never existed. You have failed.

### 375

You instruct CAIN to turn on the Variac drive to shift you into null-space and to re-engage the drive as soon as you have finished inputting the navigational co-ordinates for the timehole on Dyskra, 1985 AD. Your scalp tingles slightly as the time machine moves out of phase, and everything around you seems grey and insubstantial. You know that should you turn on the outside camera the screen would remain blank; not even blackness exists in null-space. You cast your thoughts into the void and, using your Psi Sense, locate the timehole on Dyskra. When you have translated this location into coordinates for CAIN, the Variac drive engages once more. The process of re-emerging in real time is immediate, but seems to take about an hour for you. You may spend this time in the autodoc, if you wish and *gain up to 12 Endurance points.*

The outside camera scans the terrain. It appears as a featureless red expanse of desert apparently devoid of life, but with the occasional unusually-shaped outcropping of rock against which dunes of reddish sand are piled. CAIN chimes in with a brief report on the world of Dyskra. The dominant life forms are the Repnids, intelligent beings, a strange fusion of lizard-like skin, tongue and body with a wolf-spider's legs, compound eyes and poisonous fangs, weighing about half a ton each. They burrow through the soft red rock, inhabiting cities and tunnels underground that are heated by the winds of Dyskra, a warm world with few seas.

CAIN warns that the predatory Repnids are uncivilised in this era and that he believes there is a high density of life forms nearby. You estimate that it will take five minutes to check the nearby rock outcroppings with your holo-detector to see if any of them are Speke's disguised time machine. Do you:

| | |
|---|---|
| Leave the machine to check the rocks? | Turn to **293** |
| Go to the planet Kelados in 2710 AD, where Q found a Lord of Time tampering with the past? | Turn to **418** |
| Travel to Earth in 2700 AD (if you have not done so already)? | Turn to **350** |
| Travel to Earth in the time of Alexander the Great (if you have not done so already)? | Turn to **130** |
| Travel to Earth in the Jurassic Period, the age of the dinosaurs (if you have not done so already)? | Turn to **394** |

## 376

Ripping open the ambulance doors reveals a bizarre sight – six creatures like giant ants, mandibles clicking in agitation, are backing into a honeycomb structure, their dull-red, compound eyes menacing. The honeycomb is on top of a flyer similar in design to your own. They were expecting you and two are holding small blasters in their mouthparts. Before you can move they blast you backwards out of the ambulance, killing you instantly. You have failed.

## 377

You realise that controlling two others will be difficult, but bend your thoughts to the task. One is lamenting the fact that he won't become the head of a touman, or ten thousand, if Ogedei lives. Make a **Power of Will Roll**.

If you score 8-12, turn to **97**

If you score 2-5, turn to **115**

If you score 6 or 7 roll again.

## 378

Your hand was shaking with fatigue and you have missed your target, blowing a hole in the wooden wall. The Mongol crashes into you and buries his sword in your stomach. Death is swift. You have failed and the Space Federation will never be.

## 379

### [score an F]

The monstrous crocodile has nothing that you would call a mind - you locate one instinct only, to kill and eat. It lunges swiftly, rolling out of the swamp to clamp its jaws around you. Make an **Evasion Roll**.

If you score 7-12, turn to **313**

If you score 2-6, turn to **345**

## 380

You are forced backwards against the bulkhead behind you as your blaster discharges a bolt of superheated plasma. The

Phocian appears to fuse into his free-fall couch, his body distorting horribly; the forward scanner screen is covered with a red film. You quickly leave the scene and return to your ship. You can only hope that his descendants were not to be shapers of history and that changes in the timelines will be small. You have, however, saved Korakiik, the Keladi envoy, and thwarted the renegade Lord.

You turn your ship back to the starport. As you do so you notice, on the rear scanner, an asteroid mining ship appear from behind the Asteroid Belt and your Psi Sense registers the presence of a being with great power of the mind, probably the renegade Lord. You catch a thought: *Golden Horde* and then, *self destruct*. To your surprise, the mining ship blossoms into a flowering white light, like a star gone nova, as it explodes. Is the renegade Lord dead, you wonder? You land safely at the starport a little while later. Wasting no time, you run to Falcon's Wing before starport security come to question you. CAIN tells you that he registered a Variac drive emission from the centre of the asteroid mining ship just before it blew up. Whoever it was used their time machine to wink out to safety.

Do you have a nuclear bomb? If you do, turn to **415.** If you do not, turn to **306.**

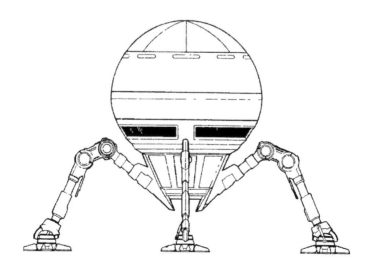

**File**

SUBJECT: Speke
POSITION: Lord of TIME
SPECIES: Earther
BORN: Pacificon, Earth 2887 AD
LIVES: Alpolis

**Personality**
A brilliant scientist, Speke, partly due to his mental powers, was one of two men largely responsible for the invention of the time machine. Like many brilliant men, he is eccentric, will not suffer fools gladly and is prone to break off a conversation suddenly, lost in thought. He is a brave man and, with Irving Klimt, undertook the first ever voyage into the past, starting from 2974. They undertook several journeys together, but Klimt never returned from an investigation of classical Greece in the time of Philip of Macedon. Lord Speke has always maintained that he was killed in a drunken brawl by a soldier, though Klimt had always been careful not to change the past by becoming involved. With the setting up of TIME Speke was the obvious choice for appointment as the Earther Lord and he has enjoyed his position ever since. He is also well known for pioneering work on the mental attack of Thinkstrike, with which he is adept. He is also Professor of Earth Archaeology at the Academy where his specialist subject is Alexander the Great.

**Homeworld**
Earth. Population: 43.997 billion.

**Diplomatic History**
Earth, as head of the Federation, has not faced a serious threat since the Hive-war in 2934. At this time the Hivers were completely defeated in space, though few landings on their homeworld, the Hive, were successful. There has been peace on Earth for three centuries.

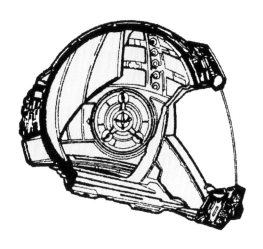

## 382

[score a G]

Realising that time travel would be invented too early if Kirik's machine was discovered, you manually set the Variac drive to engage in a minute's time and pause on your way out only to pick up Kirik's psionic enhancer. The machine winks out into null-space and it will never reappear, but at least you have preserved the timeline. The psionic enhancer carries a chip developed on the Kelados Research Station for Lord Kirik. You slip this into your helmet for it increases the power of Thinkstrike. *Add one to your Thinkstrike Modifier.*

Turn to **262.**

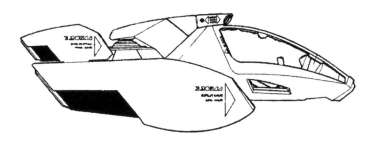

## 383

You grab him by one of his huge, blue-skinned arms and insist that he tell you where he is going. He calmly insists that you remove your arm and makes to enter his machine Do you:

| | |
|---|---|
| Apologise and return to your machine? | Turn to **119** |
| Use your Power of Will to control him? | Turn to **245** |
| Try to restrain him physically? | Turn to **266** |
| Tell him about your mission and appeal for his help? | Turn to **230** |

## 384

You walk through the hologram and see a model B time machine, that of one of the human or humanoid Lords of TIME. From the markings you guess it to be that of Lord Speke and, surprisingly, you see that the access hatch has been left on automatic, an extraordinarily careless mistake. Will you:

| | |
|---|---|
| Enter Lord Speke's machine? | Turn to **366** |
| Follow Lord Speke to the Greek encampment? | Turn to **393** |

## 385

You bring the soldier under your control and force him to discharge his musket through a crack in the ambulance's side planking. Bloodhound suddenly tenses, controlled by the renegade Lord and, drawing his blaster, takes aim at you. You are about to dive onto the ground when the musket goes off and Bloodhound regains control of himself. You run up to the ambulance, but before you arrive the front explodes and a flyer accelerates out of it. Six beings like giant ants, their red, compound eyes glaring at you balefully, are clinging on inside the honeycomb-like seats. One of them appears to have been killed by a musket ball. You realise it is the Hivers, Lord Creche 82282. The Creche skim low through the smoke of the battlefield, almost faster than the eye can see, making a sonic boom like the explosion of a powder magazine, the ammunition stores for the cannon. As they go you catch the thought that they are heading for the planet Hel. Do you:

Try to control Napoleon's mind and use
him to call off the attack of the
Imperial Guard?                          Turn to **37**
Return to Falcon's Wing and chase the
Creche to the planet Hel?                Turn to **84**

### 386

As you approach the line of battle, beneath the Russian
redoubts Davout's blue-jacketed infantry are being repulsed
for the first time, withdrawing to regroup. As they do so, a
furious cannonade opens up from the Russian guns, some of
which are firing in your direction. Make a **Chance Roll**.

If you score 1-4, turn to **364**

If you score 5-6, turn to **351**

### 387

You aim carefully from the shadows and both are felled by the
bolt of superheated plasma which seems to leap from your
hand. One is thrown backwards through the door with a crash
and the other screams horribly. A stream of twenty or more
guards come running from the building outside which the
horses are tethered. Whispering together, they look out into
the shadows fearfully. Strengthening their resolve, they fan
out towards you in four groups, drawing their swords. You
cannot use your blaster in the darkness, for you cannot see
where they are. Do you:

Run back to your flyer?                  Turn to **401**
Hide in a stand of cherry trees?         Turn to **412**

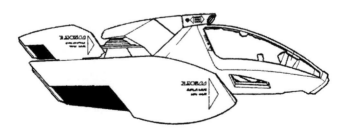

You rematerialize in the Eiger Vault. All is as you left it. CAIN informs you that the machines of Lords Silvermane and Pilota are in their bays. Lord Pilota is still on Spiro's Ringworld and Lord Silvermane is in a meeting at the Galactic Trade Centre. Will you:

| | |
|---|---|
| Travel to TIME headquarters to confront Agidy Yelov? | Turn to **261** |
| Try to track down Lord Speke? | Turn to **407** |
| Go back to the time of the Mongols, Earth 1241 AD? | Turn to **163** |
| Try to arrange a meeting with Lord Pilota, using the holophone? | Turn to **56** |

The lancers bear down on you swiftly, but the horse is an easy target. Make an **Attack Roll**.

If you score 5-12, turn to **365**

If you score 2-4, turn to **346**

Your aim is accurate and the Mongol's head disappears from his shoulders. The headless corpse takes a few more stumbling steps, the sword waving wildly, before it collapses. Acting quickly, you slit Ogedei's throat with the corpse's sword as the door swings open and several members of the Imperial Guard charge at you. You try to dive through the awning to the balcony. Make an **Evasion Roll**.

If you score 6-12, turn to **189**

If you score 2-5, turn to **8**

You tell Pilota of your mission and she says, her voice high-pitched in the thin air, 'And I am the prime suspect? I suppose you realise that if a Lastlander such as I interfered with Earth's past I might very well cease to exist. We are Earther colonials after all.'

'No, you are not my prime suspect.' Your voice is similarly

distorted. It is difficult to tell under these conditions, but Pilota's dilated pupils suggest she may be using a mild relaxant drug.

She continues, 'I noticed yesterday that somebody with a high Security Clearance has spent much time researching the history of Earth around the timehole of 1241 AD. A very great deal of time, according to the Central Library log.'

Remo, Pilota's assistant, intervenes, saying, 'Lord Pilota has been under stress, the failed attempt to travel in the future...' He indicates that the audience is at an end. You thank Pilota for her help and return to the shuttle. Within thirty minutes you are back in front of the console of your time machine.

If you have seen a man in golden armour called Iskander, turn to **114**. If you have seen a Phocian pirate, turn to **34**. If you have seen neither of these, do you:

| | |
|---|---|
| Try to follow Lord Speke into the past? | Turn to **220** |
| Follow Lord Kirik to Kelados in 3033 AD? | Turn to **284** |
| Move back into the timehole that exists in 1241 AD, the time of the Mongols? | Turn to **414** |
| Spend some time in your autodoc? | Turn to **196** |

### 392

Somehow you have only managed to hit the Phocian in the shoulder. His shoulder disappears in a hiss of reddish vapour and his arm rotates gently away from his body surrounded by a cloud of small red globules. Such is the power, however, of the alien mind which controls him that he still fires his ship's lasers, piercing the hull of the envoy ship. There is a brilliant white explosion which fills the scanner screen and then you are suddenly engulfed in blackness. You find yourself in a smoke-filled shelter, a fugitive from an alien race on your own world. The past has been changed and your memories with it. You leap out of the shelter to hurl a grenade at a strange alien craft on the street above you... As Falcon, Agent of TIME, you have failed.

You follow the figure and as you come nearer you see that his gait is similar to Speke's, but you are not yet close enough to use your power of Psi Sense to test this out. Walking briskly, he enters the camp, stopping to talk to one of the soldiers. If it is Speke, he must be fluent in ancient Greek. You soon lose sight of him in the press. The entire camp is readying for battle. The horses are being picketed in corrals and siege ladders are being brought on carts. Some of the soldiers are polishing their armour. Do you:

Head towards the largest tent to find
Alexander? Turn to **321**
Go around the camp using your Psi Sense
to find Speke? Turn to **308**

You instruct CAIN to turn on the Variac drive to shift you into null-space and to re-engage the drive as soon as you have finished inputting the navigational co-ordinates for the timehole on Earth in the Jurassic age. Your scalp tingles slightly as the time machine moves out of phase, and everything around you seems grey and insubstantial. You know that should you turn on the outside camera the screen would remain blank. Not even blackness exists in null-space. You cast your thoughts into the void and, using your Psi Sense, locate the timehole on Earth. When you have translated this location into co-ordinates for CAIN, the Variac drive engages once more. The process of re-emerging in real time is immediate, but seems to take about an hour for you. You can spend this time in the autodoc, if you wish, and *gain up to 12 Endurance points.*

You activate the camera which shows that you have landed in a tropical rain forest, full of giant ferns and primitive fir trees, weighed down with cones. Falcon's Wing settles gently into soft ooze and the holo-projector casts the image of a clump of ferns around the time machine. A great swampy lake stretches into the distance ahead. You cannot see any visual evidence of Speke but if his machine is disguised like yours, you realise that the only way of finding it, if it is here, is to take the holo-detector outside. Do you:

| | |
|---|---|
| Leave the machine to search for Speke? | Turn to **235** |
| Go to the planet Kelados in 2710 AD where Q found a Lord of Time tampering with the past (if you have not done so already)? | Turn to **418** |
| Travel to Earth in 2700 AD (if you have not done so already)? | Turn to **409** |
| Travel to Earth in the time of Alexander the Great (if you have not done so already)? | Turn to **130** |
| Travel to the alien world of the Repnids, Dyskra, in 1985 AD (if you have not done so already)? | Turn to **375** |

### 395

**File**

| | |
|---|---|
| SUBJECT: | Kirik |
| POSITION: | Lord of TIME |
| SPECIES: | Keladi |
| SPAWNED: | Kelados, 2956 |
| LIVES: | Kelados Complex, Biscay, Earth |

**Personality**

Keladi with mental powers are extremely rare. Kirik is looked upon as a mutant because of his powers and is considered 'outside caste', or classless. The metropolitan libraries all carry the rows of books needed to explain the complicated social etiquette of the Keladi. The Keladi see members of all other species, including Earthers, as having no caste. The effect that rejection by his own class has had on Kirik is unknown. It is thought that he greatly enjoys his position as a Lord of TIME and hence as a Keladi envoy, as this gives him some standing in his home world. As with all Keladi, he has a voracious appetite and a fiery temper and retains their obsession with etiquette and politeness.

**Homeworld**
Kelados. Dominant race: Keladi. Population: 4.357 billion. Habitat: temperate seas. The surface of Kelados is 95% water and intelligent life abounds within the warm seas. Kelados is rich in a great variety of marine organisms.

**Diplomatic History**
In 2664 a diplomatic mission from Earth gave the Keladi all the information they needed to become a space-faring race. Since that time there have been no wars amongst the Keladi. In 2710, however, a series of frontier incidents sparked off by Earther pirate ships almost resulted in war, largely due to the fact that the Keladi could not understand that the actions of a few criminals, the pirates, did not involve the rest of their 'clan' - Earth. The envoy, Korakiik, averted war through his realisation that the pirates were 'outside caste', not true representatives of Earth. Lork Kirik, too, understands this difference.

**396**
You walk along the edge of the forest towards the village; curls of smoke wind up from the holes in the roofs of the cottages and huts. As you approach it, your holo-detector picks up a hologram – a time machine has been disguised as trees. Your Psi Sense catches a thought as if you have discovered somebody doing something they shouldn't. *Abort reconnaissance,* you sense next. There is a click and a hiss as of a hatch opening and closing and a group of nearby trees wink out abruptly. A metre-long metal canister rolls down from the bank on which the time machine had stood. You run towards it and recognise it as a nuclear bomb. The digits on the timer are ticking past, like an old-fashioned mid-20th century fruit machine. The symbols are foreign but you guess that all of the red stars will be in line within about thirty seconds. The nuclear device appears to be of standard design and is capable of destroying Vienna and most life-forms within twenty miles of this spot. This would change history beyond recognition. As you watch, another of the red stars clicks into place on the

DETONATE line. The dials click forward one space at a time and when the middle star has clicked forward three times the three stars will be lined up on the DETONATE line and the bomb will explode. Each of the three dials has three buttons above it with which you can manually move the dials 1, 2 or 3 positions onward but you don't know which button is which. You press the buttons above the two dials whose stars are on the DETONATE line, but they are locked. You will have to move the star on the middle dial to the DISARM position without pressing a button that will make it stop on the DETONATE line. Which button do you press?

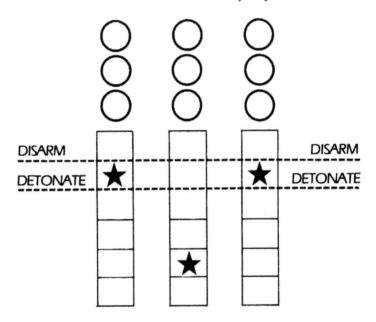

The top button.          Turn to **358**
The centre button.       Turn to **342**
The bottom button.       Turn to **327**

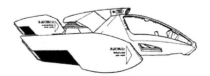

**File**

| | |
|---|---|
| SUBJECT: | Pilota |
| POSITION: | Lord of TIME |
| SPECIES: | Earther |
| BORN: | Lastlanding, 2975 AD |
| LIVES: | Spiro's Ringworld, Earth Orbit. |

**Personality**

Set apart by her mental powers, Pilota accepted her position as a Lord of TIME only when a gift of a solar-sail racer was offered if she agreed. She is highly intelligent, but seems not to take her responsible position as a Lord very seriously. She still seldom misses a race and is highly successful in the sport of solar-sailing which takes the courage to make a close approach to the sun and the fine judgement not to go too close. Before joining TIME, Pilota had been on the official list of space smugglers and was found not guilty of tax evasion after an investigation by the Lastlanding authorities. She prefers low-gravity environments similar to those on Lastlanding.

**Homeworld**

Lastlanding. Founded accidentally in 2571 when the colony ship *Utopia* crash-landed on a hospitable but low-gravity planet. It was the first outer colony. It now has a population of 0.808 billion and still attracts immigrants from Earth. It is a world of golden opportunities and great space, where it is still possible to buy unused land. Each citizen can vote on all issues via holophone in the comfort of their own home. The police force are not kept busy, but Lastlanding has become a bolt hole for those on the run, throughout the Federation.

**Diplomatic History**

Lastlanding was a founder member of the Space Federation and increases in importance. As it does so, however, its dependence on Earth dwindles. They now control their own policy towards other worlds.

**File**

SUBJECT: Creche 82282
POSITION: Lord of TIME
SPECIES: Hiver
HATCHED: The Hive, date unknown
LIVES: Hive Arkship, Sahara, Earth

**Personality**

Lord Creche 82282 is a group awareness, composed of six Hivers, These beings pool their minds in order to become a living computer. They have no personality as an Earther would describe it, but in common with all Hivers would sacrifice themselves for the sake of the Hive without hesitation. They are properly described as 'it', thinking and acting as one. Response to any question takes a few seconds as each inputs data before there is any reaction. The Hivers pioneered the Federation's studies of powers of the mind, inventing the psionic enhancer. They are thought to have developed mental powers beyond that of any other race.

**Homeworld**

The Hive. A dry, hot world, its surface dotted with cities resembling gigantic termite nests. Population (estimated): greater than 200 billion. Hiver factory workers are extremely hard working. The first to acquire weapons on their world, they eradicated all other intelligent species.

**Diplomatic History**

The Hivers were intent on conquering other worlds at the same time that Earth was building the Space Federation. They were heavily defeated in the Space War of 2934 and joined the Space Federation in the following year. They have cooperated since that date and have traded the life-prolonging drugs which give Earthers a lifespan of 250 years in return for metals.

**File**

SUBJECT: Silvermane
POSITION: Lord of TIME
SPECIES: Rigellian
BORN: Rigel Prime, 2700 AD
LIVES: Centridome, Asteroid Belt, Sol System

**Personality**
Aged, even for a Rigellian, Silvermane is the survivor of a long struggle for power on the world of Rigel Prime. Still fit and strong, he is a shrewd opponent and a pleasant comrade. He upholds the Rigellian code of honour and is proud both of himself and of his race, seeing his role as a Lord of TIME as being to further the causes of Rigel Prime. He has a liking for Spartan discomfort which is often thought bizarre by Earthers.

**Homeworld**
Rigel Prime is a large, high-gravity world covered by farmland ranges. The population is 30.131 billion. Silvermane's tribe is in power but occasional differences are settled through ritual combat, no longer to the death, between chosen tribal champions. The Rigellians' culture is based upon the code of the warrior and physical strength is still prized.

**Diplomatic History**
The Rigellians developed space travel in the 1890s and first contacted Earther spaceships in 2152. There was a long history of minor frontier wars as both Rigel and Earth staked claim to various barren planets useful only for the easily mined asteroids which surrounded them. These were eventually settled after the Battle of the Flying Coffins, notable because less than 10% of the personnel involved survived it. Rigel joined the Federation soon afterwards. The Rigellians assisted the Earthers in the great Hive war and without their help the war might have been lost.

Once safely away from the time machine you cut in the ion drive and accelerate to Mach 6 with a loud bang as you break the sound barrier. The journey takes just over half an hour and you hurtle towards the evening sky ahead of you and catch it up. The night is cloudy and dark by the time you have located the city. It is lit by torches and is a strange mixture of golden-roofed palaces, wooden dwellings and magnificent tents. You land the flyer at the mouth of a cave near the city, don the disguise of a Mongol warrior (prepared in the molecular converter), and take the flyer's homing beacon with you. As you slip into the city there are sounds of revelry everywhere. You overhear the whispered conversation between the gate guards. Through your translator you learn that the celebrations are due to the miraculous recovery of Ogedei Khan, who had been given up for dead.

Suddenly your Psi Sense alerts you. The black disc-like flyer, which you saw earlier, hisses overhead, invisible in the dark night. The Time Lord is returning to Vienna and the time machine. In the city, there is a sudden clashing of cymbals and a row of torches is brought out onto a balcony high up on the largest palace. A figure appears, flanked by guards, and you hear the cry, 'Ogedei! Ogedei Khan!' go up from the huge crowd gathered before the palace. If you do not kill Ogedei, Europe will be ravaged by the Mongols and civilisation as you know it will never have been. As you draw nearer to the palace you see two guards outside its gate. At close quarters you see that they are short and well-built. Dark, slanted eyes stare out from flat, yellow faces, marked by high cheekbones and small noses with flaring nostrils. The greasy black plaits of one of them are crawling with lice. From their smell you guess they do not wash. Do you:

| | |
|---|---|
| Return to your flyer and set it to hover over the city? | Turn to **63** |
| Walk up to the two guards and use Power of Will on them? | Turn to **51** |
| Attempt to Thinkstrike both guards in quick succession? | Turn to **40** |

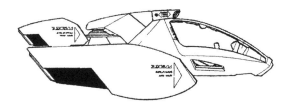

**401**

You run back towards the flyer, hoping to avoid the groups of Mongols scouring the gardens. Make an **Evasion Roll**.

If you score 6-12, turn to **11**

If you score 2-4, turn to **150**

If you score a 5, roll again.

**402**

[score a K]

You press the button and the red star clicks forward onto the DISARMED line. You breathe a sigh of relief.

Turn to **252**.

**403**

A nearby outcrop of rock proves to be a hologram. Lord Speke or another traveller in time is here! A hundred metres away a figure, dressed similarly to yourself, is walking towards the Greek encampment. Do you:

Investigate the time machine?                    Turn to **384**

Follow the figure?                                      Turn to **393**

**404**

As you turn towards the hill near Shevardino on which Napoleon has set up his Command Post, a group of horsemen gallops towards you. Marshal Ney, with some of his staff, is intent on forming a plan with Murat to combine the infantry and cavalry in an attack against the Russians in the redoubt who are commanded by Prince Bagration. Marshal Ney, 'bravest of the brave', has a fresh-faced look about him, curly hair and curling side whiskers. As he approaches, one of his aides calls his attention to a movement of the Russians. Prince

Bagration has ordered an attack. Ney reins in and curses and then sends men galloping in all directions. The speed with which he takes decisions is breath-taking. Soon he finds himself without an aide-de-camp to entrust with his next message and, seeing you in your fine uniform, he beckons you over. Do you:

| | |
|---|---|
| Ride up to him and await his commands? | Turn to **271** |
| Set spur to your horse and gallop off? | Turn to **347** |

### 405

### [score an M]

Almost deafened by the cries of battle you draw your sword and manage to force your way up one of the ladders, strong and big enough to be one of the first. As you reach the top a defender is waiting and he tries to spear you. Make an **Evasion Roll**.

If you score 7-12, turn to **160**

If you score 2-6, turn to **187**

### 406

Your punch connects and your pursuer takes a backward step. Your fist throbs painfully and with a shock you realise his face is dented, not bruised. He should have been laid out by the force of your blow but you have the misfortune to be fighting a cydroid. You have time to use your blaster. Do you:

| | |
|---|---|
| Blast to destroy? | Turn to **108** |
| Trigger a short blast at its eyes? | Turn to **269** |

### 407

Where will you search for Lord Speke?

| | |
|---|---|
| In the time of Alexander the Great. | Turn to **303** |
| Earth 2700 AD at the time of the great interstellar colonial expansion. | Turn to **249** |
| The planet Dyskra, home of the Repnids, in 1985 AD. | Turn to **373** |

## 408

Bloodhound decides to make for the hamlet of Shevardino where Napoleon is, leaving you to explore the front line of battle. Which part of the battle will you ride towards?

| | |
|---|---|
| The point where French infantry, commanded by Marshal Davout, are attacking the Russian guns. | Turn to **386** |
| The area where the French cavalry, under Murat, the King of Naples, are massed awaiting the decisive moment to charge. | Turn to **372** |
| Approach the nearest troops first, the Poles and French under the command of Prince Poniatowski. | Turn to **361** |

## 409

When you emerge on the edge of the plain there is no one nearby, just a massive throng of soldiers around the encampment. You head towards it, realising you must be on your guard as you could be challenged at any time. Will you:

| | |
|---|---|
| Head towards the largest tent to find Alexander? | Turn to **321** |
| Go around the camp using your Psi Sense to find Lord Speke? | Turn to **308** |

## 410

You throw yourself to the ground realising, too late, that they can easily pick you off from horseback using their eight-foot-long lances. You roll sideways but one of the Lancers anticipates this and pins you to the turf, his lance entering your body at the kidney. There is nothing you can do and your life slips away from you before Lynx can come to your aid. You have failed, but at least you have led Bloodhound and Lynx to the renegade Lord.

## 411

You fail to dominate the French soldier's will and he glares around the battlefield and then shakes his head. The renegade

Lord has sensed your attack on him, and the full force of that powerful mind is turned against you. You are locked in a battle of wills. It is a battle which you are bound to lose as the renegade Lord's mind is stronger than yours. All of your being is taken up with the struggle when, abruptly, the attack ceases. You shake your head dizzily, but it is only the lull before the storm. A wave of mental energy flows into you and your brain goes haywire. You seem to feel heat, cold, rain and fire all at once. It is as if you can see all colours at once and myriad voices speak in every language you have ever studied. Your brain overheats, literally burning itself out like a faulty electric motor You are a zombie, incapable of thought, and gurgling like a baby. You have failed.

## 412

As you crouch beneath the trees, you hear snuffling like that of a dog. Cautiously, you stand up ready to make a run for it but suddenly Mongols are closing in on you from all sides. You Thinkstrike two, who collapse unconscious, but the others overwhelm you. They are able hunters, used to the dark and able to track you by smell. You struggle helplessly, but they knock the helmet from your head and carry you to the pond's edge. Laughing cruelly, they force your head beneath the water lilies until your lungs are bursting. Your whole life flashes before you in the slow seconds of your death. You have failed and the Space Federation will never be.

## 413

Sweating with effort you are unable to regain control of your quivering arm and the will of the renegade Lord forces you to pull the trigger. The lightning bolt of plasma hurls Bloodhound into the wheel of the ambulance and his corpse slumps, a grotesque travesty of a human being. Your eyes are riveted on the muzzle of your death-dealing blaster as, inch by inch, you are forced to point it at yourself. Your hand is still shaking, but your finger closes on the trigger and the left half of your face and head is wiped away. You have failed.

You instruct CAIN to turn on the Variac drive to shift you into null-space and to re-engage the drive as soon as you have finished inputting the navigational co-ordinates for the timehole on Earth, 1241 AD. Your scalp tingles slightly as the time machine moves out of phase, and everything around you seems grey and insubstantial. You know that should you turn on the outside camera the screen would remain blank. Not even blackness exists in null-space. You cast your thoughts into the void and, using your Psi Sense, locate the timehole on Earth 1241. When you have translated this location into coordinates for CAIN, the Variac drive engages once more. The process of re-emerging in real time is immediate, but seems to take about an hour for you. You can spend this time in the autodoc, if you wish, and *gain up to 12 Endurance points.*

The outside camera begins to swivel, showing you the land all around. Behind you is a forest, shrouded in snow, and the hologram generator disguises Falcon's Wing as part of this forest. You are on high ground and to the right you can see a village with a few stone dwellings and many wattle and daub huts, their thatched roofs laden with snow. Ahead, the frosted ground falls away into a wide river valley. The river is frozen over, but you can plainly see its graceful curves stretching to a large walled city a few miles away. Here and there on the plain you can see parties of horsemen riding swiftly. You ask CAIN for some historical information. CAIN responds. 'It is winter, 1241 AD. The city you see is Vienna and the river, the Danube. The Mongol horde led by the general, Subutai, has conquered Russia and Poland, and defeated a western army at Liegnitz, before overrunning Hungary. They are a few miles from Vienna, poised to ravage the rest of Europe. Their ruler is Ogedei, son of Genghis Khan. He will die within the next few days and when the news reaches the Golden Horde, they must, under Genghis Khan's code of law, the Yasa, return to the Mongol capital, Karakorum, to decide who will succeed him. Vienna will not fall and Europe will be saved.'

You break in, 'And if Ogedei should live?'

CAIN continues, The likelihood is that Europe would be

overrun and the timelines changed beyond recognition. Civilisation would be set back a thousand years.'

You decide to investigate the area for signs of another time machine and CAIN programmes the molecular converter to produce the clothes of a Viennese peasant: a sackcloth tunic, woollen leggings and hooded cloak, which you put on over your uniform. You step out into the fresh clean air.

Turn to **396.**

### 415

You ask CAIN for information on the Golden Horde. He responds: 'It was a name given to Mongol tribesmen of the 12th and 13th century on Earth.' You realise this is a reference to those you saw in 1241 AD. What will you do:

Go back to the time of the Mongols

| | |
|---|---|
| once again? | Turn to **174** |
| Try to track down Lord Speke? | Turn to **407** |
| Return to the Eiger Vault? | Turn to **279** |

### 416
#### [score a T]

You can lie in your autodoc during the journey and *gain up to 12 Endurance points.* Falcon's Wing rematerializes at the same instant as Bloodhound's machine, Hunter. The digital readout shows the date: 7th September, 1812. You are at the edge of some woods and, once again, the hologram generator disguises the machine in the form of a group of fir trees. The outside camera shows an amazing sight: two colourful armies face each other along a line three miles long. It is early morning, but already the battlefield is becoming shrouded in the smoke of a thousand cannon.

You ask for a historical report. CAIN replies, 'The French Emperor, Napoleon I, has conquered most of Europe and has invaded Russia with a large army. Today, the Russian commander in chief, Kutusov, has decided to give battle, here at Borodino. The French will win a victory, but it will not be the crushing victory that Napoleon needs to force the Russians to give in before the awful Russian winter kills the

Frenchmen for them.' Thanking CAIN for his brief history, you ask him what could be done to change the timelines at this battle. CAIN responds quickly, 'Marshal Ney will win an advantage for the French, but Murat's cavalry fail to exploit this. Napoleon, unwell, will not send in his best troops, the Imperial Guard, to support Ney at the critical moment. If he were persuaded to do so he would win a crushing victory. The same might occur if Murat's cavalry were used to better effect. The Russians would be forced to surrender and Napoleon would remain master of Europe. In this case, Europe would continue to be ravaged by wars for several decades. Countless more people would die and there would be great changes in the year 3033. I do not have enough data to outline these with any great probability of being correct.'

You nod and are preparing to leave Falcon's Wing when CAIN chimes again, unbidden, 'You will remember of course, Falcon, that one of your ancestors is an aide-de-camp carrying messages for Marshal Ney.'

'Of course.' You smile and ask him to activate the molecular converter. CAIN programs a uniform into the converter and you are soon dressed in the most stylish uniform imaginable. A short white jacket, fronted with gold braid, red trousers with a black stripe down the side, a short black cape trimmed with gold, called a pelisse, and your psionic enhancer has become a bearskin helmet with a white plume. Leaving Falcon's Wing, you are amused to see Bloodhound dressed as lavishly as yourself in scarlet and blue. He suggests that you acquire horses and this you manage to do, finding the horses of some French scouts picketed nearby. Bloodhound shows you a map of the battlefield he has had printed by his own version of CAIN. The nearest troops to you are some French and Polish, commanded by the Count Poniatowski, a Pole. As you ride towards the battlefield your holo-detector bleeps. There is a time machine nearby. Do you:

Investigate the time machine?          Turn to **297**

Search the battlefield for the
   renegade Lord?                  Turn to **49**

Lynx has drawn a knife on Bloodhound and though he is very strong, he is no match for her and is already bleeding badly. They are locked together and you cannot use your blaster, neither can you use your mental powers while wearing the psionic damper. You aim a flying kick at Lynx instead but she was ready for you. With the lithe swiftness of a cat Lynx dodges and catches your leg as your boot whistles past her ear. She throws you backwards and you land on your head, breaking the psionic damper. *Lose 3 Endurance points.* Picking yourself up, you try again, as Bloodhound lunges for her knife. Make an **Attack Roll.**

If you score 7-12, turn to **339**

If you score 2-6, turn to **352**

You instruct CAIN to turn on the Variac drive to shift you into null-space and to re-engage the drive as soon as you have finished inputting the navigational co-ordinates for the timehole in Kelados, 2710 AD. Your scalp tingles slightly as the time machine moves out of phase, and everything around you seems grey and insubstantial. You know that should you turn on the outside camera the screen would remain blank; not even blackness exists in null-space. You cast your thoughts into the void and, using your Psi Sense, locate the timehole at Kelados 2710 AD. When you have translated this location into co-ordinates for CAIN, the Variac drive engages once more. The process of rematerializing in real time is immediate, but seems to take about an hour for you. You can spend this time in the autodoc, if you wish, and *gain up to 12 Endurance points.*

You emerge from the greyness of null-space and, switching on the external cameras, see a huge spaceport on an artificial island, built so that the Keladi can trade with other spacefaring races without forcing them to adapt to an undersea environment. The huge vaulted starport stretches for miles on each side; you can count more than forty different types of spacefaring vessels. The holo-generator throws the image of a large aluglass container around Falcon's Wing. The camera shows that nobody has noticed its sudden appearance. You ask CAIN for historical details of Kelados in 2710 AD.

'At this moment in time the Keladi are on the brink of war with the Earth Federation. Reason: border incidents misinterpreted by the Keladi as being a way of probing their defence systems. The Keladi at this time do not realise that many humans break the Earth Federation's laws. They suppose that if one human kills a Keladi, his "clan", or all Earthers, must approve his action. Phocian pirates are being encouraged to use Keladi starports as bases from which to prey on Earth Federation shipping.'

'What could be done to change the timeline here?'

CAIN waits for some seconds before replying. 'I can see one method of changing the timeline which would be both easy to do and disastrous in effect. The Keladi envoy, Korakiik, a telepath, regarded as insane and clanless by the Keladi, but the only one who, through his psionic power, understands the Earth Federation and the humans, is shortly due to leave Kelados orbit to meet an Earth envoy. Historically, he was responsible for preventing a war which would probably destroy both civilisations. To prevent this meeting would change the timeline to a greater degree than I can compute.'

You find yourself thanking CAIN as you pull on the uniform of a Phocian pirate which CAIN has already instructed the molecular converter to prepare. Your psionic enhancer helmet now resembles the helmet of a Phocian laser-turret operator, disguising your features. Taking your holo-detector, you set out in search of Lord Speke. Turn to **360**.

### 419
#### [score a G]
Bloodhound suggests that the first move should be to find Napoleon and as you set out with him, towards Napoleon's command post at the hamlet of Shevardino, the French troops begin to press home their attack. Davout's infantry, in massed

blue columns, storm the redoubt upon which the Russian guns are mounted and Ney prepares to send his troops against the nearby village. Smoke from the guns rolls across the battlefield and the crackle of muskets is incessant. Your fleet horses carry you swiftly towards Napoleon and his staff, who are out of range of the Russian cannon. There are perhaps fifty generals and other staff around the Emperor, many holding spy-glasses to their eyes, the better to follow the course of the battle. In the background is a magnificent squadron of twenty-five light cavalry, dressed in green, red and gold – the *Chasseurs à Cheval* of the Old Guard, Napoleon's personal escort. You rein in close to a group of aides-de-camp dressed similarly to yourselves, as if awaiting instructions. Your Psi Sense cannot find anyone else with mental powers. The Emperor looks pale and unwell, complaining of a headache and as you watch he dismounts and sits down on a folding chair. As he does so, his escorts also dismount and fix bayonets. Bloodhound turns to you and suggests that you go in search of the renegade Lord while he stays with Napoleon. Do you:

| | |
|---|---|
| Stay with Bloodhound? | Turn to **82** |
| Check out the battle lines and search for the renegade Lord? | Turn to **206** |

### 420

As soon as you arrive back at the Eiger Vault you hand Yelov over to the head of Security and your mission is completed. You return to TIME Headquarters to be debriefed by your new Section Chief, Jobanque. If you did not send Lord Kirik's Machine into null-space, he sends a team to recover it before it can be discovered in 2710 by the Keladi. On your way to your quarters you are told that Agent Lynx has returned safely to the Eiger Vault. CAIN informs you that there are slight changes to the timelines as a result of your actions in the past, but that these are too minor to concern TIME.

Two days later you stand once more in the Hall of Honours with Bloodhound and Lynx. Lords Silvermane and Pilota sit at the horseshoe table. Lord Speke is not present, having admitted to Jobanque as a result of the interest in his activities your mission has aroused that he has been breaking the First Law of TIME and living as an ancient Greek for sport.

Jobanque tells of your heroic valour and the skill with which you guarded history. He has gathered all of the evidence and tells the Lords what has been happening. 'The Hivers had intended to gain power over the Space Federation. They set out to change the past in Kelados but when this was prevented they went back to change the past in two places on Earth, in the hope that at least one would be successful. Straight after your graduation ceremony they examined the chance of using the Mongol Golden Horde to set back civilisation on Earth, before travelling to Kelados in 2710 where they hoped to ensure the outbreak of war between Earth and Kelados. Thwarted by you they then travelled to Karakorum in 1241 AD and kept Ogedei Khan alive, using drugs and the Khan's shamans, whom they controlled mentally. When you killed Ogedei Khan they tried to change history at the battle of Borodino in 1812 and were then pursued to planet Hel where they, or it, died. The Hiver membership of the Federation has been cancelled, of course. We have used the Mind Probe on Agidy Yelov. He is the traitor working with the Creche who had promised him great power under their rule. As a Siriun, he would have had an excellent chance of surviving a change in Earth's history and the Hivers were to make him Emperor of Earth. He killed Lord Kirik himself, when Kirik began to come close to finding out what was happening. Indeed, Yelov would not have sent Falcon on this mission at all, if I had not received Agent Q's final transmission while Yelov was away and insisted that Falcon act without delay. Yelov tricked both Bloodhound and Lynx into believing you, Falcon, were the traitor for a while – his deviousness is such that he even tried to convince you that he was loyal to the Federation right at the last moment by turning on the Creche.'

Silvermane shakes his head and says, 'How is it that Yelov ever came to be head of the Special Agents?'

Jobanque shrugs and says, 'He is a deadly combateer and

a clever trickster. Only a very evil man could have escaped detection…'

'And only an agent of Falcon's talents could have defeated both him and the renegade Lord,' says Pilota and she asks you to step up to her for the presentation of the Golden Wings, the highest honour the Space Federation can give.

Jobanque says, 'I thank you, Falcon. Everybody in the Space Federation owes their lives to you.'

# SCORING FOR FALCON 1: *THE RENEGADE LORD*

**Spoiler alert:** Do not look at these scores until you have completed your mission successfully (however many attempts that may take). Looking at the scores before then will tell you which decisions are the best ones, even though that should not always be obvious in the short term.

If you have played *Falcon 1: The Renegade Lord* and would like to rate your skill as an Agent of TIME, here are the victory points equivalent of the letters you should have recorded.

Q = -1   B = -1   K = +1   M = +1   C = +1   G = +1   T = +1   F = -1

If your score was:

| | |
|---|---|
| -3 or below | You are offered a job you can't refuse: tying Silvermane's bootlaces. |
| 0-3 | Demoted to cadet: 'Get back to the Academy, Falcon.' |
| 1-4 | Take a three-week refresher course at the Academy. |
| 5-8 | Congratulations, you deserve your place in the Special Agent Section. |
| 9-12 | Well done, a highly competent performance — your hologram has gone up in the Hall of Fame. |
| 13-14 | You're the best agent TIME has ever had — you're in line for promotion. |
| 15+ | As long as you are alive, the whole of spacetime is safe. |

If you have enjoyed *Falcon: The Renegade Lord*, try these other gamebooks from Fabled Lands Publishing. All available from our online store:

## astore.amazon.com/fablland-20

And be sure to drop in to the Fabled Lands blog for regular news and chat.

# THE WAY OF THE TIGER

The famous gamebook series by Mark Smith and Jamie Thomson combing ninja, battlefield tactics, politics, intrigue, adventure and horror.

Choose the skills and martial arts moves to defeat your enemy, gaining knowledge and honing your abilities to use throughout the series.

# FABLED LANDS

**A sweeping fantasy role-playing campaign in gamebook form
by Dave Morris and Jamie Thomson**

## Set out on a journey of unlimited adventure!

FABLED LANDS is an epic interactive gamebook series with the
scope of a massively multiplayer game world. You can choose to be
an explorer, merchant, priest, scholar or soldier of fortune.

You can buy a ship or a townhouse, join a temple, undertake
desperate adventures in the wilderness or embroil yourself in court
intrigues and the sudden violence of city back-streets.

You can undertake missions that will earn you allies and enemies, or
you can remain a free agent. With thousands of numbered sections to
explore, the choices are all yours.

# BLOODSWORD

An epic gamebook saga for 1-4 players by Dave Morris and Oliver Johnson. Use spells, swords, guile or secret lore to overcome your foes in a combination of tabletop tactics and interactive story.

## Golden Dragon Gamebooks

Pick-up-and-play adventures for younger readers.

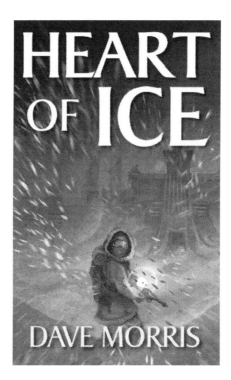

Are you ruthless enough to seize the ultimate power?
Dave Morris's acclaimed science fiction adventure of
greed, alliance and betrayal in a new revised edition.

Also these other classic Critical IF gamebooks:

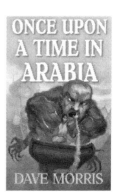

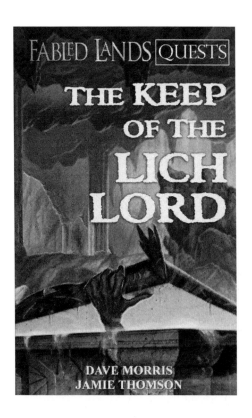

## Lord Mortis has risen!

Clawing his way back from the grave, the Lich Lord has once again set his sights on conquest. His army of corpses has already taken Bloodrise Keep and soon nothing will stand between Mortis and the ultimate victory of the zombie horde.

A cunning and fearless adventurer is needed for a vital mission to enter Bloodrise Keep and overthrow the evil Lich Lord – an adventurer like you!

Originally published as part of the Fighting Fantasy Gamebooks series, *The Keep of the Lich Lord* is back in print after twenty years in a new revised edition with new rules and all-new sections that bring it into the Fabled Lands universe.

Dave Morris's interactive adaptation of the classic tale of terror, tragedy and revenge.

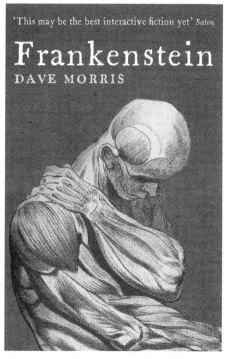

'This may be the best interactive fiction yet' *Salon*

# Frankenstein
## DAVE MORRIS

"One of the top ten book apps ever" *The Sunday Times*

"The current benchmark for high-quality storytelling via tablet." *Best of 2012, Kirkus Reviews*

In revolutionary France, young Victor Frankenstein has discovered the secret of creating life…

An interactive novel that places you right inside the story, acting as Frankenstein's confidant, guide and conscience.

Created and written by Dave Morris. Published for iPad and iPhone by Profile Books and Inkle Studios.

Printed in Great Britain
by Amazon